He was a Carlisle. Blood ties were indestructible. And instinct told Jared that little Dylan Hale was his son.

There were simply too many clues to ignore. Still, he needed more than instinct and clues before he disrupted so many lives.

He had a son. A *son*.

The word whispered through him and stole into his heart. Then he remembered Rachel, Dylan's aunt, the only mother the eight-year-old knew. He remembered Rachel's innocent blue eyes, her soft pink mouth….

Jared's lawyer shuffled some papers on his desk. "Rachel Hale, the aunt, has no legal right to the boy. If DNA tests come back positive and this goes to court, you'll win hands down."

Somehow the words didn't reassure Jared. He would win.

Which meant Rachel would lose.

Dear Reader,

Many people read romance novels for the unforgettable heroes that capture our hearts and stay with us long after the last page is read. But to give all the credit for the success of this genre to these handsome hunks is to underestimate the value of the heart of a romance: the heroine.

"Heroes are fantasy material, but for me, the heroines are much more grounded in real life," says Susan Mallery, bestselling author of this month's *Shelter in a Soldier's Arms*. "For me, the heroine is at the center of the story. I want to write and read about women who are intelligent, funny and determined."

Gina Wilkins's *The Stranger in Room 205* features a beautiful newspaper proprietor who discovers an amnesiac in her backyard and finds herself in an adventure of a lifetime! And don't miss *The M.D. Meets His Match* in Hades, Alaska, where Marie Ferrarella's snowbound heroine unexpectedly finds romance that is sure to heat up the bitter cold....

Peggy Webb delivers an *Invitation to a Wedding;* when the heroine is rescued from marrying the wrong man, could a long-lost friend end up being Mr. Right? Sparks fly in Lisette Belisle's novel when the heroine, raising *Her Sister's Secret Son,* meets a mysterious man who claims to be the boy's father! And in Patricia McLinn's *Almost a Bride,* a rancher desperate to save her ranch enters into a marriage of convenience, but with temptation as her bed partner, life becomes a minefield of desire.

Special Edition is proud to publish novels featuring strong, admirable heroines struggling to balance life, love and family and making dreams come true. Enjoy! And look inside for details about our Silhouette Makes You a Star contest.

Best,

Karen Taylor Richman, Senior Editor

Please address questions and book requests to:
Silhouette Reader Service
U.S.: 3010 Walden Ave., P.O. Box 1325, Buffalo, NY 14269
Canadian: P.O. Box 609, Fort Erie, Ont. L2A 5X3

Her Sister's Secret Son

LISETTE BELISLE

SPECIAL EDITION™

Published by Silhouette Books

America's Publisher of Contemporary Romance

In loving memory of Leo and Simonne Thibodeau
and Ellen Thibodeau Paradis

Special thanks to my husband, Frank, and my children,
Christine, Denise and Marty for always being there
through the laughter and the tears. I love you all.

 SILHOUETTE BOOKS

ISBN 0-373-24403-7

HER SISTER'S SECRET SON

Books by Lisette Belisle

Silhouette Special Edition

Just Jessie #1134
Her Sister's Secret Son #1403

LISETTE BELISLE

believes in putting everything into whatever she does, whether it's a nursing career, motherhood or writing. While balancing a sense of practicality with a streak of adventure, she applies that dedication in creating stories of people overcoming the odds. Her message is clear—believe in yourself and believe in love. She is the founder and past president of the Saratoga chapter of Romance Writers of America. Canadian-born, she grew up in New Hampshire and currently lives in upstate New York with her engineer husband, Frank.

She'd love to hear from her readers. She can be reached at: P.O. Box 1166, Ballston Lake, NY 12019.

Chapter One

It was Maine, it was August and it was hot.

The sun blazed unmercifully through the tall windows of the Henderson Courthouse. Overhead, ceiling fans whirred—the only sound as the jury filed in and took their places.

The building was old and musty smelling. The fans kept the air moving, stirring up dust, cobwebs and old memories—memories Jared Carlisle preferred buried.

Seated among the spectators, he shifted uncomfortably. He should have felt satisfaction at seeing his old rival brought to justice. Instead, he felt pity—well, perhaps a hint of satisfaction....

As if drawn, his gaze strayed to the opposite side of the aisle where a woman's glowing red hair drew him like a magnet. She sat with the Pierces, yet somehow apart. Only one person had hair that pale shade of copper—like the heart of a flame where it burns bright and true. Laurel

Hale. She was still the most beautiful girl—woman—
Jared had ever seen. And she was still with Drew Pierce.

Time hadn't changed his gut reaction—a primal urge
to challenge Drew's possession. Whether animal attraction
or conditioned reflex, it was insane. Laurel had once
taught Jared a valuable lesson about love—what it was
and what it wasn't. Now, a bright flash of her eyes and
the angry tilt of her delicate chin brought him back to the
present. Jared smiled ruefully when he realized she was
glaring at him—her exquisite face flushed with visible
resentment. Her mouth tightened; she looked away and
stared straight at the judge.

Casting a jaundiced eye on the proceedings, the judge
ordered, ''Let's get on with it.'' During the trial, he'd lost
patience with the spectators, the reporters, the defendant
and his fancy lawyers who were up from Boston. That
didn't cut much ice up here. If anything, their slick delivery probably cost Drew several points with the jury.

At a curt nod from the judge, the clerk cleared his
throat. ''Will the defendant stand?''

Drew Pierce stood, his dark head unbent. A ripple of
disapproval spread through the court. Too rich, too handsome, too spoiled…this time Drew had gone too far.

Jared searched the jurors' faces for signs of leniency
and found none. He wasn't surprised. Although the crime
was a year old, passion still burned bright—as bright as
the flames that destroyed the Pierce-operated migrant
camp and spread to the neighboring Stones End. The farm
had been in Jared's family for generations. They'd suf-
fered the loss of a produce barn and most of last year's
crop. Ironically, the crisis had brought Jared and his father
closer and signalled a new beginning for Stones End.

The Pierces hadn't fared as well.

Between hefty federal fines, civil action and legal fees,

they faced financial ruin in the community. Drew might be guilty of nothing more than following his father's orders to cut corners; but ultimately, he was in charge of the migrant camp and responsible for any mismanagement. As such, he'd made some bad decisions, risked many innocent lives and rightfully bore the brunt of the charges.

At some point, Jared stopped listening. He ran his hand over his face, recalling that dark night—the lick of the flames and blinding smoke. He'd helped in the rescue effort. Although there were several injuries, none were critical.

Finally, the list of charges came to an end. The judge leaned back in his seat and growled in a gravelly voice, "All right, let's have the verdict."

The jury foreman mopped his face with a bright white handkerchief. "Guilty."

Guilty!

Drew visibly staggered from the blow.

Like a house of cards, the Pierce family collapsed. Drew's mother fainted. Family members rushed to her side. Only one person reached out to Drew. A woman. Strangely moved when Laurel placed a comforting hand on Drew's arm, Jared admired her loyalty—even if it was misplaced.

The judge pronounced the punishment. "Five years."

At the harsh sentence, Drew's knuckles turned white.

During the trial, he'd pleaded innocent but admitted to repairing a faulty valve on a propane gas tank instead of replacing it. That one grave error in judgment had caused the explosion and sealed Drew's fate.

A few moments later, a deputy sheriff led him away. The air seemed to go out of the courtroom. Jared simply wanted out. His father was seated on his right.

"Well, that's that," Ira said. Despite a weak heart, he'd insisted on coming to hear the final verdict, which meant Jared had taken the day off from work to come with him.

"Are you feeling all right?" Jared eyed him with some concern. "Maybe you should have stayed home."

Ira drew himself up to his full height, a half inch shorter than his son. "And miss all the action!"

Jared chuckled. Despite their differences, he had to admit his old man had grit. And an eagle eye. Even at the age of seventy-one, Ira didn't miss much.

"Saw you looking at that Hale woman," Ira said. "Best cast your eyes elsewhere. She's new in town, turned up about a month ago, keeps pretty much to herself, but there's been talk."

She'd been in town a month.

Jared had been out of town most of July. Since his return, work had kept him close to Stones End, which explained why he hadn't seen her around. He would have noticed if he had. Laurel wasn't the type of woman men overlooked, unless they were blind...or dead from the waist down.

Jared knew he should drop the subject, but he didn't want any more surprises where Laurel was concerned. All right, so he was curious. "What kind of talk?"

"Seems like she's got a child with her. Folks say the boy belongs to Drew. He fixed her up with a job and a place to stay." Ira grimaced with disapproval. "Never heard of Drew doing anything unless there was something in it for him. Have you?"

"No," Jared replied grimly as he absorbed the news.

That Drew and Laurel were still involved came as no surprise; however, the fact that they had a child together came as a shock. Laurel might be a lot of things, but she'd never struck Jared as the maternal type.

Ira continued. "You might want to keep your distance. There's enough bad blood between you and Drew as it is."

Once, Jared would have taken that as a challenge; but with his father's uncertain health, winning every argument didn't seem as important as it used to be.

Jared turned toward the exit. The courtroom was full. Both sides of the aisle merged into one. As luck would have it, he became separated from Ira and found himself directly behind Laurel. The fresh, sweet scent of her perfume almost crushed his determination to ignore her. He swore under his breath, and watched her stiffen in moral outrage, which was a laugh—as if Laurel had an excess of morals, or virtue.

He recalled a sexy little tease with jade eyes—a green-eyed witch. Now, she looked almost prim in a slim navy blue dress. But if anything, her figure had grown more lush. Her thick, silky-fine hair curled naturally. It was almost restrained, held off her neck with a gold metal clasp. Tiny red-gold tendrils curled at the nape of her neck.

As they neared the door, someone pushed from behind. Jared placed a protective hand at her waist. At his touch, she released a shaky breath, and he felt his heart jolt in direct response. Damn! As if scorched, he dropped his hand from her waist, then heard her soft sigh of relief—as if she couldn't bear his hands on her.

When she reached for the door the same moment he did, he glanced at her long graceful hand pressed against the dark mahogany wood. Next to his deeply tanned hand, her skin looked soft and pale, almost translucent.

Jared pushed the door and murmured, "After you," his voice a thin mockery of politeness. She didn't have to know it was self-mockery.

He stepped outside into the unforgiving bright light of midday. The heat hit him like a brick wall.

In contrast, the coolness of her eyes met his as she turned to face him. He wasn't prepared for the up-close shock of her vivid coloring. He felt like an eighteen-year-old kid again—all hormones. Every time he saw her, it felt like the first time. Jared found himself gazing into her eyes framed in ridiculously long, luxurious gold-tipped lashes. The years had been kind to her. Nine years ago, Laurel had set his heart on fire. A spark remained.

"Hello, Laurel." He deliberately removed the slightest hint of warmth from his voice. "It's been a long time."

At his tone, she drew in an audible breath. "I'm afraid you've confused me with someone else." Her face was fine-drawn—the bones rigid with self-discipline. She was taller, more rounded, softer somehow. She had freckles. Funny, he'd never noticed that small imperfection.

He frowned at that.

The sun glinted in her hair, and Jared was struck by the memory of glorious red hair tumbling across a white pillow. He was eighteen again, waking in a strange bed with a girl he scarcely knew, and feeling obliged to ask to see her again. She'd refused, laughing as she confessed that she'd only gone out with him to make Drew jealous—why should she want a poor farmer when she intended to win Drew? In addition to the blow to his ego, her connection to Drew had come as a shock.

Now, Jared smiled at her brazen attempt at innocence. "I'm not wrong about you, Laurel." How could he be wrong? He'd spent years trying to forget her, and apparently failing from his current reaction.

"You are mistaken." She visibly recovered some poise, but almost tripped in her haste to escape him. Escape?

That seemed an odd choice of words, but the thought

lingered. Jared caught her arm before she fell down the steep flight of concrete steps. He didn't want her damaged, just a little shaken up. "I'm not mistaken about you." He smiled cynically. "How could I possibly forget? But don't flatter yourself. The memories aren't that great."

With a gasp at his deliberate rudeness, she drew back, at least as far as his hold would allow.

"You're wrong." Her gaze remained steady, almost level with his. He could see the effort it took for her to remain calm. "Laurel was my twin sister."

Was.

That one word shocked Jared.

"Perhaps you didn't know. It's been some time since it happened...." She added a few details, allowing him more grace and kindness than he'd shown her. The dark blue of her dress contrasted starkly with her pale skin. With each word, her freckles grew more prominent, ending with, "...an unfortunate boating accident four years ago."

While Jared struggled for words, something else registered. Her eyes weren't green; they were blue—soft and muted with violet shadows. Laurel's eyes were green. How could he have made such a mistake?

"I didn't know," he murmured, wishing he could retract his earlier harsh accusation, but it was too late. Hell, he was sorry—sorry he'd ever laid eyes on either of the Hale sisters. He'd never known Laurel had a twin.

She looked hurt.

Jared had a weakness for wounded creatures. As a boy, he'd found injured birds, and brought them home to heal. To his discomfort, this woman aroused the same feeling, and something more—something he couldn't quite define. He wanted to soothe her pain, remove the weight from her eyes.

But she was Laurel's twin, which meant she wasn't for him. He couldn't let some fleeting physical attraction blind him, or get in the way of common sense. He resisted the urge to apologize again. At this stage, expressing condolences would sound hypocritical.

"If you'll excuse me." She looked pointedly at his fingers that were still wrapped around her slender wrist—as if he was loath to let go.

Nothing could be further from the truth.

"My apologies." There, he'd said it. It was all very stiff and polite, very civil, he supposed. Very correct.

And yet, it felt all wrong.

With a rueful smile, Jared released her, unable to deny a small pang of regret. This woman probably needed his protection like he needed to collect one more wounded bird.

She was physically perfect, capable of holding a man captive, with fire in her hair…and ice in her veins, if she was anything like Laurel.

Jared winced, realizing how little he actually knew about the pretty young waitress from the Stillwater Inn. They'd shared a bed, but little else. Laurel never mentioned a twin—or much about herself for that matter— except that she'd moved to Stillwater to live with distant relatives. That would have made her an orphan, he supposed. Odd, she'd never invited pity. She was far too busy rebelling against her uncle's strict rules and her aunt's efforts to turn her into a lady. At the memory, Jared smiled ruefully.

There had been nothing remotely refined or ladylike about Laurel Hale.

Nevertheless, she'd taught Jared a valuable lesson— stay away from women who look as if they promise heaven, but deliver a little taste of hell.

* * *

Once released, Rachel couldn't walk away. She rubbed the spot on her wrist where he'd held her in a strong unbreakable grip. At a glance, she saw he hadn't left a mark, but it felt as if he had.

He was a total stranger, yet this man's connection to Laurel had opened a door Rachel had thought closed.

"I'm sorry, I'm not Laurel." She bit her lip, realizing how that sounded. But at that moment, she wished she shared more than a superficial resemblance to her twin sister.

She wished some man would look at her the way this one had—before he discovered his mistake. The way men had looked at Laurel. Inwardly, Rachel shuddered.

No, she didn't want that.

Of course, she'd noticed him earlier in the courtroom. His eyes had been sending her X-rated messages all day. At first, she'd found it irritating, now she felt perversely sorry because the hot glances clearly weren't intended for her. Now, when his frowning gaze swept over her, she felt wholly inadequate, something she hadn't felt in a long time. Perhaps the trial had taken more of an emotional toll than she cared to admit. Or perhaps, it was just this man; perhaps she wanted to see his eyes light up for her.

"I didn't know Laurel had a twin sister," he apologized again, stating the obvious. He was shockingly handsome—tall and lean, his skin deeply tanned, his hair longish and streaky blond. But despite the smooth features, his expression was grim, his eyes gray—not a transient stormcloud gray, but hard, like granite. There was cynicism, knowledge—as if he knew her. Or thought he did. "I'm sorry, I didn't get your name," he said, his voice crisp, like dry leaves.

She drew herself up. "I'm Rachel Hale." Though not

identical, her resemblance to Laurel was striking—an inherited alignment of features that somehow was never as attractive or vivacious as her twin. At one time, Rachel had found that shadow likeness a burden. Men had expected something from her, something she wouldn't or couldn't give.

At the reminder, her words tumbled over each other in a rush to escape. "If you'll excuse me, I really have to go."

Without waiting for his response, Rachel turned and hurried down the stone steps. At the bottom, she pressed her way through the gathering crowd just as Drew emerged from a side door, escorted by the sheriff. A police car waited.

The motor was running.

To her surprise, the Pierces weren't there. Apparently, they hadn't stayed around to say goodbye to their son. Drew spotted Rachel and reached into his pocket. He tossed her a set of car keys.

She automatically caught them one-handed. Aware of the attention they were getting—particularly from a cold-eyed stranger leaning against a pillar on the courthouse steps—she stared at Drew in dismay. "I can't take your car."

Drew threw her a mocking look. "You need a new car. I don't, not where I'm going. Take it—there's nothing else I can do for you and Dylan." Nothing.

Rachel stepped out of the way when the sheriff tugged at Drew's arm. For a brief moment, the old Drew surfaced. He looked ready to challenge Seth Powers, who simply stared back. The two had once been friends—going way back to their teens—when Drew dated Laurel. Seth was part of the crowd that hung around the Stillwater Inn. Rachel knew him well enough to know this had to be hurting Seth. Drew once mentioned that the sheriff was dating his sister. But all that had ended a year ago when Seth arrested Drew. The explosion had severed so many links.

Without a backward glance, Drew climbed into the back of the police car—a danger to no one. Except himself. He would always be his own worst enemy, Rachel thought. In addition to hiding his good deeds behind a careless smile, he was impulsive, hotheaded and arrogant. The explosion was an accident, but why hadn't he acted responsibly? Because he was Drew—always looking for a short cut, a quick fix.

Watching the police car drive away, Rachel wondered how he would survive in prison. Somehow, she couldn't see him getting out early on good behavior. She pitied Drew. For the first time since he abandoned Laurel when she was pregnant, the anger was gone. The emptiness felt worse.

The crowd slowly dispersed. Suddenly aware that she was standing alone, Rachel squared her shoulders. Somehow, she had to get through the rest of this day.

Earlier, she'd left her nephew, Laurel's son, at the summer school program. At her approach, Dylan looked up from his artwork and smiled. He was sitting alone at an outdoor picnic table while the other children played water-tag. He was the new kid in town, and Rachel worried about him making new friends. He was eight years old, no longer a baby. She couldn't shield him from life.

"Hi." Rachel smiled. However, her disappointment in the trial verdict must have shown on her face.

Dylan frowned. "Is Drew going to jail?"

She sat down beside him. "Yes, honey. He did something very wrong. And the court decided he has to be punished."

"But he said he was sorry!"

"Sometimes that isn't enough." She met his troubled eyes with what she hoped was reassurance. "Things will work out, you'll see. Let's go home."

Rachel stood and helped him gather his paperwork.

She took his hand, and they walked home—which wasn't far. They lived in a rented cottage on the edge of town. A line of thick trees started a few feet from the back of the house. The Pierces owned the house, and the woods. In fact, they owned half the town.

When she opened the front door, the dog greeted them with an excited glad bark. Dylan grinned. Like his dog, he was sunny-natured and eager to please. At times, Rachel worried that he craved acceptance too much. He craved a father even more. She wanted love and security for Dylan—more than she wanted it for herself.

Dylan ducked his head as the dog licked his face, his ears, anyplace she could reach. "Down, Sunny."

Rachel smiled at their antics. Her smile fled when she noticed Drew's flashy red sports car conspicuously parked in the driveway. Apparently, he'd ordered his car delivered to her doorstep. She found the spare set of keys in the ignition. She could send the car back, but she knew it would only return—just as the new refrigerator, stove and washer had appeared and reappeared. Great! Her reputation was already in tatters, and this would only confirm the gossip.

When she first started work at the sawmill, she'd refused several offers of dates. Since Drew arranged her job, people assumed she belonged to him.

They couldn't be more wrong.

The only connection was through Dylan. For years, he'd paid child support but never taken a personal interest in Dylan. Hoping to change that, Rachel had accepted his recent job offer and moved to Henderson, when the closing of the Stillwater Inn and the loss of her job forced her to make the difficult decision. Since the explosion was an accident, she'd felt sure that Drew would be found innocent. But nothing had worked out. While deeply immersed in the trial, Drew and his family had been kind, but understandably preoccupied, which left Rachel frustrated. Now, here she was in a strange town, and Drew was gone. The entire situation was on hold until he came home in five years—assuming he did.

Earlier that day, Rachel had felt the animosity in the courtroom. To add to her discomfort, there had been that awful man who kept staring at her. Well, maybe not so awful, she thought with a whimsical smile. He was tall, fair-haired with tanned even features. When he smiled, his gray eyes twinkled. From the fan lines around his eyes, she suspected he smiled a lot. She shook off the tantalizing memory.

In any case, his confusing her for Laurel explained his preoccupation. Laurel had had that effect on men—not Rachel, which was fine with her. She didn't need complications in her life. She had Dylan. As sole guardian, she'd quickly learned that men weren't interested in instant families.

Chapter Two

The trial of the century—Henderson style—was over. Life settled down to normal—whatever that was, Rachel thought a few days later. A morning breeze ruffled her hair, loosening a strand. She brushed it back from her face, glad that she'd gotten to work in her garden early in the morning before the day's heat intensified.

She heard a dog's frantic bark, then, "Mom, Mom!"

Hearing the note of panic in Dylan's voice, Rachel dropped the tray of tulip bulbs, and ran. She didn't stop to question her response. At first, she'd been Auntie, then Auntie Mom, and finally just plain Mom, which suited both her and Dylan. Although she tried to keep Laurel's memory alive, Dylan's childish memories of his mother were vague, colored by her long, frequent absences.

Sometimes, it seemed as if Laurel had never existed—except in Rachel's memory. Sadly, Laurel had never been able to love her son, or at least she'd rarely shown it. A little boy needed a mom, and Rachel was it in every way that counted—short of giving birth to him. From the moment she set eyes on the squalling red-faced infant, Rachel adored him. A nurse had placed him in her arms. He was hers to love.

"Mom, Mom, come quick." Dylan's voice sounded confident that she would come because—well, because she always did.

Rachel arrived breathless. "What's up?"

"It's Sunny!" Dylan pulled on the dog's collar but the yellow Labrador dragged him across the treed yard into the blackberry bushes.

Rachel caught Sunny's collar. "Stay!"

At the sharp command, the dog stopped abruptly. Tail wagging, Sunny rested back on her heels. She inched forward.

Then, a rustling sound came from the bushes.

"Uh-oh!" Dylan groaned.

With one ferocious bark, Sunny tore loose, landing Dylan and Rachel in the dirt. They looked at each other and laughed as the dog disappeared into the thick bushes.

Dylan's laughter warmed Rachel's heart. Forgetting the dog for a moment, she leaned back on her hands. A faint breeze caught in the pine trees and whispered softly. Today was Saturday, the sawmill at this end of town was closed, and blessedly silent.

The dog let out a long series of high-pitched yelps. Rachel could hear her crashing around, but couldn't see much.

Apparently Dylan could. "Sunny's got something big!" He clearly hoped it was something huge. He'd been moping around for days—ever since the end of the trial.

Rachel felt the same. A restlessness still gripped her. She felt unsettled and wondered why the memory of a handsome face and a crooked smile should linger more than all the other images. She sighed. They could use a distraction—something pleasant for a change.

She whistled for the dog. "Here, Sunny."

Dylan tried to whistle, then said, "I think it's an alligator!" He sounded thrilled at the idea.

"Dylan, this is Maine. Alligators don't live here."

"But they could. I heard about people buying them at pet stores, and letting them loose, or flushing them down the toilet. It could be an alligator. Or a crocodile."

"Mmm," Rachel murmured with a straight face. She never laughed at his stories—his dreams—no matter how wild. She knew how important dreams were. Hers were so simple, but elusive. She wanted a place where she and Dylan could stay and put down roots—probably a first for a Hale, she thought with a smile as she recalled her parents' wanderlust.

Tail wagging, Sunny came crashing out of the shrubs with a black plastic trash bag clamped in her mouth. She dragged it across the yard and dumped it at Rachel's feet.

Obviously expecting praise, the dog sat back on her haunches and grinned. Oh well, at least it wasn't a dead skunk this time. "All right, girl."

The plastic bag moved.

Dylan stared at it. "That looks too small for an alligator." He grinned at Rachel. "Maybe it's a snake."

Rachel hated snakes. With a shudder, she gingerly reached for the bag, then opened it. The inside was black, except for a couple of spots of white. Opening the bag wider, she exposed the contents.

Dylan looked over her shoulder.

"Puppies!" he breathed in shocked delight.

Rachel shared his shock. Someone had discarded an unwanted litter. She resisted the urge to cry at the careless cruelty. Weak and half-starved, the puppies were tiny, about the size of tennis balls, matted into smooth balls of fur. Their tiny claws had poked holes in the plastic bag to breathe.

When one shivered, she said, "Let's get them inside."

Dylan followed her into the house and watched as she fetched a wicker basket. "Are they going to be okay?"

Rachel lined the basket with a towel. "I hope so." She hoped this wouldn't lead to another disappointment for him. When she transferred the puppies to the basket, she noted how frail they were. One just lay there, its breathing shallow. If it didn't survive, Dylan would be heartbroken.

Dylan still looked expectant. "Can we keep them?"

"Honey, they're very young. We need to take them to the animal shelter. They're going to need special care."

The telephone book failed to yield an animal shelter, but there was an animal clinic. Rachel needed directions.

"We're located about five miles out of town," she was told by the woman who answered the phone. "Take a left at the end of Main Street, then a right, another left." This was getting more complicated by the minute.

Although confusing on paper, the directions were easy to follow. Getting lost in Henderson was probably impossible, Rachel thought as she negotiated the one thoroughfare.

Until recently, she'd lived in Stillwater fifty miles away, not far in terms of miles, but each town had its own character. Henderson was isolated and rural, a farming and logging town. Stillwater catered to tourists; the population swelled each summer when families occupied the lakeside cottages. Sportsmen came the remainder of the year.

While Rachel drove, Dylan kept up a running commentary about the puppies. "They sure are small. What if no one else wants to take them?"

Rachel answered firmly, "I'm sure they have a list of people waiting for puppies." She hoped.

The animal clinic was a surprisingly long drive out of town—uphill all the way. By the time Rachel got there, her small car was choking a bit, with that insistent knock in the four-cylinder engine that had her losing sleep at night. She could have used Drew's car, but pride prevented her from accepting any form of charity, however well-intentioned.

Stones End, the signpost read.

Very apt, Rachel thought as she turned at the sign. Stone fences lined both sides of the farm road, then rambled into the fields, framing straight lush cultivated rows of deep-green potato plants stretching into the far distance. One nearby field had gone to seed, adrift in a gaudy sea of wildflowers, as if someone had thrown caution to the wind and let nature take over.

While admiring the view, Rachel almost missed the animal clinic, which blended into the scenery. She parked the car, and they got out. Dylan carried the basket of puppies as if they were breakable. They climbed the porch steps.

Obviously new, the scent of cedar shakes clung to the building—a long low structure set against the shelter of tall flaring pine trees. In the distance, a collection of farm buildings topped the hill. The place was oddly silent, peaceful. The stillness was broken by a baby's cry.

The human sound startled Rachel. She opened the screen door and entered a reception area.

A bell stood on the receptionist's desk. One ring brought someone rushing into the room. With a baby thrown over her shoulder, the young woman smiled. "Hello, I believe we spoke on the phone."

"Yes, that's right." At the sound of Rachel's voice, the baby turned to look, and grinned a toothless smile.

His mother chuckled. "This is Nathaniel. He's not usually cranky, but he's teething."

"He's lovely," Rachel said. And he was—robust and rosy-cheeked, with dark hair. His mother had fair hair; but the infant had her soft rainwater-gray eyes.

The woman smiled. "We like him." She transferred his weight to her hip. "I'm Jessie Harding by the way. You're new in town. Welcome to Henderson. I hope you'll be happy here. Where are you from?"

Liking the woman's directness, Rachel introduced herself and Dylan. "My aunt and uncle ran the Stillwater Inn until they retired recently."

"I know the place. Isn't it closed for repairs?"

"Yes, indefinitely." Rachel didn't add any details about her move. Explanations were awkward.

When Jessie laid the baby down in a playpen, he fussed for a minute until she gave him a rattle. "You said you found puppies along the road? I don't know how anyone could throw them away, do you?"

"Well, no." Now Rachel felt guilty because she didn't want them either.

"If you'll come with me, I'm sure the doctor will see you right away." Jessie turned toward a closed door, knocked once, then opened it, pushing it wide.

Rachel was still struggling to explain, "I thought I could just drop them—" Stopping in midsentence, she stared at the man's identity, frowning at his fair hair. Several days had passed and he hadn't had it cut.

Openly familiar, Jessie teased, "Are we interrupting anything important?"

With an uneasy feeling that didn't make sense, Rachel wondered at their relationship. Was he married to Jessie, the father of her child?

Caught in the act of aiming a dart at a gameboard on the opposite wall, he grinned. "Not at all."

However, at the sight of Rachel, his smile fled. When his gaze wandered over her before finally leveling on her face, the corn flakes topped with strawberries and cream she'd eaten for breakfast curdled in her stomach. Conscious of her less-than-flattering attire—denim cutoffs and a blue cotton T-shirt—she tugged at the ragged edge of her shorts.

When a plump owl on a wooden perch behind the desk winked, Rachel jumped. She'd assumed it was stuffed.

"We're repairing a broken wing," he explained with a crooked smile. He rose and came around the desk. It was made out of oak—old, but not antique. "Hello, we meet again." His gaze fixed on her hair.

Rachel resisted the urge to smooth it back. "You're a vet!" She couldn't hide her surprise. This man didn't fit her mental image of a vet.

Folding his arms, he leaned against the corner of the desk. "It's a legitimate way to make a living."

"I only meant…" She glanced at his credentials on the wall, proof of his veterinary qualifications—even if they were fairly new. "It's such a surprise."

By now, Jessie couldn't hide her curiosity. "I didn't realize you knew each other."

"We don't," Rachel said hastily.

He corrected her. "We've met."

"I see," Jessie said with a chuckle. "Well, while you two are deciding, Dylan can help me clean the pups and set up the examining room. Shout if you need us."

Rachel hastily said, "Dylan can't stay. We have to go."

Dylan looked back. "Just a few minutes, okay?"

With a resigned sigh, Rachel agreed, fully aware of the matchmaking gleam in Jessie's eyes. It didn't match the annoyed gleam in his eyes when he said dryly, "My sister isn't long on ceremony." He held out his hand to Rachel. "I think we just got off on the wrong foot. Can we start over? I'm Jared Carlisle."

The name suited him, both gentle and hard. Of course, he would have to be both in his line of work. But what about his personal life? Rachel placed her hand in his. She didn't want an introduction, didn't want to know this man who looked at her with eyes that saw a reflection of her twin sister.

On that note of caution, she murmured, "Dr. Carlisle."

He winced at her formality. "If you insist. But I prefer Jared. And you're Rachel."

"Mmm." So, he hadn't forgotten her name. She tugged her hand free. She felt awkward, yet unable to define why.

"I need to explain about the other day." His gray gaze confronted hers.

Preferring to forget that first disturbing meeting, she shifted under that unwavering look. "There's no need."

"I think there is." His eyes clouded. Apparently intent on dredging up the past, he continued, "What I said that day was uncalled for. I didn't know about your sister."

Rachel took a fortifying breath. "You and Laurel were acquainted?" Obviously, they weren't friends.

He hesitated before saying, "I hardly knew her."

"I see," Rachel murmured, when she didn't see at all. Nevertheless, she accepted his condolences without further comment. Her thoughts were private, too personal to share with a stranger who obviously had his own memories of Laurel.

"Your son resembles you," he said.

"Dylan?" she said in confusion.

He smiled a polite sort of smile that meant less than nothing. "How many children do you have?"

"None." She had the pleasure of wiping the smile off his face. "Dylan is my nephew."

He recovered from his surprise. "Let me get this straight. Dylan is Laurel's son, not yours."

"Yes, that's right."

"I thought…"

Rachel wondered why a searing glance from this man should hurt so much. "I know what you thought." An awkward silence hung between them. He'd obviously assumed she was Drew's mistress. She didn't know how to stop the gossip, short of painting a sign and wearing it around her neck.

"He called you Mom." Jared's voice sounded almost accusing—as if he couldn't bear to be wrong about her.

"I've taken care of him since the day he was born."

"I owe you another apology." His gaze flickered over her. He didn't apologize, she noted.

"Apology accepted," Rachel snapped, making a valiant effort to contain her temper. Her head was beginning to ache from the effort. "I don't have to explain Dylan's existence to you or anyone else."

At the wounded tone of her voice, Jared could feel his indifference slipping. He'd insulted her, he'd infuriated her without even trying. Before the situation deteriorated further, he decided to take control.

"Jessie must be waiting," he said, taking the upper hand. After all, he was a vet, trained to deal with emergencies—the four-legged kind. Women, he'd discovered, were an entirely different species.

Jared opened the door to the examining room and motioned Rachel inside first. She stepped past him then stopped at the sight of some caged ferrets. The antiseptic smell mixed with the odor of animals was familiar to Jared. His lips twitched when Rachel wrinkled her delicate nose.

"Don't you like ferrets?" he asked, pointing to the playful spine-coiled creatures.

Rachel, on the other hand, had a steel spine. "Not caged ones. Are they yours?"

"We're boarding them for the owners." Jared smiled at her nephew. "Hi, Dylan."

Dylan didn't waste any more time on pleasantries. "Do you take care of sick dogs?"

Jared reached for a sterile white lab jacket. "Yes, among other things."

"Like what?" Dylan quizzed.

"Domestic animals—horses, cows, pigs. Then, there are animals who get sick or injured in the wild."

Rachel cleared her throat. "Dr. Carlisle doesn't have time for this."

"That's quite all right." Jared folded his arms, amused at her hesitation. Until now, he'd been feeling like the underdog. From her tight-lipped expression, he didn't think he'd risen very high in her estimation.

Since the trial's end, he'd tried to get the memory of a woman standing alone in the middle of a dusty road out of his mind. But the image had stuck. And here she was in the flesh. Well, not quite. Her shorts revealed a lot of leg, however. He smiled at the irony of the situation.

Jared was also aware of his sister's curiosity.

After the first year, the shine hadn't rubbed off Jessie's marriage to Ben Harding. While home for the summer, she frequently reminded Jared that he needed to find the right woman, settle down and partake in his share of marital bliss, which he had little or no intention of doing.

If he ever weakened that resolve, and that was a mighty big if, he would never consider a woman like Rachel Hale.

Would he?

"Is this the patient?" Jared eyed the basket on the examining table. Neutering livestock took up more of a country vet's time than he cared to think about. He was looking forward to a change of pace. And a challenge. Hopefully, Rachel and her nephew would provide both— strictly professional, of course.

Liar.

Jared knew he was lying to himself. Rachel intrigued him, and he was going to get to know her better. He frowned at her red hair, pale skin, and freckles. There was something about her—something innocent. So, who was he trying to convince?

Himself?

No doubt, Rachel was clearly trouble. Maybe he needed a hobby instead of a woman—like lighting firecrackers and watching them go off—hopefully without blowing himself up in the bargain. Jared grinned at the mental image and watched her bristle. He knew she was aware of him. The attraction was mutual.

So much for heeding his father's sage advice to stay away from "that Hale woman."

Chapter Three

A muffled sound came from the basket.

Reminded of her reason for being there, Rachel said, "If you could just take the puppies, we'll be going."

Jared looked into the round wicker basket. "Puppies?"

He sounded exactly like Dylan, Rachel thought, hiding her amusement. Apparently puppies brought out the kid in grown men as well as children. She stood back and watched as Jared examined a puppy, every move sure and controlled. His hands gently explored the delicate mass of flesh and bone. What had she expected? He was a trained veterinarian after all, which meant he liked animals—perhaps better than humans, she reminded herself.

Rachel cleared her throat. "What kind of breed are they?"

"Do you want a list? Could be collie, maybe setter, or a hound." He peered into the pup's eyes and smiled when it blinked and yawned. "They may not have a pedigree, but they are cute."

Rachel had to agree, but she couldn't be responsible for them—not if it meant Dylan getting hurt if something went wrong. He'd known too much upheaval in his short life. He'd lost his mother at an early age. And now Drew.

Dylan asked, "Are they going to be okay?"

Jared examined the weakest pup. "This one's dehydrated. We'll keep him and try intravenous feeding, but you can take the rest home." After placing them all back in the basket, he knelt and spoke directly to Dylan. "Without mother's milk, they don't have natural immunity, so infection is a risk. Keep them warm. They'll need a special formula. We can supply that, along with some miniature bottles and soft nipples. They can have puppy food in a couple of weeks, but for now they have to be hand fed on demand."

Dylan nodded. "Got it."

While admiring Jared's way of dealing gently with Dylan, Rachel didn't appreciate having to be the bad guy and letting the boy down. "I'm sorry, but I never said we were taking them."

Now both Dylan and Jared turned to frown at her.

Dylan pleaded, "Why can't we take them home?"

"Because we have a dog." At her response, she could see storm clouds gathering. "Besides, I have to work."

"Mary Ellen will help." Dylan was usually cooperative, but he could be stubborn when it mattered.

"I can't ask the baby-sitter to dog-sit," Rachel said, trying to find a logical excuse—one that Dylan would accept.

"She likes dogs," he argued. "She said so."

Jared stood. His height didn't intimidate Rachel—nor did his maleness. She had experience dealing with men, and keeping them at arm's length. In her current job at the sawmill, she dealt with loggers and truckers. Before that, she'd worked at the Inn, which catered to tourists and rugged outdoorsmen. She'd met all types. Men, in general, didn't affect her. This one in particular did, however.

Well, she wasn't going to let that stand in the way of her common sense. Was she? No! She was not bringing those puppies home with her—not even one. She'd done her duty, rescued them, brought them to the vet.

No one could ask more of her.

Meanwhile, Jared reeled off a list—as if she'd never raised an objection. "Keep them warm. A hot water bottle should do it. They can be adopted at eight weeks."

Rachel asked, "How old are they now?"

"Around four weeks—more or less. Is there a problem?"

"What if Dylan gets hopelessly attached?" Rachel knew her response was out of proportion, but some instinct warned her not to get involved. "What if they don't all make it?"

Jared countered in a reasonable tone, "There's always a risk, but animals can teach young children about life."

Life!

What did he know about her life? Dylan was her sole responsibility. She had to deal with the fallout when things went wrong. If anything happened to her, Dylan would be all alone in the world. Rachel's brief experience with the child care system after her parents died had left her wary.

With a persuasive note, Jared said, "Children often cope better than we think they can."

Rachel's glance fell on the puppies. They tumbled over each other, trying to scramble out. She had to admit, they were adorable. They were odd sizes with different coloring—some tan, some black, some mixed with white patches. One pup scrambled atop the others and whined pathetically. Dylan picked it up, cradling it in the palm of his small hand. It fit snugly.

"I won't get attached," he promised, his hazel eyes full of puppy love. "Honest!"

Rachel sighed. "Oh, Dylan…I know you. I wish I could say yes, but I can't."

Rachel tightened her lips, refusing to belabor the point. After all, this man was a stranger. Easy for him to voice his opinion and claim children should be exposed to some hard knocks in life, but a degree in veterinary medicine didn't make him an expert on children. Dylan was hers; he'd already "coped" too often and experienced too much loss. She knew all about Dylan's insecurities, his fear of losing the people he loved. Only time would heal his losses. And hers.

A few days later, Jared was on hand when his father passed his medical physical with flying colors.

"Keep an eye on your blood pressure and watch out for cholesterol," Dr. Peterson advised, fixing Ira with a stern look. "That's an order."

Ira calmly buttoned his shirt. "Thought that little yellow pill was supposed to take care of that."

"Only if combined with proper diet and exercise."

"Man don't need exercise if he does an honest day's work." Ira patted his chest. "Besides, this here pacemaker keeps everything ticking. Never thought I'd be wired up like a time bomb, but there you go. You know, Doc, you ought to try it. Might recharge your battery."

Doc Peterson scowled. "Oh, get out of here. You

should have enough pills for a month. Jared can bring you back then.''

Ira frowned. ''I can drive myself.''

''No, you can't! And that's final! Jared or Jessie can drive you around.''

Jared tried to defuse the situation. ''Dad, you're on the losing end of this argument.'' His father had taught him how to drive when he was sixteen. Taking away the car keys was one of the hardest things Jared had ever done.

Ira was still sputtering when he left the doctor's office. Fred Cromie had come into town with them to do a few errands. He was waiting outside. He'd worked at Stones End as a farmhand for as long as Jared could remember. His friendship with Ira went back even further. The elderly farmhand had been like a father to Jared—filling in wherever Ira failed.

When Fred heard the test results, he let out a whoop that turned a few heads in downtown Henderson. ''How about grabbing some lunch at the diner?''

With an under-browed glance at Jared, Ira said, ''Sounds good. I could use a square meal.''

Fred laughed. ''Least the boy's trying. Course there's only so much you can do with food that comes out of a box or a can.''

Ira grouched, ''Gotten so I can't tell the difference.''

''The boy'' grinned. Accustomed to his dad's crankiness and Fred's teasing, Jared ignored them both. His mood lifted when he caught sight of Rachel's bright head and long-legged grace on the opposite side of the street.

Wearing a pale lavender dress that came short of her knees with delicate string sandals on her feet, she reminded him of a long, cool, thirst-quenching drink on a scorching hot day. She was on the end of a leash, with the other end attached to a yellow Labrador. Her nephew was with her.

She stopped by a small blue car, opened the back hatch and tried to coax the huge playful dog to jump in. When a cat crossed the dog's path, the dog bolted after it, directly into the path of a passing truck.

For a perilous moment, Jared thought the dog was going to drag her along—but then she dropped the leash. Jared acted—tackling the dog, and rolling it into a nearby ditch.

Brakes squealed as the truck came to a screeching stop, missing them by inches. The driver was shaken. "Honest, I never saw the dog until it was too late! You hurt?"

"No harm done." An acrid odor of scorched tires stung Jared's eyes. His left shoulder had connected with the concrete curb. Before he could move, the dog straddled his chest and pinned him down. When the yellow Lab licked his face, Jared said with a weak laugh, "Good dog."

"Thanks for saving her." Dylan's gruff little voice betrayed bottled-up emotion as he dragged the dog off Jared.

A yellow Labrador retriever, the dog was shorthaired with a bulky chest and regal head, a soft mouth and gentle eyes. Like most of her breed, she was clearly an active, good-natured dog. The dog brought back memories of Jared's own youth, both good and bad.

Rachel's face was white as she knelt beside Jared. "I'm so terribly sorry about the dog. Today was bring your pet day at summer school. I'm afraid Sunny got a little too much attention and a bit out of control. She didn't want to leave. Are you all right?"

The color of her dress turned her eyes purple; the neckline was cut square and exposed her throat and shoulders. When she bent over him, a filigree locket on a long gold chain slipped into the mysterious shadow between her full breasts. Jared's gaze followed the movement.

He'd seen that locket before—on Laurel. He didn't want to think about Rachel's twin. Laurel was temperamental and self-centered. Perhaps Rachel was the calm after the storm.

As if she felt his warm gaze, Rachel drew back. A tiny telltale pulse beat in her throat.

Jared's pulse soared. "I'm fine." Actually, he felt a little light-headed.

"Your arm is cut," she pointed out gently.

At a glance, he dismissed the angry gash. "It's nothing."

She didn't look convinced. "Well, if you're sure?"

Jared had the distinct feeling she was treating him like a child. No one had mothered him since he was seven years old. He felt a bit bemused as a slow smile softened her perfect features. Today, she wore her hair free, curling around her smooth shoulders. Her mouth was frosty pink, and full. Her face grew flushed with concern for him, or perhaps the heat.

Jared lay there, feeling winded, yet oddly content. For the first time since they met, Rachel was looking at him with approval. Maybe risking life and limb to rescue damsels in distress—or their dogs—wasn't a bad idea.

She said slowly, "I don't know how to thank you."

He could think of a dozen ways—unfortunately, none of them were suitable for daytime exposure, let alone public display, in the middle of Main Street.

"I'm glad I was on hand." He nursed his sore shoulder.

"I thought you weren't hurt."

"Just an old football injury." He couldn't say it hurt like hell, or that sharp needle-like pains were travelling down his arm. "It acts up now and then," he insisted.

The driver of the truck left. Rachel watched him drive off as if she'd lost her last ally.

Jared got to his feet. "How are the puppies?"

"They're growing. As you might expect with bottle feedings every three hours around the clock." She sounded exasperated. Apparently she hadn't forgiven him for saddling her with the puppies. Or perhaps she was just cranky from lack of sleep.

Either way, Jared was to blame. "I thought I'd stop by. They'll be needing a checkup. And puppy shots." He had to admit it was a flimsy excuse to see her.

"I didn't realize you made house calls."

"I can bill you, if that makes it better."

Her irritation melted with a surprised laugh. "You wouldn't happen to want a free puppy as payment?"

"On second thought, forget the bill." Jared bent and scratched the dog's head. "Hey, girl. What's her name?"

Dylan replied, "Sunny."

Jared drew a sharp breath at the coincidence. "That's a good name for a dog."

"I know." The boy's smile was missing two front teeth. "My dad had a dog named Sunny. My mom told me."

With those few words, Jared's past collided with the present. He rocked back on his heels—as if he'd taken a direct punch to the midsection. He looked at Rachel. What sort of macabre joke was she playing? She stared back innocently. There had to be another logical explanation... apart from the obvious one. But why would Laurel make up something like that?

Jared had once owned a dog named Sunny.

And Laurel had known about it.

In a daze, Jared stared down at Dylan's unruly red hair,

freckles and wide hazel eyes. Of all places to find out—
in the middle of the street on a busy afternoon.

Jared shook his head, feeling as if his world had tilted
and remained permanently askew. Dylan's hair color
matched Rachel's; the boy's eyes were an indefinite hazel;
but there was that dimpled chin, and nose—so similar to
Jessie's baby.

But the resemblance was indecisive. Dylan didn't look
like Drew or Jared; he looked like himself—like a Hale.

But what about Sunny?

The dog's name could be a coincidence, Jared reasoned,
trying to maintain calm. Surely, if there was a blood tie,
he'd feel some emotional connection to the boy.

But he felt nothing; in fact, he felt numb.

Cars swept past them, reminding him that this wasn't
the time, nor the place, to get the answers he needed.

Help came from an unexpected source. At some
point—Jared wasn't sure exactly when—his father and
Fred had joined them. When Jared introduced Rachel and
her nephew, Fred merely looked curious, while Ira looked
disapproving.

"Fool chance you took," Ira said, with a disparaging
glance at the dog. "And all over a dumb animal."

Dylan frowned. "That's my dog, and she's not dumb!"

Ira issued an unrepentant "Humph."

If his father ever knew what a special dog could mean
to a little boy, he'd obviously forgotten, Jared thought. No
one could accuse Ira Carlisle of having a soft heart, least
of all his son.

With Dylan visibly upset, Jared caught a glimpse of
Rachel frowning at Ira, who was frowning back at her. It
was a clear-cut case of instant dislike on all sides. Jared
might have laughed at the situation if it wasn't such a

damn mess! The moment was surreal. They could all be related.

When Rachel felt Dylan lean against her hip, she placed her hand on his shoulder. "I'm terribly sorry, Mr. Carlisle," she said, before adding, "Dylan, that was rude. Please apologize."

Dylan looked up at her in angry appeal. "But, he…"

Her mouth tightened. "Dylan," she said, deliberately using her "no opposition" voice, which generally got a response.

Dylan hung his head. "I'm sorry."

"Better keep a closer eye on that dog," Ira returned.

When Jared said nothing, Rachel drew back in confusion. She and Dylan hadn't made a hit with Ira Carlisle, but why was Jared openly distancing himself? She couldn't deny her disappointment. Had she begun to hope for something more?

Every feminine instinct screamed a warning that he was all wrong for her. He could be kind—if and when it suited him; but then, he could turn it off without notice.

Only moments ago, Jared had been lying in the gutter, flirting with her; now he looked tense and edgy. His hot-and-cold attitude was beginning to annoy her.

Had she misread more than friendship in his warm gaze? Obviously, she had. Dylan was vulnerable; and she wasn't prepared to risk her heart. Jared was definitely a risk.

She sighed.

Even surrounded by a pair of grumpy old men, he looked gorgeous. They were all three frowning at her!

Suddenly, Rachel needed to get away from Jared's stare. Something in his eyes confused her. He'd saved Dylan's dog. She'd stood frozen and watched it happen—terrified for Jared's safety and the dog's. She owed Jared her heartfelt thanks, but couldn't quite put her heart into it. "I'm very grateful."

His eyes flickered over her, but didn't meet hers. "I'm glad I was on hand," he said, equally stiff.

Rachel lifted her chin. "Excuse me, I have to go."

She felt ridiculously let down by Jared's coolness. It must be the heat, she argued with herself as she shoved the dog into the car. She refused to admit it could be anything else.

To her dismay, Jared gave her a hand. His arm brushed against hers. She felt a trembling heat, then cold. She climbed into the car. She turned the key in the ignition.

Jared gently closed her door. "Drive safe." There, he'd done it again. Of all the miserable, phony, low-down…

How dare he be kind! She gave him a pasty smile. She was not attracted to Jared. She didn't need an added complication in her life, particularly a six-foot-two, gray-eyed wolf in sheep's clothing! She had Dylan. Love was highly overrated anyway.

Hadn't it—or its facsimile—destroyed Laurel?

Hadn't it eluded Rachel all her life?

The car started on the third try.

Rachel took a deep breath, then calmly bid Jared a cool farewell. She took pride in maintaining an even temper. Heaven knew she worked at it! The habit was ingrained. As a child she'd heard it often enough…Laurel was the extrovert; Rachel was more shy, more reflective. People always compared them. Even her mother always said, Laurel followed her heart, while Rachel used her head. Mama always laughed when she said it. But somehow, that had excused Laurel's excesses and made Rachel feel less loveable. After all these years, why did it still have the power to wound?

Dylan had the last word. He attached his seat belt, then muttered under his breath, "I don't like that man."

Which one?

Jared watched Rachel and her nephew drive away; he felt a strong urge to follow and get some answers, but knew he couldn't act rashly. He had to think.

After lunch at the diner, he drove home and wrestled with his conscience. Whether intentional or not, there was a real possibility that he'd abandoned Laurel when she was pregnant. Youth was no excuse. The years slid away...and he was eighteen again, and his dog had been fatally wounded in a hunting accident involving Drew and his friends. Jared went looking for Drew at the Stillwater Inn. Drew wasn't there, but Laurel was. She served him drinks and flirted openly. She'd listened to his anger about Sunny and offered sympathy. When her shift ended, they went down to the lake and found an empty tourist cabin. He didn't need to coax her onto the bed. She was more than willing. With her red hair spread against the pillow, Jared paused. He'd never been with a girl before, but clearly it wasn't the first time for Laurel. She'd laughed at his clumsiness.

When it was all over, he tried to do the gentlemanly thing and asked to see her again. She laughed. Why would she choose a poor farmer? He was shocked to learn she was dating Drew Pierce. She only went with Jared to get even with Drew for taking a college girl home for the weekend. Apparently, Drew's parents didn't approve of Laurel. She started to cry—hot, angry tears. At that point, Jared's fury and hurt male pride met a hollow death when he realized she was just a crazy, mixed-up kid.

He got dressed and went home, where he got into a flaming argument with his father for staying out all night.

The exchange had opened old wounds and left the family in shambles. The following day, Jared left town, humiliated over Laurel, and bitter over his father's betrayal. He never saw Laurel again. At eighteen, Jared lost his innocence. He'd never quite believed in anything since....

The truck hit a bump.

Jared glanced at his father's slumped shoulders. Ira had been silent at lunch. Fred hadn't said much, and neither had Jared, who couldn't recall what he'd eaten. Whatever it was, he had a bad case of heartburn.

They dropped off Fred, then reached the turn to Stones End. At the house, Jared swung into the driveway. The motor died, and the silence of the hills closed in around him. He looked at the old farmhouse. It needed a coat of paint and a new roof. The front porch sagged. There was work to be done. The question was, where to start?

With a mental reminder to pick up some house paint, he climbed out of the truck.

So did Ira. He stared at Jared across the cab. "I heard that boy—what was his name?"

Jared braced himself. "Dylan."

Ira lifted an eyebrow. "I heard him say his dad had a dog named Sunny. Seems to me that was your dog. Not Drew's."

Meeting that stone-cold stare, Jared knew the same hardness had crept into his own eyes. "That's right."

"I want you to tell me there's no chance that boy is your flesh and blood." Ira was breathing hard—as if he'd run a mile.

The reminder of his father's weak heart stopped Jared from snapping back and telling him to stay out of his personal life. Jared broke out in a sweat as he recalled telling Laurel about Sunny. The possibility of a child coming from that one night seemed unreal. But Dylan was real—so was the possibility that he was Jared's flesh and blood. "I can't do that."

"Then you find out!" Ira's face contorted with fury. "All these years, I saved Stones End for you...for you, and your sons. If that boy is a Carlisle, he belongs here."

Jared weighed each word. "What about the aunt?"

Ira dismissed Rachel. "Deal with her. If he's yours, she has no right to keep the boy from you. Besides, she's done her duty by the boy—she'll probably be relieved to be set free."

Somehow, Jared didn't think Rachel would be relieved. From what he'd seen, she was devoted to Dylan. But Ira hadn't seen that. Even if he did, would he care? Sometimes Jared worried about growing old and alone, but most of all he worried about growing hard...like his father. "I'll look into it."

Ira bent just enough to grunt, "Good."

Jared bit back a comment. His father probably thought he'd won. Somehow, that didn't feel so bad. Like this harsh northern land that produced him, Ira Carlisle was still a force to be reckoned with; but just then, Jared saw only a tired old man. He deeply regretted causing his father any pain.

In heavy silence, Ira walked toward the house. He climbed the porch steps and went inside.

Jared watched him go, worried about all the upheaval this would cause. He let his gaze wander over the emerald green fields and distant hills. The beauty of Stones End hurt his eyes and burdened his heart. Years ago, he'd left, weighed down by lies and half-truths—lies his father had told him about his mother—that she'd left and never asked to see Jessie and Jared again.

Eventually, Jared had hired a detective and learned she'd died in a charity hospital. But the trail didn't end

there. There was a mother's ring with three stones. Three.
He'd found a photo among his mother's things. It showed
a small child with fair hair. Her flowered dress looked too
big, a pink ribbon drooped in her hair, but nothing
dimmed her smile. She looked like Jessie...but in the
background, there were palm trees instead of Maine's na-
tive pine.

On the back of the snapshot was one word—Olivia.

He had another sister. He couldn't rest until he found
her. The detective was still working on the case and
claimed they were close. But Jared's recent trip to trace
down another lead had come to nothing.

And now, there was Dylan.

Finding Olivia would have to be put off until Jared took
care of matters closer to home.

Just then, Jared had to get back to work; but later that
evening, he walked over to Jessie's house. Made out of
log beams and glass, it stood in a clearing by the pond.

It was a summer house, which meant Jessie and her
family would be leaving when the leaves turned. Ben
Harding owned and operated a horse farm in Virginia—a
lucrative enterprise if the size of this house was any sign.
Jared found Ben and Jessie on the front porch, rocking,
as they sipped iced tea.

At her feet, Jessie's dog, Bandit, lifted his head at
Jared's arrival, then settled down again.

"Evening." Jared smiled at Jessie, then nodded toward
the man she'd married. He wasn't sure what he thought
of Ben—a hard battle-scarred man. "Where's the little
guy?"

"Asleep," Jessie responded. "Finally."

Jared looked up at the summer evening sky. "Seems
early."

She laughed. "Not if you're five months old."

"Or the worn-out parent of a five-month-old." Ben didn't look particularly worn out. He looked restless, like a caged tiger ready to spring.

Obviously, Jessie wasn't daunted. "Admit you love it."

When she reached for Ben's hand, Jared wanted to warn her not to love so much, not to wear her heart on her sleeve. But then Ben's hand closed over hers, and Jared knew their love was mutual. Jessie had won this man's heart. Ben had drifted into her life—a stranger who stayed—a willing captive.

With a warm glint, Ben smiled. "I'm not complaining."

Conversation slipped into concerns with the farm. The previous summer, Ben had managed Stones End and married Jessie in the bargain. At length, Ben stood up and stretched. "Well, I'll be turning in."

Jessie murmured, "I'll be along in a minute or two."

Jared stood. "I should be going."

"No," Jessie said, adding softly, "Stay." And once they were alone, she said, "What's up? I can always tell when something's on your mind."

Jared laughed. He'd spent years protecting Jessie from life's blows—everything from neighborhood bullies to eating too many unripe apples. When had she gotten so wise?

"I have a problem." He leaned against the porch rail, but didn't relax. He looked out toward the pond and the surrounding trees. The forest floor was green and lush. There was new growth where last summer's fire had left total devastation.

Jessie sat back, rocking gently. "So, tell me." The squeak on the porch floorboards made an easy rhythm, but it didn't make the words he had to say anything less than tawdry.

He didn't know where to begin. "It's not that easy."

"Nothing that really matters ever is."

The moon settled lower in the sky. Somehow, the words felt less awkward under shadowy light where Jessie couldn't read every expression on his face. Of course, she could probably hear the painful regret in his voice. Explaining to Jessie was hard, much harder, than he'd thought. If he could spare her, he would. At the end, she looked deeply saddened, not judgmental. "And you never saw Laurel again?"

Jared took a deep breath. "No."

Jessie came to stand beside him. "Does Rachel know?"

Jared looked down into her troubled face. "I don't know how much she knows. I need to find out before I do anything."

Wrapping her arms around her waist, Jessie nodded. "There was gossip about Drew and a girl from Stillwater." In simple words, she explained all she knew, which unfortunately wasn't much. "This girl turned up and claimed she was pregnant with Drew's child. When he refused to marry her, his father paid to keep things quiet. But there was still talk."

Jared frowned. "Why didn't I ever hear about it?"

"You weren't here."

At the reminder, Jared felt a familiar stab of guilt. At eighteen, he'd left, joined the Navy, then worked his way through college and veterinary school. Over the next eight years, he'd come back for visits but never stayed long until he came home for good last summer. He'd left Jessie to deal with his father and the farm. He felt guilty about that, too. So much guilt, so many mistakes. Hopefully, he could handle this situation without making more. He wanted to do the right thing—for everyone.

Contrary to his father's opinion, Rachel Hale was very much a part of the equation. Jared couldn't rule her out.

Reminded of Dylan's aunt, he straightened abruptly. ''Ben's waiting up for you. I should be going.''

Moments later, Jared walked away from Jessie's snug house. The windows were all lit up. Feeling more alone than usual, Jared walked down the road toward the main farmhouse. The day had started out with promise, but now the evening turned cloudy. Shadows drifted across the far meadow and crept up on Stones End. Like day into night, the past held Jared's future. In all his wanderings, he'd learned a simple truth: this was where he belonged. He was a Carlisle. Blood ties were indestructible. Instinct told him that Dylan was his.

There were simply too many clues to ignore. But he needed more than instinct before disrupting so many lives.

He had a son.

Son.

The word whispered through him and stole into his heart. His son. His. Then, he remembered Rachel. He remembered her blue-violet eyes, her soft pink mouth.

She was going to hate his guts.

Chapter Four

The sun poured through a large window overlooking Main Street. Pierce Sawmill was emblazoned across the glass in gold-edged letters.

Rachel worked in accounting. Her job wasn't glamorous, but she enjoyed it—usually. Today, the air conditioner was broken. Despite a requisition, no one had come around to repair it.

The metallic scream of a saw biting into hardwood drowned out the sound of Jared's arrival. Only the stirring of warm air, the office door opening, alerted Rachel to his presence. She looked up from her desk, wondering how long he'd been standing there watching her. The thought sent a forbidden shiver down her spine—one she quickly rejected.

"Can I help you with something?" She felt the heat in her face rise as she lifted her voice above the noise.

"Jessie mentioned you worked for Drew." His voice seemed to echo and bounce off the four walls.

Unable to suppress the defensive note, Rachel said, "I work for the Pierces." Another log tumbled with a deafening crash. To her relief, Jared closed the door. Her relief lasted about a second. He'd shut himself in with her. Her office was small. It shrank with Jared Carlisle in it.

He apologized. "I should have called first."

"Did you want to see Evan?"

Rachel assumed he wanted to see Drew's brother who managed the sawmill.

"I wanted to talk to you," he said, as if she hadn't interrupted. "Could we go somewhere for coffee?"

"I'm sorry. We're short of staff. I can't leave the office unattended." At her refusal, the air crackled between them. What were they playing, cat and mouse? Hit and miss? Who was keeping score? Rachel sighed. She wasn't very good at this male-female game.

"What about after work?" he said.

Rachel latched on to a ready-made excuse. "I'm sorry. Dylan will be expecting me home at four."

He raised an eyebrow. "Look, if it's about the other day. I'm sorry if my father upset you."

"He didn't upset me," she insisted. "In any case, he was right. Risking your life for a dog was foolish."

He winced. "Ouch."

"Is there anything else?"

"Actually there is," he said with quiet intensity. "Is there any reason why we can't be friends?"

The request caught her off guard. "Not really," she said after a moment's hesitation.

"Good." He smiled. "If you recall, the puppies are due for their shots. You forgot to give me your home address."

That wasn't surprising; she'd hoped he'd forget all about her, and the puppies. She gave him the address, adding, "I'm sorry if I inconvenienced you."

"Not at all." There was a gleam of amusement in his eyes—as if he knew she wasn't sorry at all. "I had to come into town. The sawmill isn't that far out of the way."

The office door opened. "Rachel—" Her boss, Evan Pierce, frowned at Jared's presence. "Am I interrupting?"

Jared replied, "I was about to steal your assistant away, but she resisted." He walked out, saying, "I'll be in touch."

After Jared left, Evan said, "Whenever you have time, please log this in." He handed her a thick file. "By the way, my mother sends her regrets. The family left town after the trial, but she's very anxious to get to know Dylan better. She's expecting you both to join her." Evan didn't smile.

Rachel could never tell whether he approved of her or not. "I'd like that, too. But Dylan still needs to adjust to this move, and school's starting soon—then, there's my job."

"There are schools in Bar Harbor," he said dryly. "And as far as your job is concerned, we have connections there. It shouldn't be too difficult to line up a job."

Rachel stiffened, refusing to let Drew's influential family take over her life. "Please thank your mother. Dylan and I would love to visit sometime, but not now."

After he walked out, Rachel tried to concentrate on work. She stared at the figures on her computer screen and watched them blur. The numbers didn't add up. The trial had left the Pierces in debt. And with no funds to buy new timber, cut or standing, the situation at the sawmill was only bound to get worse.

With the migrant camp closed since the previous summer, the local farmers were in trouble. Henderson relied heavily on the lumber industry. Hundreds of jobs depended on the sawmill remaining solvent, including Rachel's.

When she finished work, Rachel walked home—surprised to find Jared there. He and Dylan were in the yard playing catch.

While she stood unnoticed, Jared threw a long one, and Dylan missed. The ball flew into the woods, and Dylan and Sunny took off after it. The dog was barking with glee, Dylan was laughing, so was Jared. The scene was so normal, so rare...everything she wanted for Dylan.

At that moment, Jared saw her. Unable to tear her gaze away, she watched his easy grace as he crossed her yard. She pushed her hair back, aware of a certain expectancy.

He spoke first. "I got here about half an hour ago. Mary Ellen explained you were running late, so I told her she could leave. I hope you don't mind," he said with a crooked smile some women might find endearing.

Apparently, he'd charmed the baby-sitter. But Rachel wasn't an impressionable teenager. She frowned, refusing to be swayed by his rampant masculinity. "She should have called me and let me know."

He raised an eyebrow. "And what would you have said?"

"That's hardly the point."

At her tone, he looked surprised. "You're upset."

"Of course. I'm responsible for Dylan."

Jared's mouth tightened in a flash. "And you think I might do something to harm him? Believe me, you have nothing to fear in that department."

Not reassured, she decided to drop the subject, but felt

compelled to add, "Next time, please let me know." Assuming there was a next time.

He nodded toward the sign on the lawn advertising free puppies. "Have you had many takers?"

She nodded. "We've got a waiting list."

"I gave them their shots, they're ready to go. You'll be glad to get your life back," he said, as if her life was filled with thrills and excitement whenever she wasn't dog-sitting.

Nothing could be further from the truth.

Rachel hadn't had a date in more months than she could remember. "I'd still feel better if you'd accept some kind of payment." Her mouth went dry when his gaze slid over her lips.

When she blushed, Jared felt like a fraud—a lecherous one at that. The urge to kiss her soft pink mouth had come out of nowhere. He cleared his throat. "It's not necessary."

When Dylan turned up with the ball, Jared said, "Before I forget, there is one other thing. I waited for your mom to get home." He'd left a box in the back of his truck parked in the shaded driveway. Now, he reached in and pulled out a squirming ball of fur. Jared set it on the ground where it shook itself into a floppy-eared black and white puppy. "Remember this little one?"

"He made it!" Dylan's voice held awe.

At the tone, Jared's grin grew wider. "He had a little trouble at first, but he's a fighter." He didn't reveal the lengths to which he'd gone to save the puppy. There was little he could do for Dylan, but using his veterinary skills was a start.

Dylan nodded in agreement. "Yeah, he's a fighter."

Sunny trotted up. Nose to nose, the big dog and the

little one got acquainted. "Sunny adopted the pups," Dylan explained.

The new pup broke away to explore, sniffing at the long grass, darting into the pansies and coming out with yellow pollen on its black nose. When the pup started to dig, Rachel picked it up. "Oh no, you don't," she scolded, laughing when a silky pink tongue licked her thumb.

A moment later, she set him down at a safe distance, and the curious pup found another patch of flowers.

Dylan promptly named the puppy "Digger."

Rachel gave a resigned sigh. Despite all his promises— "not to get attached"—Dylan had given each puppy a name, which Rachel knew would only make it harder when the new owners came to take them away in the next week. There was Bear and Tony and Cindy and Cookie and Pepper—and now Digger.

Just then, a car pulled up, and a rough-looking man got out. "Sign says you got dogs," he said. "I need a good watchdog. Are they going to be big?"

Jared said, "Small to medium-size." He didn't like the man's attitude and was tempted to send him on his way.

Rachel beat him to it. "I'm sorry, they're all taken."

The man nodded toward Digger. "What about that one?"

Rachel scooped up the puppy. "We're keeping him."

At that, Dylan grinned from ear to ear. Jared just stood there as a slow smile crept over his face. Damned if she hadn't surprised him. So Rachel had a heart—she was just afraid of losing it—but under the right conditions, she would take a risk and "get attached."

After the man left in a huff, Dylan threw his arms around Rachel. "Thanks, Mom!" The boy was obviously delighted, and Jared could see why. Rachel was the kind of mother any boy would love, which only made Jared's dilemma worse.

Rachel was conscious of Jared's undivided attention. He warmed her with a smile that she imagined meant approval.

"I'll have to send more of my patients to you for some TLC."

"No, thanks, I think we've met our quota." Rachel set the puppy on the ground. "Supper is in one hour," she called after Dylan as he ran off with Sunny and the pup trailing behind.

She turned back to Jared. "Would you like a cup of coffee?"

When he accepted, she hid her pleasure. The feeling came from deep inside, a warm tide, like a well that couldn't be emptied. He followed her into the house.

Her voice even, she said, "How's business?"

"Things are slow. We've got one in-patient, a turtle with an infected shell. He's on antibiotics. The ferrets went home last week. However, there is a prize pregnant cow that's gone past her delivery date."

A laugh escaped her. "Sounds promising."

He grinned back. "Could be twins—that would mean a bonus."

"One would hope." Disarmed by his humor, Rachel relaxed her guard. He obviously liked children—he was saving turtles and owls. How dangerous could he be?

Jared looked around the small front hall with its neat coatrack. Curious about the way she and Dylan lived, he felt like a fraud, a man on a mission to uncover the past. A narrow flight of stairs wound its way upward on the right; and to the left, an arched door opened into the cozy living room. Dominated by shades of yellow accented by pale greens and blues, the room was filled with plants. A partially finished jigsaw puzzle took up most of the coffee table. Tropical fish swam companionably in a fish tank. The glass sparkled. "Nice," he said, taking in the bright atmosphere, slowly absorbing the meaning. Home.

Aware of the breathless quality of her voice, Rachel said, "The kitchen's through here." Why had she weakened and invited him inside? Now, she didn't know what to do with him. She reached into a cupboard. If only she had instant coffee…but all she had was regular ground.

While he wandered around, looking at Dylan's drawings displayed on the refrigerator door, Rachel measured coffee grounds and water. It took a while for things to percolate. She wasn't sure what they talked about, but eventually the coffee was done. She reached for her mother's fine cups and saucers—thin china decorated with cabbage roses, etched in gold, and breakable. They weren't valuable—except to Rachel. In fact, she usually reserved them for very special occasions. Feeling bemused at the realization, she stopped, then firmly reached for a pair of solid earthenware mugs.

She poured coffee. "Sugar, cream?"

"Yes, please."

Rachel joined him at the round wooden table. Set in a cozy alcove, it suddenly felt much cozier. She lifted her cup to her lips, and took a cautious sip.

He took a swallow, lifted an eyebrow. "This isn't bad."

"What did you expect?" She needed to lighten the atmosphere, which had grown oddly heavy.

"Not a great cup of coffee," he countered with an easy careless smile that didn't quite reach his eyes.

Rachel suspected a lot of things came easily to Jared Carlisle, perhaps too easily. "I'd almost forgotten," she said, searching for a safe neutral topic. "Earlier, you said you wanted to discuss something."

At the reminder, Jared hesitated. "It was nothing important," he said at last. He'd almost forgotten his mission. Was he prepared to reveal his suspicions?

His gaze returned to the drawings on the refrigerator. He could remember his own mother displaying his childish artwork. He supposed that's what mothers did. Funny, how he'd forgotten that. But he'd never forgotten coming home from school one day and finding her gone—and no one pinned his drawings up anymore. At the time, he was seven years old, not much younger than Dylan. All these years later, he still felt a pang of regret. A boy needed a mother. Jared knew firsthand how it felt to lose one. If Dylan was his son, Rachel was part of the package.

Turning away from that troubling thought, trying to sound casual, he said, "Raising a young boy on your own can't be easy. Have you always been responsible for Dylan?"

Suddenly the focus of all his attention, Rachel cautiously reached for her own cup. "Yes." The cup was warm. She wrapped her fingers around it. Nevertheless, his next words sent a chill up her arm—straight to her heart.

"What about Laurel?"

Her mouth tightened. "What do you want to know?"

He cleared his throat. "Where was she?"

Rachel took a moment before answering. "After Dylan was born, Laurel was very unhappy. She needed to get away."

"So she left Dylan?"

"She left him with me. She came to see him whenever she could." She added a few details.

Jared learned that Rachel's aunt and uncle had been

wonderful; they'd helped her finish college. She'd taken advantage of on-campus daycare while attending classes. Apparently she'd had no social life. Although Jared didn't discover anything new about Dylan, he learned that Rachel had sacrificed her youth for the boy. She didn't seem to realize how unusual that was.

With each question, he watched her withdraw further and further. He felt like an interrogator...like an unfeeling brute pulling the wings off a fragile butterfly. And for what? So that he could take Dylan from her?

Before making a move, Jared needed to get acquainted with the boy, to lessen the shock when it came—to know whether this odd tenuous bond he felt with this child was real, or all in his mind—or his heart.

Jared glanced at his watch. "I should be going, I've still got other cases." He pushed away from the table. He had to see Rachel again—for more than the obvious reasons. "Thanks for the coffee. Maybe we could do this again."

"Mmm," was her noncommittal response. She collected the used mugs, then set them in the sink.

As far as refusals went, hers left Jared with no room to argue. He'd heard Rachel use the same tone with Dylan, which didn't do much for a man's ego. Of course, his masculine ego wasn't at stake here...was it?

Over the next week or so, a green pickup truck could be seen parked in Rachel's driveway with enough regularity to start tongues wagging. One day, when Mary Ellen wasn't available to stay with Dylan, her mother volunteered to fill in. "Are you sure you don't mind?" Rachel asked when she dropped him off in the morning.

"Not at all," Nora insisted. "Dylan's a joy to have around." She was a kind, warmhearted woman, naturally friendly and inquisitive when it came to her new neighbors. The entire O'Neil family had taken Rachel and Dylan under its protective wing—for which Rachel was grateful, except when it came to answering questions concerning her personal life.

"Have you got time for a cup of tea?" Nora said.

Hoping to avoid one of Nora's "heart to heart" talks, Rachel refused politely. "I'm running late for work."

Nora just smiled. "Mary Ellen tells me Jared Carlisle's been spending a lot of time at your house."

"Just to see the puppies." Rachel eased her way from the kitchen, down the hall, to the front door.

Nora followed. "That's not what Mary Ellen said."

With one hand on the doorknob, Rachel stopped. "What did she say?"

"Well, I don't know about you, but it seems like Dylan's got a huge crush on the man. He needs a father. Seems like he's decided Jared's a good candidate for the job."

Rachel closed her eyes. "Oh, God."

Smiling, Nora said gently, "Maybe I shouldn't ask, but were you in love with Dylan's father?"

"He's my sister's child, but he's always been with me."

"Is that why you never married?"

"Not really. At first, Dylan and school took up every minute of the day," she admitted. "Then, when I finally came up for air, I discovered all the suitable men in town were taken, and the rest were too old, too young or too married."

Nora laughed. "Well, you could do a lot worse than Jared. The Carlisles are good people. Ira's a little testy at times, and there was all that trouble years ago with the mother, but Jessie and Jared turned out okay."

Rachel shook off the urge to ask for more details. "I really do have to go...." She made her escape.

But she couldn't escape Nora's words—Dylan had decided Jared would make a good father.

Thus, a few days later, when Jared stopped by with the casual invitation, "I thought we could go out for pizza, you, Dylan and I," Rachel balked.

She was thinking of Dylan when she said, "I don't think that's a good idea."

Jared raised an eyebrow. "Why isn't it a good idea?"

"This is difficult to put into words, but you may have noticed that Dylan is a very friendly little boy."

"He's a great kid. You must be proud of him."

"Yes, well." Rachel took a deep breath. "Of course, I'm proud of Dylan, but his openness often leads to his getting hurt. He puts his faith in people too easily."

"I'm not sure I follow you. Why don't you spell it out?"

"He likes you," she said. "I don't want him getting ideas."

"Let me get this straight. You're turning down a date with me because I included Dylan in the invitation."

"Please understand, he'll read more into it." She sighed. "He has a habit of getting attached to people, then he doesn't understand when they drop out of his life."

By "people" Jared guessed she meant men. Although he didn't like it, he had to admit she had a point. He had no serious intentions toward Dylan's lovely aunt—not honorable ones.

Rachel was simply a means to get at the answers concerning Dylan. Wasn't she?

Considering himself well-warned, Jared said, "Are you protecting Dylan? Or yourself?"

She stiffened. "It doesn't really matter, does it?"

Jared shrugged. "I suppose not. But just as a matter of interest...you did let Drew get close."

"That's different. He's Dylan's father."

Jared caught the ring of conviction in her voice. It made him pause—she was so sure that Drew was Dylan's father.

Could she be right?

Hours later, after making a couple of emergency calls, Jared got home. Stones End felt empty, silent, unlike Rachel's house which was crowded, lively, warm—like her. He held the screen door so it wouldn't slam and wake his father.

He needn't have bothered.

Ira was up, sitting in his usual chair by the window, listening to his favorite music—Scottish marching bands. Along with Ira's Scots-Welsh ancestry, the Celtic music was bred into his bones. Jared had grown up with the pipes and drums, drilled with the knowledge of what it meant to be brave and honorable and true. His father accepted nothing less. Now, Ira stared at his son. "You went to see that Hale woman." A low rumble of drums accompanied the words.

"Her name is Rachel," Jared responded tightly.

Ira's eyes narrowed. "What's that got to do with it? Have you talked to her?"

"I'm handling things my way." Jared hid his confusion. What the hell was he doing? Why was he feeling defensiv ? He was growing fond of Dylan, which was fine, but falling for Rachel wasn't part of the plan. What plan? No matter how much he tried to deny it, Rachel wasn't like other women he'd known; she stirred emotions he'd never felt before.

He frowned. What was he thinking? Why was he letting

his feelings for Dylan spill on to the boy's aunt? Rachel wasn't for him. Physically, she was everything he admired in a woman, and then some. But then, he wasn't looking for a woman. And if he was, she would need more than silky hair, soft skin, and softer eyes—eyes that reminded him of delicate, blue-violet chicory blossoms.

A blunt, "Did you learn anything?" reminded Jared of his father's presence. It also reminded him that love had turned Ira into a bitter man.

Jared had no intention of going down that dead-end road. His mouth tightened. "No. It's too soon."

Ira rose wearily. "That boy is eight years old. Seems to me enough years have passed without dragging this out." As usual, Ira had cut to the basic truth—no matter how unpalatable.

Nevertheless, Jared held his ground. "There's too much at stake." He couldn't explain his feelings. Frustrated by Rachel's apparent distrust of men, her need to maintain her independence, and her protective attitude toward Dylan, he didn't know why he was hesitating.

"Humph, have it your own way." When Ira switched off the music, the silence felt heavy.

Jared watched his father leave the room, knowing he'd let him down again. In truth, they'd let each other down. He wished he had a ready answer, but the question of Rachel and Dylan wasn't that easy to resolve. They had feelings.

Jared had feelings—too many.

His father needn't have worried about his getting at the truth about Dylan. Even if Jared's conscience allowed evasion, the years of upheaval in the Carlisle family was a lesson. The situation with Dylan was hauntingly similar, with one exception—there was still time to learn the facts,

to stake a claim. Above all, Jared wanted the boy to know
he was loved and wanted.

Wasn't that what everyone wanted?

Over the next days, Jared had to face facts. So far, his
acquaintance with Rachel had yielded no new details concerning Dylan's birth. Left with little choice, Jared asked
his lawyer to make some discreet inquiries.

At the end of the week, the man handed Jared a copy
of his findings. Although inconclusive, there was nothing
to refute Jared's suspicions. The record showed that Laurel Rina Hale had given birth to Dylan Graham Hale on
August fifteenth at two-twelve in the morning—nine
months, give or take a few days, from the day Jared and
Laurel made love—one more piece of the puzzle. The
father's name was blank. For one long moment, Jared
stared at that empty space and felt the weight of the past.
Because of one reckless act, a child had been cheated of
his birthright. Jared felt guilty of neglect and so many
other emotions that had no name—they were too new.
Belated and raw. But no amount of breast-beating would
change the situation. He could never regain the missing
years. He could only be there for his son in the future. If
Dylan was his son....

Jared's gaze ran down the remaining facts, weight:
seven pounds, fourteen ounces. Height: twenty-one
inches. Blood type didn't reveal anything. A smudged
footprint measured the length of Jared's thumb. With a
slight smile, he traced the delicate imprint—so tiny, so
perfect—faded with time. It blurred as Jared blinked away
a surprising surge of emotion. He couldn't afford senti-
ment, he had to think.

His lawyer said, ''You could simply walk away from
this.''

Jared grit his teeth. "No." There were some truths he couldn't evade—blood ties were one of them. He couldn't walk away from his son—not when he'd experienced a family split. He knew what it was like to search for a family resemblance in a face in a crowd.

The lawyer reshuffled some papers on his desk. "The aunt has no legal right. If DNA tests come back positive and this goes to court, you'll win hands down."

Somehow, the words didn't reassure Jared. He would win, which meant someone had to lose.

Chapter Five

Change was in the air. August drifted into September; Indian summer weather set in. Dylan started school.

And Rachel's job came to an abrupt end.

The Pierce Sawmill filed for bankruptcy. In a daze, Rachel accepted her lack-of-work notice. She'd recognized the signs of financial failure weeks earlier, but she wasn't prepared. As the dust settled in the old post-and-beam building, the silence was unnerving. For the first time since Rachel met Evan, he wore an air of failure.

"The loans came due all at once." He looked as if he hadn't slept. "In the end, we simply ran out of time." He sorted through a pile of correspondence—much of it red-inked. "If anyone comes looking for me, just tell them I'm out. Damn Drew for getting us into this mess!"

Rachel sighed. "Don't you think he's paying?"

Evan laughed harshly. "Maybe spending some time in prison will knock some sense into him!"

Or maybe it would break him, she thought sadly as she handed more correspondence to Evan.

He threw it into a box. "My mother still has her heart set on you joining the family on the coast. I hope you won't disappoint her."

Rachel could feel the power of the Pierces closing in on her. They wanted Dylan. "Can I think about it?"

"You haven't got much time," he apologized. "I'm afraid the cottage is part of the sawmill property. We bought it for the land, and never got around to expanding. It's yours until the end of the month, but that's the best I can do."

With a second unexpected blow, Rachel felt at sea, as if her life had gone adrift. "I'll have to make arrangements."

"If you need anything—job references, relocation— call me. I'll be in town for another week or two." Evan handed her a business card with his home phone number. "We've got several real estate projects going. I'm sure we could find a place for you."

Rachel accepted the card, even though she didn't intend to use it. Nevertheless, when she returned to her desk, she tucked it into her purse—just in case. She had her pride, but she had to think of Dylan as well. In less than four weeks, she would have no roof over her head. She'd thought she'd found a home in Henderson, but like so many things in her life, the situation proved temporary. Moving on, starting over, had been a way of life while growing up with her parents.

Orphaned at twelve, she'd arrived at the Stillwater Inn with all her worldly possessions in one small suitcase. She'd done her very best to belong. And there, she'd stayed—while people came and went. Some were more friendly than others, but they were strangers nonetheless.

Her aunt and uncle were generous, loving. Rachel had a room at the Inn, but it was never home. Sometimes, she wondered if such a place existed. In any case, she'd survived a disruptive childhood, but she wanted so much more than that for Dylan.

Rachel spent the next hour cleaning out her desk. She hadn't worked there long enough to accumulate many personal items. Everything fit into her tote bag.

Half an hour later, she left the building.

To get out of the millyard, she had to cross a phalanx of disgruntled men. Earlier, she'd handed out final payroll checks with lack-of-work slips. The men were understandably angry and frustrated. Her involvement with the Pierces made her an obvious target. She almost turned back to the safety of her office.

Instead of moving aside, one man took a threatening step toward her. A crude pass drew laughter. "You're wasting your time," someone taunted. "She's Drew's woman."

Rachel heard footsteps; she took a hasty step and felt her ankle twist. Someone grabbed her arm. In shock, she turned to find Jared. Her breath came out in relief. It lasted a second before he started to drag her away.

"Come on," he said, "let's get out of here."

Before Rachel could respond, she found herself lifted onto the seat of the dilapidated green pickup truck. He'd left the motor running.

Jared climbed in and started off. "I heard there might be trouble. Did they hurt you?" His voice had an edge.

Concern?

"No," she gasped, alarmed at the thready sound of her voice. Inwardly, she burned with humiliation, aware that Jared must have heard the taunts and laughter linking her and Drew. He probably believed it. She hadn't seen him since she turned down his casual invitation to dinner.

He hit the brakes at the traffic light. ''You should have turned back. That was a damned fool thing to do!''

''They wouldn't have touched me.''

Jared gave her a disbelieving look. ''You think not? Some of those men believe in an eye for an eye.''

Feeling the color rush out of her face, Rachel said, ''If you're trying to frighten me, you've succeeded.''

''Good.'' He returned his gaze to the empty crossroad. ''So, that puts an end to your job. Have you made plans?''

''I haven't had a moment to think.'' Rachel felt no need to share her fears—or Evan's offer of a safety net—with a near stranger, no matter how drawn she felt to Jared.

She glanced out the window. The view of the sawmill did nothing to lift her mood. Spread out over several acres, the lumberyard was the size of several football fields, littered with timber in varying stages of processing, from harvested trees to processed hardwood. Trucks and heavy equipment made up a good chunk of the Pierce inventory. Today, it lay idle. There were several buildings—all closed up.

The traffic light turned green. In silence, they drove the short distance to Rachel's house.

Jared was aware of her tight-lipped silence. Despite the bravado, she looked tense and frightened. He regretted his harsh words, as well as the fact that she'd lost her job. Without a doubt, it complicated everything. He pulled up in front of her house and stared at the neat white cottage. It was part of the Pierce property. Was she?

A child's bike sat in the driveway…along with Drew's bright red sports car.

She spoke, a slight quake to her voice. ''I should thank you. I seem to be doing a lot of that lately.''

Jared heard the nervous tremor and turned to look at her. "Don't thank me. I just happened to be there. You should call the police." Feeling unexplainably protective, Jared reminded himself that she belonged to Drew. The men had shouted it, and Rachel had made no attempt to deny it.

"That's not necessary, nothing happened. In any case, I'm sure I could have handled it."

Jared smiled. She didn't give an inch—he liked that about her. In her straight black skirt and white knit top, with her bright hair smoothed back from her face with a wide black hairband, she didn't fit the image of any man's mistress. "Those men could be dangerous. They're just looking for an excuse to start trouble."

She glanced away. "Yes, well..." Her hand shook as she reached for the door handle and pushed. When nothing happened, she pushed again.

"That door sticks." Jared reached across. His hand covered hers on the handle, and the move brought them in close proximity. Too close.

Rachel felt the brush of his hard shoulder against hers and tried to make herself small. She was tall and not exactly reed slim; and right now, there didn't seem to be enough room to breathe, much less claim her own space.

Jared heard her breath catch, felt the soft flutter against his face, and knew she was just as affected by their closeness as he was. Trying to ignore the heady, elusive scent of her perfume, he held her startled gaze for a long moment. Her eyes were blue and innocent, shaded by lush eyelashes. He wished her vulnerability didn't touch him. He was going to hurt her—there was no way around it. The truth about Dylan would have to come out. With the mill closing, his timetable had just stepped up. She was enchanting. What if he kissed her? What if he simply drew her into his arms and kissed her fears and all her objections away?

If the situation were different, he might pursue Rachel for real. But she was Laurel's twin—Dylan's aunt—and too much stood between them. He wrenched his gaze away from the tempting sight she made. One push and the door opened.

Rachel slipped out.

A moment later, Jared followed. He noticed her limp, then swore under his breath and lifted her in his arms. "Why didn't you say you were hurt?"

At his accusing tone, the color drained from her face. Nevertheless, in that stubborn, tight-lipped voice he was beginning to recognize, she insisted, "It's nothing. Just a twinge." She sounded annoyed, then subsided when his arms tightened their hold. "This isn't necessary. I can walk."

Inwardly, Rachel fumed when he ignored her. Creating a scene would only make her feel foolish. Besides, her ankle did hurt. She hated to admit a weakness, but it felt good to have someone to lean on, if only for a moment or two. For some reason, Jared made her feel safe and secure—something rare in her experience of men. He bore her weight with ease. Either her latest diet was working miracles, or he was stronger than he looked. In any case, he wasn't breathing hard as he carried her up the walk, then up the porch stairs.

At the door, she reached to turn the doorknob. "Please, put me down."

"I intend to—in a minute. You really should lock your doors." Why this need to protect her? Jared wondered. Under the circumstances, it was damned inconvenient.

Jared walked into the house. It felt good to be there. Water gurgled in the fish tank, hamsters scratched in sawdust—Rachel's house was full of life, love and laughter. Everything Jared could possibly want in life was here— under one solid roof, within four impenetrable walls.

Like a lone wolf, lured yet repelled by a flame, he felt drawn to her and Dylan—not sure what he was looking for—yet aware that whatever it was, he'd found it. Now, he was afraid to lose it. He wanted Dylan. Maybe Rachel was part of the package. Was that so bad? Or did it have a certain appeal? He'd never given a moment's thought to "courting Rachel." Now that he did, it seemed logical.

Maybe it was the answer to all his problems—marry Rachel and adopt Dylan. The truth could remain buried, his father would just have to accept it—Rachel and Dylan need never know. Jared frowned at that. Could he build his life around a lie, even if it was well intended?

Gently, he set her down in the small kitchen. She leaned back against the table and gingerly tested her foot.

She took a breath. "I think I just twisted it."

With the shades drawn against the sun, the house was dim, shadowed, a cool welcome after the heat outside. Jared didn't feel particularly cool. He meant to leave. Instead, he offered to get some ice for her ankle, adding, "Sit."

Rachel sat, irritated at the barked order. "I suppose," she bristled, "that bedside manner works on your patients."

He looked up, his startled gaze quickly gave way to a wicked gleam. "Be careful, or I might demonstrate."

Rachel blushed fiery red. Embarrassed, she had only herself to blame. Their relationship was so platonic, she'd begun to wonder if there was something wrong with her— or him. Deciding she needed the reminder, she said, "Dylan should be home from school any minute."

He ignored the warning. "I should check to make sure

you haven't got a serious injury. I'm only a country vet, but I do know anatomy. A sprain is a sprain.''

She sat back. ''All right.'' What was the point of arguing? When he knelt down at her feet, she took a deep breath and slipped off her shoe. She felt foolish and unsure, wondering why the mere thought of his touching her made her pulse race. The first contact was just as she feared—electric. Leaving a scorching path, he gently cupped the heel of her foot, then ran an exploratory thumb over her instep. Trying to remain immune, she tried to imagine him checking a horse's hoof or a cow....

With his head bent in concentration, she couldn't see his expression and had no idea if her response was totally one-sided. He was obviously experienced with the opposite sex, while she'd never had time for men, never trusted one to get this close. Jared's hands were firm and gentle. His touch felt familiar, which was insane.

He rotated her ankle—she winced, welcoming the slight pain when it pulled her out of a sensual haze.

''Did that hurt?'' He glanced up, and their glances locked.

Some inner reflex made her deny it. ''No.'' She didn't blink an eye—afraid any reaction might betray how she felt. How did she feel? Like her bones were slowly dissolving and rearranging her into someone new.

Jared observed her heightened color with interest. ''The swelling's gone down. It might be a little sore for a couple of days.'' Before he could add anything, the door flew open.

Dylan called out, ''Mom, I'm home.''

Jared dropped Rachel's foot. Dylan's arrival tore them apart—as if they were guilty of something lurid.

Jared recovered first. ''Hi, Dylan.''

Rachel stood, putting weight on her ankle, and winced, unable to disguise her painful reaction.

Dylan noticed. "What's wrong?"

Rachel said, "Nothing, it's only…"

Jared interrupted her midsentence. "Actually, your mom hurt her ankle. It will be fine by tomorrow." He smiled reassuringly at Dylan. "How about us guys making dinner while she gives it a rest?"

Before Rachel could object, she found herself sitting in a comfortable chair in the living room with her leg propped up on a footrest. When Jared searched though some magazines on the coffee table and handed her one on hooked rugs, she snapped, "I'm perfectly capable of making dinner."

Jared leaned over her, challenging softly, "So am I, and Dylan's going to help. Do you have a problem with that?"

With one glance at Dylan, who looked delighted, Rachel subsided. "What are we having?"

"Hamburgers are my specialty."

Wordlessly, she nodded.

Half an hour later, Rachel gave up on the magazine. She tossed it aside, feeling an odd discontent. Jared was so clever—manipulating her into accepting his presence, then taking over. He'd invited himself to dinner by offering to make it. He and Dylan were hard at it. From the sounds coming from the kitchen, they were having a hilarious time. Jared's masculine laughter mingled with Dylan's little boy giggles. Rachel leaned her head back and closed her eyes.

A man in the kitchen cooking dinner, keeping Dylan entertained, while she sat and relaxed with her feet propped up—it was a fantasy come true. Why was she fighting it?

Who was she trying to protect—herself or Dylan?

Why couldn't she accept her good fortune? Was she so conditioned to expect the worst from life? She frowned, hating to admit it might be true. Life had dealt Rachel her share of blows, but that was no excuse to stop believing in love. Was it?

Rachel resolved to do better, which got her through dinner—scorched hamburgers and cold french fries. Ice cream for dessert. At eight o'clock, Rachel sent Dylan to brush his teeth and get ready for bed.

Aware that he'd outworn his welcome, Jared was loath to end the evening. They hadn't discussed Dylan.

Again.

Jared had waited for the right moment, which never arrived. Would there ever be a right time to break Rachel's heart?

To his surprise, she walked him to the door. "How's the ankle?" he asked.

She looked down at her foot—as if she'd forgotten all about it. "Just a twinge. It's fine."

He knew he should leave.

Something held him there.

He wanted to kiss her; the urge was strong, deep and damn near irresistible. But there was that blasted red sports car parked in her driveway—a reminder of Drew.

They were in the front hall. He lowered his voice to keep it from drifting upstairs and disturbing Dylan. "Before I leave, there's just one thing I'd like to know."

She stopped. "What's that?"

Jared reached and slowly drew her forward, surprised when she didn't resist. "Were those men at the sawmill right about you?" When her body stiffened, he felt it.

"About what?" she whispered, obviously sensing a trap.

"Do you belong to Drew?"

She shook her head vehemently. "No!"

Her silky hair brushed his hand. "Good—because I made a rule a long time ago that I'd never tangle with Drew's possessions, and I was just about to break that rule."

Jared gave her time to turn away.

Rachel wanted to turn aside...but something kept her rooted, even when he pressed her closer. Her blouse was thin cotton, so she could feel his heart pounding against hers, a startling discovery that made her heart pound in the same rhythm. His mouth slowly lowered over hers, gently stealing her breath, taking her mouth, and shattering her conception of Jared Carlisle. He might be impossible, interfering, and confusing at times, but she didn't dislike him after all.

Jared's eyes were dark, almost black, when he raised his head. "I've wanted to do that from the moment I saw you."

The first time?

At the reminder of their meeting outside the courtroom, Rachel drew away. "Are you still confusing me for Laurel?"

When her words sank in, Jared drew in a sharp breath, then searched for a way to reassure her, but there was none. "I guess you'll have to decide that for yourself."

She blinked, visibly confused. "What is that supposed to mean?"

"It means I was barely acquainted with her," he admitted, which was true...as far as it went. Rachel's mention of her twin was the opening Jared needed to bring up the subject of Dylan, but suddenly, he couldn't take that next step. She'd just lost her job, her future was unsure—how could he add to her burden? "We need to talk.'' He captured her soft blue eyes, took a deep breath, then added, ''But not tonight.''

Rachel gazed at him, waiting for a further explanation. When none was forthcoming, she bid him good-night with a sense of frustration. He'd left so much unsaid.

How could she trust a man who kissed her as if he meant it, but still remained a total enigma? Though she tried to put all the doubts out of her head, she wondered if his relationship with Laurel had been as casual as he claimed.

Was she a fool to let that matter?

Later, Rachel tucked Dylan into bed. She leaned over and kissed him, loving the clean little boy smell of soap and gel toothpaste.

Dylan said, ''I like Jared. I think he likes you.''

''Mmm.'' She smoothed the covers over his chest.

''I think I might be a vet when I grow up.''

''And I think you think too much,'' Rachel kissed him with a light laugh. ''Now how about going to sleep?''

She went to her own room where she undressed. She unbuttoned her blouse. Underneath was a locket on a long thin gold chain, a gift from her parents on her twelfth birthday. Laurel had always worn an identical one.

When Jared looked at Rachel, who did he see?

He'd kissed her, but who had he kissed? And why did it matter so much? Why did Jared resurrect all the old insecurities she'd thought long resolved?

Tonight, she'd deliberately placed the reminder of Laurel between them—to test him? If so, he'd failed. He'd given Rachel no reassurance, he'd asked for nothing from her, and promised nothing in return.

At the thought, Rachel felt chilled. She took a long warm bath, then climbed into bed. A slight breeze stirred the sheer curtains at her window.

A harvest moon—round and pale, more silver than gold, bathed her bedroom with a white light and searched out shadows, making her aware of the emptiness.

Until lately, she'd always felt safe in this room, this house. Tonight, she felt alone.

Rachel didn't sleep well.

She dreamed of Laurel. It was always the same—they stood on opposite sides of a choppy river with Laurel daring her to cross, and teasing when she wouldn't. Mama had forbidden them to play there, which only drew Laurel more and more. When they went home, Papa was waiting, leaning against his car. He swung Laurel around. "How's my best girl?"

When he saw Rachel, he held out his hand and she went. His car was still warm, almost humming, and for a moment, Rachel felt warm too. Mama was there, worrying as usual.

"Did you girls go down to the river?" She looked at Rachel for answers—because Rachel was supposed to look out for her twin.

Laurel's green eyes dared her to tattle. Rachel's eyes were blue—true blue, Mama always said.

Sometimes, it was hard to love Laurel, but Rachel didn't want to get her twin in trouble. Besides, Laurel always got even. "No, Mama," Rachel lied, and felt her soul shrivel up at the disappointment in her mother's eyes. And she vowed she'd never tell another lie as long as she lived.

And Laurel just laughed....

The blaring sound of the alarm shocked Rachel awake. It was early, the day had broken, yet everything seemed so gray, so unfinished. Her eyes felt scratchy and dry with unshed tears. She felt exhausted; she'd dreamed of Laurel—an old recurring dream that came whenever she felt troubled. Her sister's life was so unfinished—sometimes Rachel felt she was living it, as if her own life hadn't started yet.

Breakfast at Stones End was strained.

The Carlisles always gathered in times of trouble. Jared was the center of attention. The scrambled eggs turned cold, the toast dried, and no one noticed.

"You didn't tell her," Ira said, furious at what he clearly saw as another delaying tactic.

Jared had counted on his sister's support, but even Jessie shook her head in disapproval. "You should have told Rachel the truth when you first suspected," she said, "before you got to know her and Dylan."

Jared hedged. "I was hoping to soften the blow."

Jessie's expression held little sympathy. "Well, there's no way you can avoid hurting her."

When Jessie looked at Ben, silently communicating her concern, Jared realized he'd probably never have that soul connection with anyone. Ben simply offered, "Anytime you need to talk, Jared, I'm willing to listen."

"Thanks." There was only one person Jared needed to talk to and that was Rachel. Hopefully, she wouldn't hate him too much. What could he say—that he'd slept with Laurel and suspected he was Dylan's father...that he had no excuse except that he'd been eighteen years old at the time, and stupid and reckless and selfish...that he'd left town the following day and never set eyes on Laurel again...that she'd never told him she was pregnant? And if she had, what would he have done about it? But she hadn't told him, and he'd never had to make that decision—until now.

Youth, ignorance, lust—nothing justified his behavior. No matter which words he chose, he was guilty as hell.

Would Rachel understand? Would she forgive?

He thought of the honesty that shone from her eyes. And the vulnerability. How could he cushion the blow? How could he get at the truth without inviting Rachel's hatred? He needed her cooperation. He needed her trust.

But which came first?

Jared had to admit he didn't have a clue. Nothing in life had prepared him to be a father—a belated one at that. His own father hadn't exactly set a shining example. If Dylan was still an infant, Jared might grow into the role; but an eight-year-old was an entirely different deal. Yes, Rachel was going to hate him. He despised himself.

Looking at the half-eaten remains of breakfast, Jared pushed his plate aside and started to leave, but Ira's next words stopped him cold. "And now she's leaving."

"She's leaving!" That bore repeating.

Ira nodded. "She's planning to go…" He still refused to use her name. "That Hale woman" had become "she" or "her"—anything but "Rachel." Jared had given up on trying to reshape his father's opinion—uncomfortably aware that he'd inherited the same stubborn streak. Now, Ira's voice rose. "I heard she's going to the Pierces. Evan offered to take her with him. It's all around town."

It was all around town.

Jared frowned. Why was he always the last to hear the gossip? Perhaps he didn't mix in the right circles. He'd been spending all his free time with Dylan and Rachel. And she hadn't said a word. Last night, he'd kissed her and felt her lean into him in an all-too-brief moment of surrender—yet she hadn't revealed that she was leaving town!

Why did women always cut and run?

Chapter Six

Jared needed to see Rachel. The sky looked low and bruised. Black thunderheads gathered against the hills and rolled into the valley.

Confusion, anger and disappointment drove him to Rachel's house. He turned into the driveway.

Instead of getting out immediately, he cut the motor and stared at the small white house surrounded by tall pine trees and low, trim barberry shrubs. It looked safe and secure, bounded by nature, tranquil and unruffled, and he was about to invade it with an ugly revelation that would cast a cloud over so many innocent lives.

Jared climbed out of the truck, unsure of his next step, except that it had to be taken. Waiting for an ideal moment to confront his past was no longer an option.

The dog started to bark, instantly shattering Rachel's peaceful morning. She was alone; Dylan was in school. She was gardening, trying to stay busy and not panic about the loss of her job. She was planting a mix of tulip and daffodil bulbs in small clumps of three or four instead of rigid rows. Gardening always soothed her. Earlier, she'd done some laundry, then made a few calls, beginning the painstaking process of finding new employment. Faced with necessity, she didn't have the luxury of thinking in terms of a career move. There was an opening at the bank, but with so many layoffs, the chances of getting the job were slim. The Stillwater Inn should be reopening soon. But work there was seasonal, another temporary fix. She needed something more secure. Evan's offer could be the solution.

Moving closer to Drew's family didn't have to mean giving in to their demands. It was the practical solution, perhaps the only one. But somehow, she couldn't make that decision. It would mean leaving northern Maine, with its wild beauty and untapped resources, and all she'd grown to love. It meant leaving Jared.

Jared was in her thoughts when he arrived. Lately, he was seldom out of them. Frowning at that admission, Rachel pushed herself up from the mulched bed.

Although their relationship had never gone much beyond friendship—except for one not-so-casual kiss, she couldn't deny that the thought of never seeing him again left an aching emptiness in her heart. Watching him cross the lawn, Rachel wanted him to go away, she wanted him to stay; in all honesty, she didn't know what she wanted, but suspected it was about six-foot-two, with chiseled features, fair hair that needed a trim, and eyes the color of granite. Wearing faded blue jeans, he cut his long stride at the sight of her.

She'd never seen him take an awkward step. Something was wrong. He stopped under the shade of the oak tree, his eyes shadowed. There was something hard and determined about him.

Last night, he'd said they had to talk.

She broke the silence first. "What's wrong?" She took a step toward him.

Recalling her hurt ankle, he asked, "Are you okay?"

"I'm fine."

"I heard some crazy story about Evan offering you a job." Jared drew in a deep breath and slowly released it as he took in Rachel's appearance—her worn jeans, the gardening gloves, the cultivated bed of brown earth behind her. His father was wrong. Why would she plant flowers if she was leaving? "They said you were moving away."

Head bent, Rachel slowly pulled off the gloves. "I have to look for a job. Evan offered to help. That's all."

"When were you going to tell me?" His voice was hard.

Visibly startled at his tone, her gaze flashed back to him. "I don't know. At this stage, nothing's definite."

Jared looked for a handy target—besides Rachel. His gaze landed on the tulip bulbs. Although brown and dry in a dormant stage, once planted, they would survive the winter frost and bloom in spring…but Rachel wouldn't be there. Everyone knew—but him. The mere thought infuriated him.

He exploded, "If you're leaving, then tell me—why the hell are you planting tulips?" None of this made sense. It was too sudden, too abrupt—as if someone had cut off his lifeline. A heart line.

She glanced at the flower bed. "It's time, I always plant tulips in the fall." She shrugged. "Anyway, even if we leave, someone else will be here to enjoy them."

Jared's blood pressure rose another notch.

Someone else would be there. Not Rachel. Would spring come, would flowers ever bloom for Rachel? Didn't she ever think of herself? For once, he'd like to know what Rachel wanted. She obviously hadn't included him in her plans, or even thought to keep him informed. Admittedly, he'd never given her a solid reason to place her faith in him, but that small piece of logic escaped him at the moment.

Suspicious of a woman's staying power, he refused to accept any form of evasion. "So, where will you go? What will you do?"

Surprisingly, she had an answer to both. "I have some savings to tide me over for a while. The Pierces would like time with Dylan, which is long overdue. We might stay with them while I look for a job on the coast."

"Did Evan offer you a position?"

She stiffened. "Evan offered, but I didn't accept. I have experience in hotel management, not real estate."

So, she wasn't financially dependent on the Pierces. Somehow, that didn't relieve Jared as much as it should. He asked, "Why didn't you mention any of this last night?"

Gloves off, she tucked them into her jeans pocket. "The subject never came up."

"You knew I'd be interested."

Rachel didn't appreciate his possessive tone. She shook her head in confusion. "Why should I?" They were little more than friends. He'd kissed her once, which hardly qualified as a relationship.

"I don't want you to leave." His blunt admission drove the breath from her lungs. "I care about what happens to you—you and Dylan."

Rachel stared, bewildered. He cared? What did that mean? All morning, a storm had been building. The sky took on a more ominous gray, thunder sounded closer, a few scattered drops of rain struck the ground. Her face. She tried to ignore them as she replied, "That's very kind of you, but we've been on our own for a long time."

Apparently determined to have his say, he continued, "If it's a job you need, I can use an assistant at the clinic. Think of it as something temporary if you like—until we can come up with something more permanent."

After sorting through all that information, Rachel was more puzzled than ever. "But what about Jessie?"

He had an answer for that. "Jessie and her husband will be leaving in the fall, after the harvest. They have a horse farm in Virginia."

Apparently he had this all worked out. She wished he'd let her in on his plans sooner. "But I don't know a thing about animals."

"You could keep the books, answer the phone."

Rachel smiled at that generic job description, unable to accept, no matter how tempted. When her parents died, she'd become the object of charity at the age of twelve, forced to depend on strangers for her survival. Since then, she'd struggled to make her own way. Accepting help from Drew had been a mistake. "You don't have to create a position for me," she said, determined to maintain her independence.

"Then, what about Dylan? I thought he liked it here."

"He does, but..."

"Then don't go," he said quietly.

When he added nothing, she laughed shakily. For one insane moment, she'd thought he was going to say he'd fallen in love with her. It happened, didn't it—love at first sight? But not to her. Stifling that small hope, Rachel insisted, "I have to do what's best for Dylan."

A touch of sarcasm crept into his voice. "And you

think dragging an eight-year-old boy around the state is best.''

''No, of course not, but I don't have a choice.''

Choices.

Faced with a difficult one, Jared felt the weight of responsibility. The next step was entirely up to him.

By now, the rain was falling in earnest. Rachel's hair glistened with dampness, curling around her pale oval face. With her blue cotton sweater clinging to her, emphasizing the generous curve of her breasts, she looked ravishing, and wary and vulnerable. Jared looked away, knowing what he had to say next would change the way she felt about him—forever.

He said heavily, ''Let's go inside, you're soaked.''

The move granted him a brief reprieve.

While Rachel changed into some dry clothes, Jared made coffee—just to give himself something to do.

The storm struck overhead, and wind rattled the windows, closing out the rest of the world. While Jared waited for the coffee to perk, he took a seat at the table. He stared out the window. Drops of rain washed down the glass.

Gradually, small puddles formed…undoing Rachel's efforts and turning her flower bed into soggy ground.

Jared heard her moving around, doors opening and closing, then her footsteps hurrying down the stairs. He didn't want to hurt Rachel, she obviously loved her twin sister.

He wondered how much—or how little—he could tell, and still get at the truth.

Rachel found him in the kitchen. She tried to smile. ''Ah, coffee. It's almost noon, I could make sandwiches.''

''No, thanks…I can't stay long.'' He stood, slipped his

hands into his back pockets. "We have to talk. I've put this off, but I guess there's no right way to say this."

She held his glance. "Whatever it is, please, just go ahead and say it."

He nodded. "When I first met you, I had no idea Dylan existed. I hadn't heard from your sister in years."

"What does Dylan have to do with you?"

She gasped when he said, "I think he's my son." The words shocked her to silence. He continued, "I met Laurel nine years ago...around the time you were away at college. I went to the Stillwater Inn...."

Rachel backed away. "I don't want to hear this!"

He reached for her hand and felt it tremble. "I need to tell you. You need to know."

Pulling free, she shook her head. "No! No, I don't."

"Yes." And the words followed.

She went into the living room, and sank onto the couch. Jared sat beside her—not close.

"Sunny was my dog," he said. "Not Drew's. Laurel must have known I'd find out someday."

He spoke in a low-toned voice, as if each word was torn from some deep, private place inside. Even in her own pain, Rachel realized he was hurting too. With each additional revelation, she felt her heart breaking, crushed, until the pain numbed. At length, she watched his lips move, but his voice grew more distant—she couldn't make out the words.

The details meant nothing.

When he stopped, the silence was deafening.

Rachel couldn't bear to think about Jared's intimate involvement with Laurel. After a moment, she found her voice. It broke over the words, "I don't believe you," but she didn't cry. Anger flashed, then disbelief.

"Why would I make this up?"

She shook her head. "I don't know why, but it's not true. I asked you once, and you assured me there was nothing between you and Laurel," she argued. "You told me the two of you were barely acquainted."

"That's true."

As his meaning sank in, she whispered, "Oh God!"

"I'm not proud of that fact. I can't make any excuses." Nevertheless, he tried. "We were both young, careless."

"Why are you doing this? Why now?"

"Isn't it obvious?" When she shook her head, he stood, paced away, then turned back. "Because I don't want you to leave and take my son with you. I want him in my life."

Rachel gasped in horror. "You want me to give him up?"

Jared's eyes held pity. "I never said that. I don't want anyone hurt, but what if he's my son?"

Unable to bear the meaning of that, Rachel stood up, confronting him. "What if he isn't your son? A few dates. A dog named Sunny. That's all you've got to go on. It could all be coincidence. You can't be sure."

"There are legal methods," he said. "DNA tests. The law covers situations like this. You'd be surprised how common it is."

Only one thing registered. "You spoke to a lawyer?"

"Just a preliminary investigation," he confessed, obviously aware that this betrayal, above all the others, cut into his credibility.

How could Rachel trust him? How could she ever believe in him again? All along, he'd pretended friendship, while he was plotting to take Dylan from her. He'd shattered her trust—what was one more betrayal? Everything she'd felt for Jared was built on lies.

When he tried to speak, she covered her ears in denial. "Get out, get out, get out."

"Rachel." He grabbed her hands, forcing her to listen. "I didn't want to hurt you. If there was any other way—"

She tore free, rubbing her palms together, as if she could obliterate his touch. "You said you aren't sure. What if you're wrong about this?"

"What if I'm right?" He braced himself. "Don't you see? I have to know."

Rachel shook her head. "I want you to go."

"I realize this has been a shock. When you've had time, we can talk some more. You can't run from this, Rachel," he said with some urgency. "Neither can I."

Before walking out, he said, "I'm sorry."

After he left, Rachel couldn't think. She tried to shut everything out…Jared and Laurel, Jared and Dylan. Jared. Jared. Jared. It went round and round in her head. She looked around. How odd—the laundry basket was still where she'd left it earlier…everything looked so normal, as if nothing had changed. Yet everything had. Past, present and future—nothing would ever be the same.

Rachel had built her life around the fact that Dylan was Laurel and Drew's son. Was it all a lie? As a teen, Laurel had been rebellious. She'd found a perfect match in Drew—the typical bad boy opposing his family's dictates. Dylan was the result of that match—or so Rachel had always thought.

What if she was wrong?

What if Jared was right?

Dear God, she couldn't bear the thought of what that could mean! She would lose Dylan. Panic struck at the thought. She couldn't lose Dylan. She couldn't. An icy calm swept over her. Determined to prove Jared wrong, she welcomed the pain-numbing detachment. She would go to Drew, he would explain and all would be back to normal.

The following day, making arrangements to see Drew proved easier than Rachel expected. A call to Evan brought quick results. Without revealing any details, she told him she had to see Drew about an important personal matter.

She was grateful when Evan offered to use some family connections to arrange a meeting between her and Drew who was awaiting an appeal date before being transferred to a federal facility. Two days later, Rachel travelled to Caribou—a distance of some seventy-five miles.

Evan was waiting for her outside the lawyer's office in a brick two-story building. He was openly curious. "Perhaps now, you'll tell me what this is all about."

"I'm sorry, you've been so helpful, but I need to discuss this with Drew." Rachel glanced up at the tall brick building. "Is Drew here yet?"

"They haven't arrived. We can go in and wait." He held the door open, motioning her through with a polite nod. "Look, if my little brother's gotten himself into some kind of jam, I'd like to help."

When his eyes dropped to her slim waist, Rachel felt an almost hysterical urge to laugh—or cry. Obviously Evan believed the lurid gossip about her and Drew, and thought she could be pregnant with Drew's baby. How easily people jumped to all the wrong conclusions!

She found her voice. "It's nothing like that. You've already helped by arranging this meeting."

He shrugged. "Well, if you're sure. Drew should be along in a few minutes. You can wait for him."

The office was on the second floor. Together, they

climbed the stairs and went inside. After saying he'd see her later, Evan left Rachel with the receptionist. The woman showed her into a small conference room. There were several leather chairs arranged around an oval mahogany table.

The room was very masculine, official—obviously meant to impress or intimidate depending on the circumstances.

When the woman left, Rachel took a seat. She wanted this to be over. Trying to find a distraction, she looked around the room, clinging to the small details—the hunting scene on the wall, the thick velvet drapes, the brass clock, the crystal brandy snifter and glasses....

She jumped when the door opened.

Dark and brooding, Drew came in, escorted by a man in police uniform. The two men didn't exchange a word as the guard removed the handcuffs from Drew's wrists, then said, "One hour," before walking out.

That was when Drew turned to Rachel. She gasped at the bruise on his right eye. He touched it self-consciously. "I tripped on some stairs."

"Are you all right?"

He laughed, still cocky, still Drew. "Sure, things couldn't be better." He'd lost weight, but if anything, he looked more handsome than ever. "How about you? And Dylan?"

He took a chair opposite and stared at her, his gaze unwavering. Rachel's spirits sank like lead when she realized there wasn't a hint of curiosity in his dark eyes, not a question as to why she'd come, and she knew—she knew with absolute certainty—that everything Jared had told her about Laurel was true! Deep down inside where Rachel buried all her disappointments, fears and tormenting doubts, she'd always known. Laurel had never been faithful to anyone, not even Drew.

Rachel clenched her hands. "You know why I'm here."

At the statement, he nodded. "It's not hard to guess."

"You knew about Sunny!" Her voice shook. "You knew Jared would eventually learn the truth about Dylan when we moved to Henderson." It wasn't a question. "And yet, you let it happen. Why on earth would you want all this information to come out after all these years?"

Drew leaned back. "Because it was time to end the charade. It's gone on long enough."

Rachel sighed at his terse reply. "Please explain. There have been so many deceptions. I need to know the truth. What really happened?"

"Are you sure you're ready for this?"

"Yes." Rachel folded her hands on the table and waited.

"Nine years ago, two months after we broke up, Laurel claimed she was pregnant with my child. Without going into details," he said dryly, "I knew better, so I got the truth out of her. She admitted that Jared is Dylan's father."

Once said, the words couldn't be recalled. "Why did you wait so many years to tell anyone?" Rachel said in despair.

His mouth twisted, and she realized this was tearing him up. "Because it wasn't my story to tell," he said, his eyes shadowed with regret.

"Please, tell me now."

He hesitated, then shrugged. "I suppose I still had a grudge against Jared, and no one knew. Laurel had kept silent. Finally, when Jared came home to stay, I decided it was time to right old wrongs. The best solution seemed to be to put you three together and let fate take a hand.''

"You decided! What about me?'' Rachel felt betrayed, frightened. Drew had deliberately set her up; he'd never considered how it would affect her. She had no legal right to Dylan. She'd trusted Drew and look where it got her. Jared was the same—stealing beneath her reserves, giving her a false sense of security. "How dare you play God, manipulating the situation!''

At her accusation, Drew's face darkened, but he held on to his temper—maybe jail was teaching him a thing or two. "Dylan is Jared's son.''

"He's mine.'' Rachel's voice shook, but even as she said the words, she knew it wasn't true. She didn't own Dylan. He wasn't hers to keep or give away. She had an obligation to grant Dylan his birthright. Any denial would only lead to more unhappiness.

There were still a few details she needed to clear up.

"Why are you doing this?'' she asked.

For once, Drew didn't have a ready response. When he spoke, his voice held regret piled upon regret. "Maybe because I'm partly to blame for the entire mess. We broke up over a ridiculous argument. She was hurt when I didn't bring her home to meet my parents. So she got even.''

Could Laurel have been that vindictive?

Rachel didn't have the answers. "And yet, all these years, you've made support payments, you let everyone believe Dylan was yours. Why?''

It took him a moment. Drew had probably never examined his own motives too closely. Nevertheless, his confession bore the ring of truth. "Because he's Laurel's son,'' he said huskily. "You know, the irony is that I probably would have agreed to marry her if she hadn't lied.''

"Because you loved her," Rachel whispered. How terribly sad—Drew had loved her, and Laurel had never known.

Drew didn't deny his feelings. Instead, he said, "You can walk out of here, right now. Pick up Dylan, and leave Henderson and Jared behind. Evan will see that you have money." He stood, leaving her to make a decision. "Or you can go back and tell Jared. I have no intention of telling him, or anyone else. It's your choice, Rachel, that's the best I can do," he ended quietly. "I'm sorry."

Rachel stood. With a few words, he'd put an end to a painful chapter in his life—and opened a new uncertain one in hers. There was nothing she could say or do to change things. The past had caught up with the present, and the future was still unknown.

Without a word, Rachel left him there.

Moments later, she found Evan waiting outside.

From the expression on her face, he obviously guessed her meeting with Drew hadn't gone well. "We can discuss it over lunch," he said.

They had lunch in a downtown restaurant overlooking a small park. There was a fountain. Over crab cakes and fresh tossed salad, Rachel talked, and Evan listened. At the end, he offered to break the news to his family.

Rachel conveyed her regrets to the Pierces and thanked them for their kindness. "If it had to happen, I'm relieved this all came out into the open now. Before your family and Dylan formed any close emotional ties." Perhaps Drew was right, she thought wearily, the truth had to come out sometime. But at what price?

Sounding sincere, Evan expressed concern for both her and Dylan. "That job is still open if you need it." When he offered his hand, she took it. "Good luck."

Rachel was surprised at his kindness. But then, the

Pierces were always surprising her, she thought with some resentment as she drove home later. Drew had deliberately turned her orderly life upside down to salve his conscience, "to right an old wrong," as he put it.

Was she supposed to give Dylan up? The boy was her heart, she'd lived for him. Was she predestined by fate to lose, to sacrifice everything, and live her life in Laurel's shadow? With today's revelations, Rachel had to admit there was a side of Laurel she'd never known. Along with that sad admission, Rachel faced the possibility of losing Dylan.

How would she bear it? How would Dylan bear it?

But Drew had given her a choice. She could take Dylan, pack her things, and leave town—just keep going and never look back. Or—she hesitated before completing the thought—she could face Jared. If she did, she knew she couldn't look into his gray eyes and lie.

After dropping a bombshell in Rachel's lap, Jared felt the only decent thing to do was give her a few days, long enough for the fallout to settle. He'd told her the whole truth, everything he knew. He almost hadn't. Luckily, fate—in the form of the sawmill closing—had saved him from making that irreparable mistake. Rachel might be angry and disillusioned for awhile, but he hadn't destroyed her trust completely, he could rebuild it—he hoped.

Waiting was never Jared's strong suit.

Why wait, when a simple phone call to Rachel would set the next event in motion? After finishing with a patient, he stared at the phone on his desk, picked it up, then dialed Rachel's number. "I want to see you," he said, relieved when she answered on the fourth ring.

If she sensed his urgency, it wasn't apparent in her voice when she replied, ''Where?''

He'd expected an argument, and took a moment to think. He could go to her house, or she could come to the clinic, but he wanted this conversation to take place on neutral ground. He frowned, realizing that sounded as if he was preparing for battle.

''If you're free, we could go for a drive,'' he suggested. ''I can pick you up in half an hour.''

''Yes.'' The phone went dead.

Jared stared at it—as if the buzzing dial tone could somehow bring her back. He frowned. So she wasn't going to make this easy. But at least she was talking to him.

Chapter Seven

Jared found Rachel waiting when he got to her house. Apparently, she was anxious to get this meeting over with. She looked pale, carved out of ice. She greeted him with just about the same level of warmth. Ignoring his help, she climbed into the truck. He drove down Main Street and took a left at the light.

For the first time, she looked at him. "Where are we going?"

"Where we can talk," he replied.

"But Dylan will be home from school at three."

Jared glanced at his watch. It was just past noon. "That should give us plenty of time."

She pursed her lips. "You insisted on this meeting. As far as I'm concerned, we don't need a drive. We can settle things right now. I'm not giving Dylan up without a fight. I plan to contact a lawyer."

Jared set his mouth to keep from arguing. "Can this wait until we get there?"

She subsided in abrupt silence. He could feel her irritation coming at him in waves.

They drove out of town, the farms growing farther and farther apart. The road kept climbing. Finally, Jared turned onto a dirt road. Eventually, he stopped on an old abandoned logging road in the middle of nowhere.

Rachel looked around, openly puzzled. "Where are we?"

"We need to talk uninterrupted," Jared explained. "I thought Stones End was the best place." His voice was quiet, tense. "Let's get out, we can walk the rest of the way."

Rachel simply nodded and started to walk. Jared fell into step.

She was wearing a simple skirt and blouse. The print was a mix of blues and greens. The colors swirled together against a blue sky. A pale sun clung to her, gilding her red hair. The earth seemed to fall away behind her, and there was only sky, and clouds and Rachel. He wanted to touch her—to see if she was real. Could any mortal woman be that bewitching?

"I talked to Evan and he arranged a meeting with Drew," she said, staring down at the ground as she walked along the rough path, a steady rise. It was so peaceful, she could almost pretend her world wasn't about to shatter.

"And?"

Rachel ignored the impatience in his voice, delaying the inevitable. "I needed to talk to him. It seemed only fair to listen to his side of the story. Besides, it's pointless to go through all sorts of tests when Drew knows the truth."

Side by side, they walked up the trail to the top of the hill where the trees had been clear-cut and new ones planted.

Jared felt annoyed. Despite her claim of non-involvement with Drew, she'd gone directly to him for answers. "Considering Drew's record," he said, "how could you think he'd tell the truth, even if he knew what that was?"

"I don't know," she admitted. "Maybe I know another side of Drew than you do. Or maybe I just hoped he'd tell me what I wanted to hear."

"And what's that?" Jared asked, impressed by her directness. He didn't know Rachel very well, but nothing had ever led him to believe she was anything less than honest—even when it hurt—which probably meant he could believe her feelings for Drew were little more than friendship. "What did you hope to learn by going to Drew?"

They'd reached the top of the hill, and Rachel felt winded from the climb. "I hoped he'd tell me that you're mistaken." She turned to face him. "That Laurel didn't lie, that you couldn't possibly be Dylan's father."

"And did he confirm or deny it?" His eyes flickered once, but his voice was strong and firm, demanding answers.

They stood on a grassy knoll overlooking a fertile green valley separated into halves by a swift-flowing river. The scene was idyllic, but Jared hadn't chosen it for the view.

They were alone—two people on top of a lonely hilltop.

They stood apart.

In this isolated place, Rachel felt trapped and knew why Jared had chosen this spot—she couldn't run from the truth. But neither could he. Here, on this hill, with the past like a wedge between then, they had to decide Dylan's future.

Rachel couldn't reveal her fear, couldn't show weakness. Dylan was hers, and she was prepared to fight for him.

"He didn't even try to deny it," she said, unable to glance away from the demand in his eyes. "Laurel told him the truth years ago—you are Dylan's father. But that doesn't mean you have any moral right to him." With the words, she raised an obstinate chin, claiming the child she thought of as her own. "He doesn't know you. I raised Dylan since birth, and I think a court might uphold my rights."

At her answer, Jared caught his breath. She was fierce and defiant, a tigress defending her young.

How could he deny her claim?

"So, it's all true," Jared said, his mind racing at the implications. He was Dylan's father. The knowledge filled him with new determination. God willing, he would have time to earn Dylan's love. But he had only these few precious moments to secure that future.

"Yes, it's true," she said quietly.

Jared was deeply aware of missing so many years with Dylan. Through no will of his own, through one senseless, irresponsible act, he was a father. The irony of the situation didn't escape him.

After his parents' poor example, he wasn't sure he believed in family—a mother, a father, a child. Children. Yet, here he was, blessed with a ready-made one.

Rachel didn't appear too happy about it.

At his silence, she clenched her hands. "I can't let you have him. I'll fight you in court."

"Is that the way it has to be?" Filled with unbearable guilt for not being a dad to Dylan, for hurting Laurel,

Jared looked at Rachel and knew he couldn't take the boy from her. Was there time to undo the harm? "The only way?"

She shook her head. "You're giving up your claim?"

"No, I'm not giving up." He spoke evenly, measuring each word. "You've jumped to a lot of conclusions. Can we agree that we both have Dylan's best interest at heart?"

At a brisk nod from Rachel, he continued, "I don't want to drag him through the courts. A little boy needs a mother and a father."

"What are you saying?" Her voice was thin.

Jared hadn't given this much thought, certainly not as much as it deserved, but this was the only way to repair the past without destroying everything in its wake. "I never intended to take him from you. I thought we could work something out."

"What are you talking about?" she snapped, losing control and revealing some of her tension. "Shared custody? Visits? What?"

Nothing could make this easy, so he just said it, "I thought we could get married. It's the obvious answer."

Rachel's entire body recoiled. "It's not obvious to me! Next, you'll be claiming you had this in mind all along."

Jared felt his face heat up. "I did think of courting you."

She gasped. "I don't believe you."

"Believe it!" Holding back his temper, he held both hands up, palms outward. "How about a truce? Just think about it, and you'll have to admit, marriage is the ideal compromise."

Marriage a compromise? That didn't make sense to him, much less to Rachel apparently.

She looked horrified. "Marriage! My God, I wouldn't marry you if you were the last man on the planet!"

The last man.

At that, his mouth tightened. "I know this all comes as a shock. It's not exactly easy for me either. Just think of it as a practical live-in arrangement between two adults."

"What about love?"

Jared didn't blink. "We both love Dylan. I have a lot of respect and admiration for the way you've raised him. A lot of people don't start with as much going for them. There are worse reasons to marry."

If there were, Rachel couldn't think of any at the moment. She was too caught up in her own unhappiness. She dreaded losing the only thing she had left—her heart. How could she protect herself from this helpless attraction to Jared? With the sun beating down on her head, she couldn't think straight. "I don't know." She felt dizzy.

"We both know it's the only solution."

Rachel didn't know any such thing! She didn't even know if he intended their marriage to be real or in name only.

All the tender feelings she'd felt for Jared were frozen. He'd used her to get information, to get close to Dylan. He'd pretended friendship. How could she consider marrying him, knowing the truth about his motives?

Besides, he was probably offering marriage out of a sense of duty, as a salve to his conscience. Duty was no substitute for love. Neither was sex—no matter how attracted she was to Jared.

Deeply torn, Rachel wrapped her arms around her waist. This was insane, but she was actually considering his proposal! While he waited for an answer, she considered all her options, which didn't take long. There weren't any. Of course, his offer was a practical solution. And wasn't she the practical one? She could marry Jared and keep Dylan.

But could she live without love?

Love.

What did she know about love? Rachel thought of her parents' marriage, the parts she didn't like to think about—her father's restlessness, always searching for something just out of his reach, his apparent dissatisfaction with each new job, and her mother's tears with each new move.

Laurel had loved Drew. But their youthful troubled relationship had resembled an unhealthy obsession more than love. On the other hand, Aunt Grace and Uncle Charlie were still devoted and in love with each other after fifty-three years together, but they were from another generation when people revered home and family above all else.

Rachel sighed. Perhaps Jared was right—love didn't have to be part of the equation after all. But marriage lasted a long time. She wanted to be fair, to do what was right for everyone. Did she have a real choice? She had to do what was right for Dylan.

Yes, Jared was right, it was time to put personal feelings aside, and create a family for Dylan.

"Yes," she whispered.

He cleared his throat. "You won't regret it."

She already did.

"I think we should make it soon," Jared insisted, unwilling to give her time to change her mind.

She frowned. "How soon?"

"Next week," he said firmly. "Getting a license won't take long. We could keep things simple...unless you want a lot of ceremony and something bigger."

"No." She didn't flinch from his words. "Not really."

"Then, it's settled?"

"Yes," she said with a lift to her chin.

Jared released a breath at her agreement.

They climbed back down the hill. When Rachel lost her footing, he reached out a hand and steadied her. Jared felt her hand tremble in his, shocked at the icy cold texture, and his reaction. He wanted to never let go.

On the drive home, they were both silent, full of the enormity of the decision they'd just made, except for a brief exchange when Rachel suddenly turned to Jared.

"Won't people think this is rather abrupt?" Her smooth brow wrinkled into a frown. "What will we tell them?"

"The truth. There have been enough evasions as it is," he said, glancing at her. "No matter how we go about this, there'll be talk, so why not go with the simple truth?"

Talk about evasions. His answer only frustrated Rachel. He'd uttered a lot of words, but hadn't really answered her question. "And what exactly is the truth?" she asked.

"That you've spent the last eight years raising your sister's son—my son—and that we're getting married."

"Yes, of course." How could he make their marriage sound so logical, when it seemed unfathomable to her?

That evening, they broke the news to Dylan. Rachel sat on the couch next to the boy, while Jared stood at a small distance. She'd witnessed Jared in several moods, but never this one. He appeared nervous—unsure—his shoulders tense, his body rigid. Apparently, this wasn't easy for him either, which was some comfort.

Until this moment, she'd prayed for a reprieve. There was none. No gallant knight on a white charger to save her from herself. There was only Jared. And he didn't look any happier than she felt. If things were different, this could be the happiest moment of her life—instead of the lowest. Nevertheless, she'd promised her support.

The next few moments would set the tone for their future—hers and Dylan's. And Jared's. How odd to link them all together! She held her breath when Jared spoke first.

"I've asked your mom to marry me," he said, with a smile she felt sure was intended to reassure Dylan, rather than Jared's intended bride since he wasn't even looking at her. "And she said yes. I hope that's okay with you."

From the first word, Dylan's eyes grew rounder and rounder. He sat up straight. "Does that mean you get to live with us, mow the lawn, and take out the garbage, and stuff like that?"

Clearly taken aback as the list grew, and grew, Jared said, "Since you put it that way, I guess so."

"Mom's car needs a new muffler...and a tune-up."

When Jared good-naturedly agreed to the negotiations, the bride price, Rachel stared in amazement. Why hadn't she thought of that? She was acquiring a handyman—a man around the house—not a husband. Somehow, that wasn't comforting.

Dylan frowned. "My friends have dads who check their homework and make up all kinds of rules."

Jared raised an eyebrow. "Like what?"

The boy shrugged. "Like no television after supper, and no video games and no..."

With a smile, Jared interrupted. "Sounds like you know a lot on the subject. I'll tell you what, since I'm new at this, you can guide me along. When it comes to making up rules, your mom is doing a fine job. For now, let's just worry about all of us getting to know each other better, and learning to be a family. Think you can handle all of that?"

Dylan broke into a huge smile. "Okay. Are you going to live here with us?"

Rachel hadn't thought of that either.

"Actually, I'm hoping you'll come live with me at Stones End." Before adding anything else, Jared drew an audible breath, surprising Rachel with the announcement. "I'm going to be your dad. I hope that's all right with you."

His gaze went to Rachel's in mute appeal.

Taking pity on him, Rachel broke in gently, "Dylan, there's something else you should know." When the boy turned to look at her, she smiled and gently smoothed his hair back from his brow. She swallowed back the tears, wanting to make this as easy as possible for Dylan. "It may be hard for you to understand at first, but Drew isn't your real father."

Dylan's face cleared and the tension went out of him. "I already know about all that." He sounded very grown up for an eight-year-old.

Wanting to be very sure, Rachel said, "What do you know?"

"About Drew not being my father," Dylan answered with a child's simplicity. "I just asked him one time, and he said he wasn't my dad. But that he wished he was."

"You never mentioned this before."

"I thought you knew."

"Oh, I see," Rachel said, grateful for Drew's delicate handling of the situation. She took a deep breath, then another one. "Well, there's something else you need to know. You see, Jared is your father. He never knew about you until very recently. But now that he does, he…"

When Rachel paused, Jared took over. "Now that I do know about you and Rachel, I want us to be a real family."

Dylan looked puzzled. "Like a real dad? I thought you only got one of those when you get born."

At the words, a look of anguish crossed Jared's face.

When he said nothing in his own defense, Rachel found herself rushing in to explain, "Well, Jared wasn't around then, because he didn't know. You see, he went away and your mom didn't know how to find him. But he's here now. What do you think of that?"

His eyes still troubled about something, Dylan obviously didn't know what to think as he said, "I guess that's okay."

Although visibly disappointed, Jared had to be satisfied with that. Rachel knew the subject wasn't closed.

Jared didn't stay long.

Dylan prepared for bed.

After bathing, and putting on his pajamas, he came to find Rachel in the kitchen where she was putting away the last of the clean dishes.

"How about a glass of milk and some cookies?" she asked.

"Chocolate chip?"

"Mmm." She set the snack on the table. But before Dylan sat down, she noticed he'd buttoned his pajama top wrong. She drew him close. "Here, let me fix that." As she unbuttoned the row, she said, "You like Jared, don't you?"

"I like him." He spoke around a mouthful of chocolate chip cookie. "But do you think he likes me?"

"Oh, honey, of course he likes you."

Dylan gave her a straight look that stopped her heart midbeat. "Just because I'm his kid?"

She slipped a button into a hole. "You and Jared became friends the first time you met at the clinic. Remember how nice he was about the puppies?"

He looked doubtful. "I guess so."

"I know so. The point is, he didn't know you were related to him that first day. He found out later." She sighed, doing up another button, trying to find the right words, but how could she explain what she barely understood? "I know this is all very confusing. But, I also know that he's going to love you. He is your father. You and Jared are meant to be together."

"And you."

Rachel groaned inwardly at her unconscious slip. How could she convince Dylan when she felt so insecure? "Yes, of course. We're going to be together. All three of us."

For Dylan's sake, she was marrying Jared. The adjustment had to be smooth, or the boy would guess something was wrong. In the future, she had to guard every move, every word. According to Jared, they were going to be a real family. A real one.

But was that possible, given the circumstances?

Rachel couldn't deny one simple inescapable fact—the only love binding her and Jared together was their mutual love for his son.

His son.

His family.

Rachel felt like a mere appendage—an unnecessary one.

The following day, Jared didn't expect his father's blessing, which was just as well, because Ira heartily disapproved of his son's plans to marry a woman he'd known such a short time.

"Marry in haste, repent at leisure," Ira doled out the ominous warning, adding a few new inventions he'd thought up on the spot—such as his own experience with wedded bliss. "If you're dead set on going through with this," he said, finally recognizing his son's determination, "we're not having some hole and corner affair."

Thus, plans for the wedding created a stir and a flurry of excitement in the Carlisle family—and a welcome diversion from unpleasant reality. However, it still left time for Jared to have doubts. A wedding could mean family unity or division. In this case, which would it be?

Jared wasn't sure.

For one thing, there would be a new bride at Stones End.

Jared took one good look at the peeling white paint on the old farmhouse and realized how dismal and unwelcoming it looked. He wanted Rachel to love Stones End— unlike his mother who had hated it at first sight.

The grim reminder ate at him, forcing him to admit that he had hopes for this marriage. He wasn't exactly sure what those hopes were, but the knowledge was there— buried under a more prosaic outlook. He didn't love Rachel, and she didn't love him, but he wanted her....

He took a second look at the house.

His marriage was a gamble, only days away; but here, at last, was something he could do. With only a few days to do some cosmetic repairs, he got out a bucket of white paint.

Jared hadn't gotten very far on the front section before Ben pitched in to help. Jessie took up a paintbrush while Nathaniel was napping. Fred helped. Ira just stood back and shook his head at all of them.

Three days later, they were only two-thirds around the entire house when it started to rain—huge wet drops washed away half a day's work. For the next three days, it rained.

The painting never resumed.

Jared hoped it wasn't an omen.

On the eve of the wedding, Ira was all gloom and doom. He was sure that his son was marrying for all the wrong reasons, including being trapped by a certain redhead.

The rush to the altar raised quite a few eyebrows. Explanations had raised even more. The wedding rehearsal had proven awkward and stiff.

Later, the Carlisle family were gathered together. Rachel and Dylan were supposed to be there, but she'd called to say Dylan had a slight cold. Rachel had made their excuses; she was putting him to bed early, and hoped he'd be better in time for the wedding. Jessie had baked a glazed ham with raisin sauce—Jared's favorite.

As he cut into a slice, he felt like a condemned man eating his last meal.

Ira shook his head in disapproval. "Girl's flighty and has no clear understanding of country life."

Like Avis. Ira didn't have to say the words. Jared knew that he was comparing Rachel to his mother. That worried him, in addition to the fact that Rachel didn't even pretend to love him. He had no emotional hold on her whatsoever.

Nevertheless, he defended his bride. "You've only spoken to her once."

"Once is all it takes. Look where she comes from. Everyone knows the Stillwater Inn is a tourist trap. No local worth his salt would be caught dead there," Ira said with visible disgust. When no one commented, he continued, "She's bound to be soft. What's she going to do when the snow blows and she can't get out for a week? Or two," he added. "What will she do come winter at Stones End, when the days are cold and long? And the nights are even longer. She'll have to pull her weight."

"You're wrong about Rachel. She's not going to run

at the first sign of trouble,'' Jared said, hoping he was right, while resisting the tempting thought of all those long cold lusty winter nights with Rachel.

"Humph. We'll see."

Until then, Jessie's husband had been listening with a vague smile. Now, Ben got straight to the point. "I've only got one bit of advice…flowers. Get the woman some flowers. Oh, and a ring can't hurt."

His eyes met Jessie's, and she smiled.

At the reminder, Jared was glad he'd remembered to have his grandmother's wedding ring polished and the stone reset.

But he'd forgotten the flowers. "Thanks," he said, well aware that he wasn't prepared for any of this.

How could anyone prepare to share the rest of their lives with someone? Shouldn't there be some basic training attached to marriage? Even under ideal conditions, it was a gamble. This union seemed to have all the cards stacked against it. But win or lose, Jared was in for all he was worth. For what was the worth of a man if it wasn't his heart? His soul? Before Rachel was done with him, she'd probably have both. However, he had no intention of letting her know that until he was good and ready—or she was.

Hell, this was confusing! What did he know about men and women, love and marriage, and all the rest? His personal experience of women hadn't given him much reason to trust the "weaker sex." As a result, he'd left women before they left him. Not that there had been that many women. He was bound to blow it—just as his father had. But not without giving it all he had…Jared knew no other way.

With a scowl, he refused to admit to pre-wedding jitters. Now that he thought about it, maybe he should be worrying! Ben had mentioned flowers.

So, on his wedding day, Jared rose at daybreak and went out to pick some flowers for his bride. He trudged through a field, knee-high in wildflowers.

There were plenty to choose from. Too many. Damn it, he'd never thought to ask what kind of flowers she liked. He hadn't thought about Rachel—her likes and dislikes. What did he know about flowers? He was a Carlisle— which meant he was hale and hardy, strong and tough— and insensitive.

Eventually, he cut a few delicate tea roses from the bush Ben had planted for Jessie. Hoping some of their good fortune would rub off, he made up a small bouquet of roses and wildflowers—Queen Anne's lace, purple loosestrife and buttercups. Then, he frowned at the collection. It was missing something.

There was one more flower he had to pick—chicory weed. The delicate blue-violet blossoms bloomed for only a few short hours each day—from morning till noon. He found some along the roadside, then dropped the flowers off at Jessie's. "Will these do?"

Jessie nodded. "They are lovely. I have just the thing to set them off nicely." She fetched a blue satin ribbon, cut a generous length, then wrapped it around the flower stems. She tied it into a bow, then stood back to admire her handiwork. "There, that should do. I'll see that Rachel gets it."

"I was going to do it, but Fred reminded me that it's bad luck for the groom to see the bride before the wedding."

"I'm glad to help." Jessie reached up and kissed his cheek. As brother and sister, they were still close. They'd always been there for each other. At times, there had been no one else, forging an unbreakable bond. "Be happy," she said, obviously aware of his inner turmoil, the risk he was taking with his heart. "I love you."

"I love you, too."

Be happy.

That was a tall order. Jared wondered if anything good could come of such a muddled beginning.

Chapter Eight

It was Rachel's wedding day. She stared into the mirror and saw a stranger, a woman in a delicate white dress.

A bride.

The vintage dress was romantic, shimmering lace with a dropped waist, short scalloped sleeves and a layered skirt. It had belonged to her mother...and her mother before her.

To Rachel's amazement, Aunt Grace had saved it all these years in an old trunk stored at the Inn. When informed of the wedding, Grace had sent instructions on where to find the trunk, along with her sincere regrets that she and Charlie couldn't get there in time for Rachel's wedding. They were exploring the Rockies, and by the time they packed up their campsite and started home, they'd barely make it in time for Halloween, much less the wedding.

Rachel loved them dearly, but she was relieved they

weren't coming. She couldn't have fooled them into thinking this wedding was anything more than a sham. Grace would be upset, Charlie would be somber and worried, but they would support Rachel's decision—they always had. Grace understood the meaning of family.

Yes, Grace would understand and support Rachel's decision, even though it was made out of a sense of duty, rather than love. Rachel had succeeded in giving Dylan a family. Then why wasn't she happy? Because duty wasn't enough? Selfishly, she wanted more.

Jared had sent flowers…wildflowers, not the hot-house kind. Was that significant? Had he picked them himself? Rachel knew so little about him. They'd never been alone for any length of time, yet she was marrying him in one hour and seventeen minutes.

Tonight, they would be alone.

Dylan wouldn't be there as a buffer. Nora O'Neil had offered to keep Dylan overnight to give the newlyweds some privacy. Rachel had tried to protest, but then she'd felt foolish. After all, she was marrying Jared. Heaven help her if she couldn't spend one night alone with the man! She shuddered at the thought—not totally from fear.

Plagued by last-minute doubts, Rachel could only hope she'd made the right decision when she agreed to marry Jared.

As if touching a talisman, she pressed a hand to the gold locket at her throat. With a pensive sigh, she slipped it under her neckline and felt the metal warm against her skin. With her mother's pearls around her neck and tiny pearl studs in her ears, Rachel stepped back from her reflection in the floor-length mirror.

Something was missing—a veil.

She wove a few wildflowers into a wreath and placed it on her head. The soft pastel blossoms contrasted with her bright hair, which she wore up. The effect was bridal, but not overly formal. Thank goodness Jared had agreed to a simple outdoor ceremony! She frowned at her paleness and tried to pinch some color into her cheeks.

Fortunately, the dress wasn't pure white. Gently aged over time, the lace was creamy white, but it was white. She hoped Jared understood what that meant.

She hoped he would be patient.

Oh, she hoped for so many things. Like a child, she wanted to close her eyes before she jumped—so she wouldn't see where she fell.

After leaving Jessie, Jared went back to Stones End. All was quiet. He was running late, but still had time to dress and make it to the ceremony on time.

Keeping his bride waiting at the altar would amount to a monumental mistake—and he'd already made too many of those. Rachel didn't expect much from him. As a result, he wanted their marriage to be perfect—at least the ceremony part, he thought with a frown. Going beyond that point didn't bear thinking about.

He checked his watch again, and took the stairs two at a time. His bedroom door was open. Someone had obviously been there before him, and they'd stolen his pants!

Jared stared into the empty closet then ran his hand through his hair. He couldn't believe this was happening. This was no joke! Furious, he spun around. And there on the back of a chair was his wedding gear—traditional Highland dress—a Black Watch Regiment plaid wool kilt, complete with a Prince Charlie jacket and Barathea vest, black bow tie, dress sporran—the works. He recalled seeing his father and grandfather in full regalia at special family occasions, and guessed this was one of them.

A wedding, after all, was a family event.

Left with nothing else suitable for the ceremony, Jared dressed, then stared into the mirror. At the reflected image, he let out a hard laugh, a bit self-conscious at a sight of naked knees, yet oddly moved by his father's adherence to tradition.

A moment later, Ben knocked on the door. "Hey, is there a bridegroom in the house?" He didn't even crack a smile when he saw Jared's kilt. Apparently he was in on it.

So was Fred Cromie. "Let's get a move on." He eyed Jared with approval. Fred took a deep breath, obviously moved, yet his words held only bracing humor. "Well, aren't you pretty? Never saw a bridegroom in a skirt before. Hope you don't outshine the bride."

Jared thought of Rachel in all her feminine glory. "Not a chance," he said, feeling a little weak at the knees.

Fred grinned. "Well, come on, we're going to be late."

They drove to an empty hilltop.

Preoccupied and unaware of his surroundings, Jared got out of Ben's car, but when the others stayed put, he realized they intended to leave him there—nearly a mile from the church—with the ceremony due to start any moment.

As the car pulled away, Jared started after it. "Hey, wait a minute." The joke wasn't funny anymore.

Then he heard it—the wail of the bagpipes.

In full-dress kilt with his bagpipes slung over his chest, Ira crested the hill. If his father had appeared in drag, Jared couldn't have been more shocked.

The thin reedy notes died, and Ira cleared his throat. "It's family tradition—piping the bride and groom."

Jared's reply was thick with emotion. "Thanks, Dad."

"Families have to stick together, even when the going gets a little rough. You know, there's still time to change your mind." When Jared remained silent, he said gruffly, "Well then, if you're determined to go through with this, let's not keep the girl waiting."

Jared swallowed hard, more touched than he cared to admit. He didn't know much about tradition, but just then, he felt part of something bigger than he was. He felt the love a father bestowed on a son. And he knew that one day, he would do the same for his son. With a nod, Jared murmured, "Let's go," and fell into step with his father.

They moved slowly.

A path wound along the tree line, down into the valley where a small white steepled church waited.

Guests mingled outside where the ceremony would be performed. Ira took a deep breath and raised the pipes to his mouth. The somber notes carried the weight of the Highland Wedding Song, mixing sunshine and shadow, a pledge of fidelity and the promise of tomorrow.

The morning mist seem to rise up and meet the clear pure notes. The wind carried them through the valley.

Just as the sun pierced the dark clouds and set the rolling green hills aglow, Rachel heard the pipes. The haunting love song sent chills down her spine.

The barbaric ancient sounds made her aware of all she was giving up to ensure Dylan had a family…a clan. All this tradition would be his. Jared would own her.

Was it worth the price?

Then she saw Jared—tall and straight, his hair streaked with gold, his eyes gray but unwavering as he came over the hill and down into the sun-filled glade where she waited.

Her soul grew still.

And she listened, and waited. A sense of peace and inevitability flowed over her. Until that moment, she'd wanted to run, now she felt grounded, rooted in one spot.

This was where she belonged. With this man about to claim her unto eternity...if only he felt one ounce of what she was feeling.

She watched as Jared took his place beside Reverend Matthews who was officiating at the ceremony. Then everyone turned expectantly toward her. The center of all those eyes, Rachel took a fortifying breath.

Dylan gave the bride away.

He placed her hand in Jared's.

Rachel felt Jared's strong grasp. She dropped her eyes, afraid to reveal how he moved her. Her heart thudded with discovery. It was too soon to feel this way. Too soon, too much! But her heart wasn't listening.

"Do you take this man," the Reverend said moments later.

The words shook her.

Rachel clutched at the small bouquet of flowers. Blue satin ribbons fluttered around her, a few petals drifted away with the wind...and she felt utterly carried away at the thought of binding herself to this man.

For once, she allowed her heart to speak for her.

"Yes," she whispered, irrationally fighting down all her doubts and fears, binding herself, taking strength in this new feeling of unity, hoping she'd find a way to belong.

Yes, she would dare to dream. Maybe she and Jared could build something together.

They exchanged traditional vows since neither had felt capable of coming up with something more original and uniquely suited to their situation, which probably wouldn't be sanctioned in a church if they had.

Rachel felt a moment's guilt. Did she really mean to love, honor and cherish? She would cooperate, and never break faith, but heaven help her, she had no intention of loving Jared unless he loved her back.

With a few brief words, Rachel was tied to him.

The ritual went on.

They exchanged wedding bands—ties that bind a man and a woman for all time. Or should. Jared wasn't sure of anything, much less his bride's loyalty. Did a marriage of convenience allow for devotion—"'til death do us part?" Or were they just words whispered into the wind, carried away on a breeze, weightless, meaningless?

Jared couldn't recall what they'd rehearsed, but after he slipped the ring on Rachel's finger, he held her hand until the end. She had slender delicate hands, elegant—just like the rest of her. It was time to kiss his bride. She looked like something he'd dreamed up. Everything and everyone dulled beside her.

She looked outwardly calm, filled with resolve, but he could feel the faint tremble in her fingers. His eyes held hers for a long moment before dropping to her lips.

At that point, she closed her eyes—probably to block him out, he decided with an ironic twist to his mouth.

But as his gaze drifted over Rachel in her lace and silk dress, he knew he'd never seen such a vision of beauty.

Instead of a bridal veil, she wore flowers in her hair.

His flowers.

His smile softened as he saw the pale blue chicory blossoms woven between the pink-and-cream roses.

Rachel didn't see the tenderness in his eyes, but she felt it in his kiss as his mouth took hers gently. There was hunger as well; she felt it…and trembled.

He released her, obviously as shaken as she was.

Rachel felt flushed and hot.

He frowned, as if unsure what to do with her—now

that he'd acquired a bride—a blushing one at that. But she should have known his hesitation wouldn't last long.

He smiled, a wicked gleam entered his eyes. "Well, shall we try that again?"

She had no time to respond—verbally, that is.

Her physical response to his kiss was totally unplanned, unscheduled, uninhibited and about as inconvenient as it could be. She wanted to hold him and never let go, melt into him, and feel the earth move under her feet.

When he released her, she noted that he looked a little flushed as well. They turned, as one, to greet their wedding guests.

Rachel had invited a few friends from Stillwater, plus a couple of former co-workers from the Sawmill. Apart from the O'Neils, she hadn't formed any close friendships in the short time she'd lived in Henderson. She was surprised at the large turnout. People had come out of curiosity—or affection—she wasn't sure which. With Ira and Jared at her side, everyone was pleasant. Apparently, Ira had stamped her with his seal of approval, and that was that.

Jared now wore a wedding band on his left hand; but on his right, he wore a ring with a Celtic knot—a symbol of family loyalty. Ties that bind.

Ben and Jessie stood nearby, lending their approval to the event. If either had reservations about Jared's hasty nuptials, it didn't show. In fact, Ben appeared totally distracted by his lovely fair-haired wife in her blush-pink dress. They were obviously in love. Rachel looked away, aware of all the elements lacking in her own marriage.

Their baby sat happy and content on a blanket nearby. When a bright yellow butterfly flew by, Nathaniel reached for it and toppled into the grass. Before crumpling with tears, his face registered surprise as the grass tickled his nose.

Rachel went over and picked him up, hugging him to her, allowing the small warm body to ease the chill in her heart. Suddenly, like fizzy champagne when exposed, all the sizzling sexual attraction between her and Jared seemed to go flat. It wasn't enough to sustain a marriage. Aunt Grace's words of wisdom came back: "marriage should start with friendship."

Rachel didn't like Jared very much at the moment. From their first meeting, he hadn't been totally honest with her. Too bad, she had to keep reminding herself.

From a short distance, Jared watched Rachel holding Jessie's baby. He couldn't keep his gaze from straying in her direction—an admission he found difficult to accept.

Jared wasn't prepared for her effect on him. He felt protective and possessive. He felt married. Rachel looked so natural holding Jessie's infant son. They'd never discussed having more children. Their marriage was real—they'd both agreed.

How real?

Within hours, he'd know the answer. Jared swallowed hard and went to find a glass of punch.

The ceremony was over, people started to mingle.

Rachel found a quiet moment alone with Dylan.

He'd given the bride away—not too sure if he liked the sound of that. "You're still my mom, right?"

Closing her eyes, Rachel hugged him tight. "Always." He'd never know the sacrifice she'd made this day.

Dylan stood at her side, watching over the proceedings with a worried frown on his small face. "It's that man!"

His angry tone startled Rachel. "What man?"

"That one." He pointed to Jared's father. "He was mean to my dog in the street that day. Remember?"

"Oh." How could she have forgotten that first meeting with Ira Carlisle glowering in disapproval?

In all the upheaval of the wedding, she'd failed to explain Ira's relationship to Jared. How was she going to tell Dylan that Ira—that awful man—was his grandfather?

Not one to waste time on ceremony, Ira marched toward Rachel and Dylan with a determined air—obviously prepared to get this unpleasantness over with. From his great height, he looked down on Dylan. "So, you're Jared's boy. That makes you my grandson. What do you think of that?"

At the news, Dylan's eyes rounded; he looked to Rachel for confirmation. When she nodded, he turned back to Ira with a serious look. "I don't know, sir. I never had one before. What does a grandfather do?"

Clearly taken aback, Ira laughed. "The boy's no dummy!" He sounded pleased. "Tell you what—we'll work on it. I got one grandson in diapers. Guess I can figure out what to do with another one."

To Rachel's amazement, Ira's eyes were twinkling when he noted Dylan's red hair. "There must be some Scots blood in the boy." He threw Rachel a thick glance, adding in a gruff voice, "And in the lass."

"On my mother's side," Rachel said, wondering why his approval should matter to her.

There was a certain strength and dignity to Ira that demanded her respect—if not her affection. Her spirit fell when he muttered an indecipherable, "Hmm," and stomped off.

Apparently, Jared had overheard the exchange. "Is there really some Scots blood, or did you make that up?"

"My mother was a MacBain." Did he imagine she'd make it up merely to get into Ira's good graces? If he did, Jared's opinion of her was pretty low. "Does it matter?"

"Not to me. But congratulations, you managed to score a point with my father."

Somehow, Rachel managed to hold on to her smile.

Scoring points with Jared's father had never entered her head. But now it did. Was that the way to win Jared's approval as well? Considering the few times she'd observed the strained relationship between father and son, she didn't think so. She sighed, wondering if there was a way to win Jared's love, and wishing it didn't matter. But it did.

He didn't need her to gain custody of his son. So why had he gone through with this wedding? Would she ever understand the man?

Surprisingly, he stayed at her side. Theirs wasn't a love match. Under the circumstances, she could only be grateful for his support.

She didn't know what to expect from the Carlisles and their neighbors and friends—certainly not the outpouring of kindness and acceptance she and Dylan received. They'd brought casseroles and salads. Tables overflowed with fruit punch and desserts. Nora had insisted on baking a wedding cake.

The ritual of cutting into it couldn't be missed.

Rachel pinned on a smile and kept it there—even when Jared fed her a small piece of cake. His fingers brushed her lips. The sweetness lingered long after she swallowed the iced confection.

Music started, thrumming through her veins.

The men joined hands, forming a circle. Someone pulled Rachel in with the women—a circle within a circle. They went round and round, stopping at random partners. Rachel danced with Dylan, then several others, before Jared came around to her.

When he placed both hands at her waist and swung her

around, Rachel almost forgot the steps from her childhood. She felt lightheaded, her heart raced ahead of her brain, then landed her on her feet when he released her to reel with the next girl. And on it went. They danced three and a half times—she counted them—before the music stopped.

As the music died, she was in Jared's arms, and he was looking at her with a bemused smile on his face. And then, he kissed her—very softly. And she knew he was just as confused as she was. With a mere legality, a few words exchanged in front of witnesses, she was his, and he was hers, and neither knew what to do about it. It shouldn't change a thing, but it did.

She wore his ring—a circle of love. It had no beginning, and no end. Rachel looked down at the gold wedding band and felt a tight constriction around her heart.

There was a last flurry of excitement as the bride and groom prepared to leave. Rachel tossed her bouquet, but kept some of the blossoms as a keepsake—she wasn't sure why.

Seventeen-year-old Mary Ellen O'Neil caught the bouquet. Mary Ellen smiled—as if she had the groom all picked out. And maybe she did. Rachel suspected Mary Ellen had her entire life all mapped out, which couldn't be said for Rachel. At the moment, she felt like a chess piece, maneuvered from place to place. And she didn't play chess!

Under the circumstances, a honeymoon would have been a farce. Ira had offered to stay overnight at Jessie's—to give the newlyweds some privacy—for which Rachel was grateful. She couldn't imagine play-acting the part of the happy bride for one moment longer.

She was relieved when it was time to leave.

At Stones End, Jared turned at the mailbox.

The road climbed, then leveled off. They reached a sharp curve where a canopy of trees seemed to swallow her up.

Rachel looked back and couldn't see where she'd been.

Chapter Nine

The house was around the next curve.

It was actually quite pretty, Rachel thought, admiring the sparkling white farmhouse. A porch went across the front, then wrapped along one side—where Jared parked in the driveway. And there the prettiness ended. Only half the house was painted. The rest was gray and dingy.

"We started to paint," he said. "I was hoping to get it done before you came. Then the rain came."

"I see." Unable to hide some of her dismay, Rachel wondered how many more surprises lay in store for her at Stones End. Then, she saw a rosebush in a sheltered spot by the porch. It gave her something to cling to—hope.

They got out of the car. The evening sky was gray, like embers left over from a warm fire. The day's heat had given way to a light rain. She turned her face up to the mist. The moon was up there, probably behind that huge black cloud.

As they climbed the porch steps, she wasn't prepared for Jared's next move. He swept her off her feet, pushed the door open and carried her over the threshold. Forced to hang on to him, Rachel swallowed her breath along with her nerve. His nearness overwhelmed her, making a mockery of her efforts to remain immune. His hair was like silk. His shoulder muscles rippled with strength.

He spoke with just a tinge of humor. "I heard it's bad luck if I don't do this."

With her resistance failing, she couldn't pretend a moment longer. "We wouldn't want that," she said icily. Putting on a show for Dylan was one thing, she saw no need to continue the act now that they were alone.

Jared set her on the floor none too gently. "What's that supposed to mean?"

The rough let-down loosened the flower arrangement in her hair. She pulled it out and tossed it aside. "Oh, please! You can stop pretending! You're not any happier about this situation than I am." Her voice shook slightly, risking his anger, yet driven to have her say.

The kilt certainly did nothing to dim his masculinity. Hands on hips, he looked tall and threatening, like an ancient Scottish raider, a ravisher of innocent maidens—not that he was guilty of either—yet. But he had that all-conquering air about him.

He laughed harshly. "Thanks for the reminder. So, you've made up your mind to hate me. I had wondered."

She squirmed, feeling very small and petty, under his angry glance. "I didn't say that."

He ran a weary hand through his hair. "I'm trying to do the right thing." He looked as fed up as she felt.

"I know." She should have realized this charade was

equally difficult for him. Did marriage have to be so hard? Would it always feel so strained—almost to the point of breaking? She let out a breath. "I'm sorry."

"Hell!" His mouth went taut. "So am I."

They stared at each other—both confused and unsure about why they were apologizing. It was too soon to have regrets, which didn't bode very well for their future.

Jared broke the silence first. "Look, let's try this again." Shocking her, he scooped her up and walked back out to the porch. He laughed into her reddening face. "This time, be nice. Remember, you're the bride, I'm the groom. You're supposed to admire my rugged manhood, and I'm supposed to tell you that you're beautiful."

Feeling helpless, Rachel clung to his broad shoulders. "This is insane." She laughed shakily.

"No, it's not." His voice dropped to a husky note. "You are beautiful."

Her smiled wobbled. "Thank you." So was he—but she couldn't say that. He smiled as if he saw right through her. She watched his eyes darken to charcoal as his head bent. She swallowed, unable to subdue a clamoring pulse.

"Now, I think this is the part where I'm supposed to kiss you," he said huskily, removing some of the awkwardness with humor. Oh, he could be charming....

She couldn't let that blind her to reality, she thought, then promptly forgot when he pressed her into his hard chest and lowered his mouth onto hers. Rachel hadn't been kissed that often, or that well, but she recognized seduction when she encountered it. It was there in Jared's kiss, the soft coaxing texture of his tongue against her closed lips, the satisfied groan when she opened to him....

She was breathless when he released her. She felt ruffled, and a little light-headed. Too much punch? Or not enough, she wondered as she recaptured her composure with the reminder that their marriage wasn't based on love. They'd both agreed. Was Jared making the best of the situation by accepting a bride he hadn't chosen? Or was he genuinely attracted to her? How could she trust him? She had no idea.

This time, he set her gently on her feet.

Rachel smoothed down her dress. The fabric felt fragile—like the many lives it had lived, and the marriages it had witnessed. Wordless, they stared at each other.

The silence made her uncomfortable.

He'd grown up on this farm, he was a vet. Apart from that, she knew so little about him. And she'd already used up her meager knowledge of animals.

"I forgot to thank you for the flowers," she said, wondering what they were going to find to say to each other for the next fifty years—if they lasted that long.

He smiled. "You're welcome."

"And Dylan…I think he was pleased." She was trying to be friendly—but not too friendly, after that kiss.

"Dylan's a great kid. You should be proud of him."

This was the part where she had to learn how to share— no matter how difficult. "So should you. He's your son."

"I've missed so much. I hope you'll help me catch up."

She tilted her head. "What do you want to know?"

"Everything there is to know."

"Now?"

"No." Jared smiled. "Not right now."

"Oh."

"We have some time to ourselves before the family invades the place. May I suggest we use that to get to know each other?"

Rachel wasn't going to ask how he planned to accomplish that in one or two days—the possibilities were all too obvious from the gleam in his eyes.

"Yes, well, we have plenty of time," she said.

When threatened by emotion, Rachel reached for a safe practical topic. She looked around. With the wedding so rushed, there hadn't been time for an earlier visit. She was seeing the house for the first time. The furnishings were limited, which would leave room for a few of her things. She hoped that would make it feel more like home.

Home.

Rachel stood in the middle of the room and slowly turned, trying to take it in, trying to find an acceptable emotion—besides dismay. She searched for something to say.

"This place is…" What was the polite word—rustic? The room was nicely proportioned, large and square, with paned glass windows. There were a few pieces of uphol-stered furniture, a sturdy recliner, an antique oak side-board. The wooden table and chairs just looked old. And tired—as if no one had really cared about the place in a long time. To her surprise, Rachel felt drawn to the house.

Jared said, "It could use some brightening up."

That was putting it mildly, she thought. "I have a few pieces, if there's room." From the little she'd seen, the house was sparsely furnished, but Rachel didn't want to intrude. After all, this was Jared's home.

Jared looked around, seeing it through her eyes. This room was the center of a working farm. "We can make room for your things." He'd never taken interest in the house or the furnishings. His wedding night seemed an odd place to start.

She tapped the satin toe of her shoe on the linoleum floor. "I suppose there must be real wood under there."

"I'll get your things." Jared escaped before she got around to stripping and refinishing the oak floors.

Once outside, he drew in a frustrated breath. He smiled at the irony of the situation. He was thinking of bed and she wanted to rearrange the furniture and redo the hardwood floors. Next thing he knew, she'd be complaining about the pickup truck, and buying his clothes.

She was moving too fast.

Rachel was thinking like a wife, while he was thinking like a new bridegroom, understandably curious about his bride. This was their wedding night—his and Rachel's.

The ceremony was over, let the marriage begin!

All right, so he wanted to make love to his wife. Delaying would only add to the tension and possibly add to Rachel's resistance, which wouldn't do any of them any good.

He smiled, wondering if Rachel was reaching the same conclusion…somehow, he doubted it. He'd discovered she had a temper, but she got over it just as quickly. She couldn't be pushed or coerced. In fact, she was extremely strong-willed; so was he. Married only a few short hours, they'd already had their first fight—a minor skirmish with no clear winner, which put them exactly back at square one.

Jared suspected the battle wasn't over.

If nothing else, their marriage promised to be full of excitement…hopefully, with a little passion thrown in for good measure when the time was right. Ah, and there was his problem. How would he know when the time was right?

He had no intention of rushing his bride off to bed and giving her more reason to resent him. With their entire lives ahead of them, one premature step on his part could ruin everything. Admittedly, Jared didn't know about love, but he knew he didn't want his marriage to fail. He didn't want Rachel to hate him.

A house divided was no way to raise a child.

Jared's mood took a dive when he reached for Rachel's luggage and discovered she'd brought one small suitcase—just enough for a short visit. Wasn't she planning on staying?

And that's when it hit him! He wanted her to stay, he wanted her to plant roots so deep that she'd never leave.

Not terribly pleased at the discovery, Jared lifted her bag and carried it upstairs. He found Rachel in Jessie's old room. She was at the window, gazing out at the view from the second story. He knew what she could see— fields that stretched fertile and green; thick woods crisscrossed with silvery streams, an overgrown apple orchard, all of it fenced in with miles of stone walls, shrouded and threatening as the daylight settled into dusk.

At his entry, her hand fell from the lace curtain. She looked nervous, obviously unaccustomed to having a man invade her bedroom. At some point, they would have to share the same space and learn to live together—in more ways than one. He dropped her suitcase on the bed. "Will this do?"

She nodded. "The room is lovely."

It was icy blue with white lace curtains—a perfect foil for her bright coloring. She looked like a princess in a fairy tale—and just about as untouchable.

"It used to be Jessie's. I hope you'll be comfortable." A couple of steps brought him within touching distance.

She leaned back against the windowsill. "I'm sure I will." Her gaze wandered to the big brass bed. The quilt was turned down invitingly. "Where will you sleep?"

As if pulled by an invisible string, his gaze followed

hers. His voice taunted her. "I can use my old room for tonight; that is, unless you prefer I stay."

"No, no," she hastened to say.

He ran his finger down her arm. "I want to make love to you. Would it be so terrible to just let it happen? You know it's bound to sooner or later. Why not sooner?"

She bit her lip. "I don't know, I really think it would be better to wait until we know each other better."

"There's one surefire way of accomplishing that."

His mouth sought hers.

With a small moan, Rachel leaned against him—all the tension of the day dissolved as she sought to find some reassurance from him. She wanted him to convince her that he was right. Why wait? Was it any wonder her voice sounded weak when she gasped, "I'm not sure, you never..."

"Not that I didn't want to." He slowly undid the small buttons on the back of her dress. He ran his thumb across her bare shoulder. "Don't you know how you affect me?"

"No, I don't," she whispered. She felt cool air against her flesh when he lowered her dress to reveal a camisole top.

His voice grew gentle. "Each time I see you, I want to touch you, to see if you're real, to see if the fire and gold are all on the outside."

"This is too soon." Much, much too soon.

So why did it feel so right—as if she'd waited all her life for this one moment? This one man. She was a virgin. She wondered if he'd guessed. It might be old-fashioned and romantic, but her aunt had advised her to save herself for the right man. Now, Rachel wanted Jared to be that man!

She wanted him to convince her that their marriage

wasn't a complete sham, that they could make it real in a physical sense and perhaps an emotional one.

Before she could formulate another objection, Jared leaned over and kissed the tender place where her throat curved into her shoulder. Just then, the moon broke through the clouds and cast a warm glow across Rachel's pale skin.

At the sight, Jared caught his breath. In the silvery moonlight, she looked flawless...flaming red hair...bare white shoulders. His gaze fastened on a thin chain with a gold locket around her elegant throat. And suddenly, Jared was thrown back in time—and Laurel was there with that same hair, that same locket—and she was seducing him with her witchery. He closed his eyes, recalling it all— the disillusion and regret. Laurel had taught him one thing, sex without love was an empty wasteland—an exercise in delusion.

And now he wanted Laurel's sister, and she didn't love him, and the cycle went on. When he opened his eyes, he saw Rachel, he saw confusion in her eyes.

Jared released her. "This is too soon." He ran a hand through his hair. "I'm sorry, you're right. We'll wait."

Rachel felt each word with a physical pain. The moon disappeared. She stood there, numb and cold—despite the warm night. Of course, Jared was right. It was too soon. No, she had said that, and he agreed. She rubbed the pain between her eyes. Oh, who cared who was right—or wrong! Being right was little comfort now. All she could think was—she'd saved herself for this!

She saw his gaze on the locket and pressed her hand against it. "This was a gift from my parents on my twelfth birthday. Laurel had one like it."

Jared lifted his gaze from the locket. "I know."

Rachel's swift intake of breath revealed her shock. Of

course, he'd seen the locket. He'd made love to Laurel. His words starkly reminded Rachel of her position.

She still wore the locket out of loyalty. She was raising her sister's child, now she'd married Laurel's former lover. Sometimes it seemed as if she was living Laurel's life—instead of her own.

His mouth twisted. "We can't pretend it never happened, Dylan is proof." He'd made love to Laurel first.

The knowledge would always be there between them.

"Yes," Rachel whispered, feeling hurt and humiliated, and wishing he would just go. With a few words, he'd reminded her of their circumstances. Their marriage was less than ideal. Was he warning her not to expect too much?

"I'm sorry," he said huskily.

The light brush of his lips against hers did nothing to warm Rachel or remove the ache in her heart.

Rachel spent her wedding night alone.

With all the unspent emotion surrounding the wedding, she slept poorly, falling into a fitful sleep around dawn. She woke to the sound of silence. Disoriented, she opened her eyes to blue walls and oak furnishings. Despite light-filtering shades, the room was filled with early-morning sunshine. The brass bed was wide, the mattress was soft, big enough for two, but she was alone. Her mood plummeted.

Last night, Jared had walked out.

And she had let him go.

She looked around the room—just to make sure he hadn't come back. He hadn't. After he'd left, she'd gone from anger to confusion and back again. She'd gotten ready for bed. Now, her eyes widened at the mess she'd left in her wake. Her wedding dress was where she'd left it, neatly folded over a wooden ladderback chair, but her satin shoes lay tipped onto the floor. She'd left a trail of satin underwear across the room, and sheer hose draped over one brass bed rail. The only item missing from the abandoned scene was a bridegroom.

As if on cue, a light rap on the bedroom door startled Rachel. "Just a minute," she called out, running a hand over her tangled hair as she climbed out of bed, then reached for her bathrobe. She was tying the belt into a knot when she opened the door. "Yes, what is it?"

It was Jared—in a white towel.

A very small towel.

And he was red-faced.

"Um...I'm sorry. It's early. Did I wake you?"

She shook her head, trying to recover from the bare tanned width of his shoulders...the thick fair hair sprinkled on his chest. Last night, they had agreed to respect each other's space. Was he changing the rules? So soon? Golden stubble covered his chin. In her opinion, fair-haired men seldom looked rakish, but he did.

"I was awake." She tightened her belt another notch. Only her feet were bare, but when his gaze drifted lazily over her, she felt naked—every nerve and fiber exposed. The thin peach silk of her nightdress and matching robe suddenly felt heavy on her breasts.

His eyes, shaded gray and overcast with slumberous passion, came back to meet hers. Unshaven, he looked as if he hadn't slept much more than she had, but it looked better on him. "I'll only be a minute. I need my clothes," he said.

"Clothes?" she repeated, as if she'd never heard of the convention.

"I can't find them," he explained. "Rita must have moved my things when she was cleaning, assuming Dylan would use my old room. The house only has three bed-rooms. This one, one across the hall, and Dad has the one downstairs.''

While all that registered, Rachel wondered where he intended to sleep, and all she could say was, "Rita?"

"Ramon's wife." When she looked blank, he added, "He manages the farm, she helps around the house. They have a teenage daughter who works part-time at the clinic, and a boy who's about Dylan's age. They're practically family."

More family!

She raised an eyebrow. "And where do they live?"

He smiled. "They have a house down the road. I never got around to explaining the setup here. We'll get around to that. For now, if I could just get my clothes..."

"Yes, of course." Rachel opened the door wider.

Jared walked in, apparently taking in the scene in one quick glance, then letting his gaze drift more slowly over the bits and pieces of underwear. With his attention focused on a lace camisole, he stumbled over one of her shoes.

The towel slipped.

Rachel held her breath, but he caught the towel in the nick of time. "Ah, sorry about that," he murmured. His face turned red. She didn't know why she was blushing, too.

He rubbed his stubbed toe against the opposite ankle, dragging her attention to his muscled calf. "I guess while we're at it," he said, "we'll have to discuss some practical living arrangements." Clutching at the towel with one hand, he reached into the closet with the other and drew out a pair of jeans and a shirt. "I keep a cot at the clinic for when I have a patient staying overnight. I could sleep there until we…that is, until you and I come to some arrangement.''

More decisions.

Married less than twenty-four hours, Rachel faced the reality of her situation—the intimacy of being married, but not being a wife. Apparently, Jared was claiming a husband's right to stroll through her bedroom whenever he pleased.

What about a wife's privileges?

''I see,'' she said, trying to sound more sophisticated than she felt. She might be twenty-six years old, but years spent raising Dylan, coupled with her own sense of natural reserve, had left Rachel with little experience with men.

He frowned at that cool reply. ''But until then, it would be more convenient if I could store my clothes here.''

''Of course. There's enough space in the closet.''

So, this was to be only the first of many towel encounters, Rachel realized—not quite sure how she felt about that—certainly not awful.

In fact, after Jared left, she found herself humming.

With no clear idea of their plans for the day, she dressed casually, then tied her hair up on her head. A few curls escaped at the nape of her neck and around her ears. She dusted a light powder over her nose; then, with a shrug, gave up trying to hide the freckles. No matter how she tried, she could never be glamorous.

By the time they met again over breakfast, Jared had regained his dignity along with his clothes.

She was wearing jeans and a soft yellow sweater, but an image of her in a peach robe remained fixed in Jared's mind.

She'd cooked eggs and sliced some leftover ham she found in the refrigerator. Toast and coffee made up the rest. They sat at a large claw-legged wooden table situated near a window overlooking the apple orchard. The trees looked heavy, their branches bending low, almost touching the ground, with ripe red fruit—Macintosh and Northern Spies.

Trying to find a way out of eating the runny fried eggs, Jared forked them around his plate. He cut into a piece of ham and tried to ignore the burned edges. About the only thing she hadn't ruined was the toast, and the coffee.

Jared chewed through a charred piece of ham and failed to hide his amusement. "You're a lousy cook."

She set her own fork aside. "I've never had much practice," she admitted, honestly. "The Inn had a full-time cook. I'm trying to learn, but Dylan's not very demanding."

"For a moment I thought—" His voice broke off, unsure of what he meant to say. He'd seen her house, she seemed like such a nest-builder, he'd naturally assumed she could cook. His mistake.

At his unfinished sentence, she tilted her head. "What?"

Setting his fork down, he met her curious gaze. "I thought you'd ruined the meal on purpose."

"That's a pretty cynical attitude," she said, obviously feeling provoked, and trying hard not to show it. "When I decide to play underhanded games, I'll let you know."

At her spirited response, Jared leaned back in his chair and grinned. "I'm sure you will." Rachel, all lit up, was like a wet firecracker—all fizzle and no pop. Even her anger was restrained. Someday, he'd like to break through her inhibitions to reveal the woman—the passionate redhaired firebrand—hidden beneath the thin layers of reserve.

She was full of surprises. Last night, a reminder of Laurel had served as a wedge to control his baser instincts.

Unfortunately, Rachel didn't appear as grateful as she should be for his forbearance—not to mention the cold shower—which created a whole new dilemma for Jared. Since Rachel didn't love him, making love to her would only make her despise him more—wouldn't it?

Last night's awkward reminder of Laurel, no matter how ill-timed, had slowed things down. Now that he had time to think, Jared knew that seducing his bride on their wedding night would have been a mistake. She might have accepted his lovemaking, then regretted it later. The mood of the wedding had obviously affected them both and held them captive.

Being a newlywed was a heady business, and heaven knew Rachel went to his head like fine wine. But the feeling would be better if allowed to age.

Chapter Ten

Rachel wasn't sure if this was the right time for this conversation. Nevertheless, she was willing to listen.

Jared had more to say. "I know this setup is awkward. But I want you to be happy here. I messed up badly when I didn't tell you everything I knew about Dylan, which wasn't much at the time. I'd like us to try and be friends. Who knows where that will lead?"

"I agree. I want Dylan to feel secure. That's why I'm here," Rachel said, no longer sure if it was the only reason.

He stood up, looking relieved. "I should go down to the clinic and check a couple of patients, but I won't be long. How about if we drive into town and pick up Dylan? When we get back, I'll give you both a tour of the place."

She smiled at his suggestion. "I'd like that."

His gaze swept over her in her long-legged jeans, stopping at the flimsy sandals on her feet. "Those aren't too practical for trudging around the farm. We'll have to get you some boots.''

So, she was going to be trudging around the farm, more than once. Why did something so mundane hold an edge of danger and excitement?

The farm tour scored a hit with Dylan.

His face flushed with excitement, he hadn't stopped smiling since Rachel and Jared picked him up at the O'Neils'.

The day was warm and dry. A light breeze stirred the tall grass and riffled through the lush, green fields of produce—mainly potatoes—in various stages of harvest.

''This is the busiest time of the year. We hire extra help.'' Jared nodded toward the seasonal farmworkers in the potato fields. When several lifted hands and waved, he stopped and introduced Rachel.

Ramon Morales politely removed his hat. ''I wish you both well on your marriage.''

Rachel thanked him, adding, ''I understand you have a little boy. I hope he and Dylan can be friends.''

''Si, that is good.'' Ramon smiled back. ''I will tell my wife. And Miguel. He will be pleased.''

The men went back to work.

Dylan ran ahead, while Jared and Rachel followed more slowly as Jared pointed out some of the farm buildings and their uses.

''I didn't realize this was such a large operation,'' Rachel said at one point.

''Farming is big business. If you can't haggle price with the brokers, you're out of the game.''

There was a cow barn, and the rest were packing and storage sheds. Some had been damaged in last summer's explosion at the neighboring migrant camp. A shell and bare foundation remained where one barn had once stood.

Jared explained that instead of rebuilding, his father had insisted on using the insurance money to help finance the clinic.

Dylan waited for them to catch up. He climbed up the wood fence and hung on to the top rail. "Wow, look at this!"

Cows.

Sharing his enjoyment, Rachel leaned against the fence. "This is wonderful, all this freedom," she said. "You were lucky to grow up here."

His eyes shadowed, Jared looked around, as if seeing it from her eyes. "I suppose I took it for granted. It's all I knew until I left home and discovered other places. At eighteen, I couldn't wait to get away. I did a short tour of military duty in the Middle East, before getting stationed on the West Coast where I eventually got my degree."

"But you came back."

He smiled. "I missed it."

They walked on, with Dylan exclaiming at every turn.

Jared took him for a tractor ride around a pasture dotted with bales of hay, maneuvering the large piece of machinery with ease. Rachel refused a turn—unable to tell whether Jared was serious or teasing. In either case, she preferred to keep both feet safely on the ground.

Leaving the tractor behind, Dylan discovered a creek filled with all sorts of creatures.

"The creek is usually shallow," Jared explained. Ankle deep, the water trickled between the exposed rocks. "As a kid, I used to come here a lot and catch tadpoles and frogs. But it's not always safe. After a storm, this can fill up with enough water to carry a pickup downstream." There was also a pond stocked with trout, and a rowboat.

"Don't come out here alone," Rachel worried out loud. "And no swimming unless you have an adult with you."

"Yes, Mom."

They walked through the woods, and Rachel worried about wild animals. She started to say, "Don't..."

"I know," Dylan said. "Don't go in the woods by myself."

She smiled sheepishly. "Am I being overprotective?"

Jared chuckled. "You're being a mom. A reminder of staying safe can't hurt. Right, Dylan?" He gave Dylan one of those man-to-man looks Rachel had seen only in the movies.

Dylan got it. He stood a little taller. "Right."

Realizing she was being humored, Rachel wasn't sure how this co-parenting was going to work. Obviously, Jared intended to be a hands-on father.

"I guess that's it," Jared said when they came to a low stone fence marking a boundary line. "At least for today."

"There's more?" she asked, dropping onto a fallen log.

Jared sat beside her. "We can't see it all today. The perimeter around is several miles. Are you hungry?"

"Starving," she admitted.

Dylan said, "Me, too."

"Then, let's go home. We can pick some apples on the way. The orchard's just the other side of those trees."

Filled with boundless energy, Dylan ran ahead with Jared, while Rachel preferred to follow more slowly. By the time she reached the orchard, Jared had filled half a bushel basket with apples, but Dylan was nowhere in sight.

Jared bit into a ripe red apple and handed it to Rachel. "Have a bite," he said, offering to share, tempting her with a warm intimate smile that made her wonder if Adam in the Garden of Eden had been as innocent as he proclaimed.

Nevertheless, she bit into the apple, murmuring, "Mmm, delicious. Where's Dylan?"

"Up here, Mom!"

Rachel looked up and nearly choked. He was grinning down at her through the branches, ten feet up in the tree without a ladder. "Dylan! Be careful!" She turned on Jared. "I thought you were looking after him. Why didn't you stop him? If he falls…"

"He won't fall," Jared said calmly. "He's safe."

"He's only eight years old!"

"And old enough to climb a tree. Rachel, he's a curious little boy; you can't protect him from everything. I know that's a mother's job. Maybe I'm wrong, but I think it's my job to give him some room and make him believe he can climb that tree. And to be there to catch him if he falls."

Staring back at him, Rachel took a deep breath and slowly released it, along with some of her fears. But one remained. Maybe he was right about Dylan. But what about her? She looked down at the half-eaten apple in her hand. She was in serious danger of falling deeply in love with her own husband. Who would catch her if she fell?

It was all a matter of trust.

A little boy's voice called down, "Hey, Mom. This one's a beauty. Here, catch." Dylan tossed down an apple.

Rachel caught it. Now she had two apples. She didn't know whether to eat them, juggle them or toss them both at Jared's head. Or take another bite of the apple. She had to admit the man stirred some ambivalent emotions. How could she understand him? He obviously didn't understand her.

Putting her trust in someone was foreign to Rachel. For so long, she'd cared for Dylan on her own. It was hard to let go, to share, to stretch without breaking.

Later, as they walked back to the house, Jared firmly warned Dylan, "A farm is fun, but it's full of hazards as well. Unless you're with an adult, or you have permission, stay out of the woods. You could get lost. You also have to stay away from the fields and the machinery, the barn, the pond..." There was more, which left Dylan with free access to the grassy, partially shaded area surrounding the house.

Rachel was grateful that Jared had set some boundaries. No matter how she felt about their personal situation, she knew he had his son's best interest at heart.

That evening, Jared hoped to avoid a repetition of the previous night's awkwardness over sleeping arrangements.

He excused himself when Dylan went to bed. "I've got to check on a patient." Jared left the house.

Outside, like a night shade coming down, the evening skies had darkened, clouds hovered. The air was cool. He did have a patient to check. He was also tired, but for some reason, he was in no hurry to seek his lonely bed. Instead, he lingered, forced to acknowledge that a sense of loneliness gripped him and held him captive. The feeling wasn't all that new, but the intensity was. He didn't let people get close. But that was changing—like a thirst that couldn't be quenched with one draft, like a hunger that couldn't be sated with one taste. He saw a light go on in an upstairs window.

Rachel.

Eventually, the light went out.

Only then, did he find his way to the clinic.

On Monday morning, Rachel made another adjustment.

Ira arrived, along with Sunny and Digger—then there were the hamsters and the fish.

Ira took one look and exclaimed, "The place is turning into a zoo." He added a few choice words.

Fortunately, Dylan was out of hearing range. Jared looked exhausted—so did Rachel—which seemed to satisfy Ira. To all outward signs their marriage was real.

Jared gulped down the rest of his coffee. "I have to go." Under his father's watchful eye, he aimed a kiss somewhere in the vicinity of Rachel's mouth. However, his hand on her shoulder left a scorching trail. "I'll be at the clinic if you need me," he said on his way out the door.

Ira shook his head and went back to his morning paper.

Rachel had a few errands to do. First, she drove Dylan to school. She'd spoken to Dylan's teacher and the bus driver about the recent move. Nevertheless, she felt the need to remind Dylan one more time. "Remember to take the bus home."

He waved. "Bye, Mom."

"Bye," she said, biting her lip as she watched him skip up the walk. She wished she had somewhere to go, something to do. She could start the process of packing and moving her things out of her old house; but somehow, she wasn't ready for that. Instead, she picked up a few items of clothing for her and Dylan, and left the rest for another day.

Maybe tomorrow.

The long day stretched ahead. Jared had plucked her out of her simple life and thrust her into a new situation. While he went about his usual routine, apparently she would have to deal with Ira on her own.

She went back to Stones End.

When she walked into the house, Ira said, "I'll stay out of your way." For the rest of the morning, he sat in his recliner by the window and watched every move Rachel made—as if she was going to make off with the family jewels.

Jared came home at noon.

The meal was strained.

Ira's contribution added to it when he asked his son pointedly, "Dylan's a Carlisle. When are you going to get around to signing the papers and making it legal?"

Jared managed an even reply. "There's no rush."

Feeling invisible when both men ignored her, Rachel looked from one to the other. "What papers?"

The elderly man rose from his chair. "I think I'll turn in for a nap. You two need to talk."

And talk fast.

Rachel clenched her hands. "Since you've obviously discussed this with everyone else—your lawyer and your father—when were you going to tell me?"

Jared admitted, "I planned to break it to you after you got accustomed to Stones End."

"In the future, I wish you'd stop protecting me from the truth. It only makes it harder." She should have realized Jared wanted Dylan to bear the Carlisle name, but the announcement still came as a shock. And the fact that Jared had left her out of the decision process hurt.

"He's my son," Jared insisted quietly, as if she still needed convincing.

Rachel bristled at his tone. "You can't own him!"

"Dylan is a Carlisle. Nothing on God's earth can change that. I'm sorry, Rachel. I've tried to give you some space and consider your feelings when it comes to this marriage, but this is one area where I can't. Dylan needs to know who he is, he needs to be part of a family. This family."

"Your son! Your family!" Unable to hide her feelings, she poured all her resentment into those four words.

He looked shocked. "It's your family as well." His mouth tightened. "I'm sorry you can't see that, but it doesn't change anything. Dylan is a Carlisle. Making it legal is only a formality, but a necessary one. I'm not trying to leave you out. I'm asking you to trust me."

"How can I when you never tell me anything? From the first, you've kept the truth from me."

"I know we started all wrong. I still think we could have something special. Just give me a chance."

"How do I know you're not lying now?"

His eyes darkened. "I guess you don't." Where that admission would take them she would never know because the phone rang. Openly frustrated at the interruption, Jared answered. "An accident?" he said. "Where?"

Rachel watched his face change as he wrote down some directions. When he hung up, with just a few words, he shut her out. "I'm sorry, we'll have to finish this later. I have to go." He was already miles away from Rachel.

Accepting that he was urgently needed somewhere, and that he apparently wasn't going to share any of the details with his new wife, she nodded, then watched him leave with everything between them so unsettled. Briefly, she'd dared to hope, but now she knew. Stones End would never be her home. It belonged to Jared, just as everything did, including Dylan. Who was she kidding? Including her. At least part of her...her heart.

Over the next few days, Rachel discovered that Stones End was a busy place. The main farmhouse served as headquarters for a thriving produce operation.

The phone rang constantly. That afternoon, when someone named Olivia called, Rachel answered. "Can I help you?"

When told that Jared wasn't available, the woman asked, "Is this Jessie?"

"No, this is Jared's wife, Rachel."

"Oh, I'm sorry." Olivia sounded young, but not that young, and a little unsure. "I didn't know he was married." The confidence faded with each word. She laughed nervously. "I guess there's a lot I don't know."

"It was fairly recent." Assuming Olivia must be an ex-girlfriend, Rachel tried to convince herself that Jared's past didn't concern her. "Would you like to leave a number?"

"No, that's all right." The voice sounded smaller, more distant. "Just tell him I'll call back."

Rachel hung up. Something in the woman's voice made her uneasy. If there was another woman in Jared's life, someone he genuinely cared about, he wouldn't have married Rachel. Would he? She stared at the phone, wondering exactly how far Jared would go to carry out his sense of duty.

That evening, when Rachel gave Jared the message, he stared at the name on the yellow notepad.

"Did she leave a number? An address?" He stared at the note, then at Rachel. He looked shaken.

At his reaction, Rachel clenched her hands. "No, I'm sorry, she didn't. Is there a problem?"

He crushed the note. "No, it's okay."

When he failed to add any details, Rachel assumed the worst. For days, she couldn't put the woman's voice out of her mind. It stayed with her, buried under a heap of worries, both old and new.

For the remainder of that week, the routine at Stones End didn't vary much from day to day. Rachel saw little of Jared. He was still sleeping at the clinic using a sick calf as an excuse. Apparently, his veterinary business must be booming—or else he was avoiding her. At times, she felt invisible.

On Friday, she'd planned a light lunch, but Ira asked her to plan a meal, and to set some extra plates.

"For how many?" she asked.

"Six…maybe seven, if the broker turns up." His voice held a challenge; he obviously knew he'd shocked her. "Once a week, we review the farm business over lunch. Ramon's wife usually puts a meal together, but now we've got a woman in the house, I told her not to bother."

Rachel knew he expected her to fail; she was just as determined to prove him wrong.

Fortunately, Jessie had dropped off a large pasta salad and fresh rolls. She'd picked apples and baked a perfect deep-dish pie. With a sinking heart, Rachel wondered how she could live up to such high standards. If Jared expected anything like it, he was in for a major disappointment.

Nevertheless, pride had Rachel digging up a roast out of the freezer. Without a microwave, she couldn't thaw it out, so she tossed it into a pot of water, seasoned it and brought it to a boil. There wasn't time to let it simmer.

Lunch was a disaster.

Fred Cromie was polite. "She sure brightens up the place." He said nothing about Rachel's cooking.

Ramon Morales thanked her, but never asked for seconds. Ben was clearly the silent type. And the broker never turned up. Neither did Jared.

Ira clearly enjoyed himself. After eating a piece of pie, he set the last slice aside, saving it for his afternoon snack. He yawned. "Time for my nap."

Later that afternoon, Rachel walked down to the corner to meet Dylan at the school bus stop. The air was filled with the scent of fresh earth, wild grasses and flowers.

She had to admit Stones End had a wild primitive sort
of beauty that intrigued her. Just that morning she'd found
animal tracks by the back doorstep. Now, each time the
bushes stirred, she imagined a rabbit lurking, or a deer—
or something worse. There must be bears and wolves, but
she didn't need wild animals to alarm her. Since the mysterious phone call from another woman, she'd felt Jared's
restiveness and wondered—who was Olivia? And what
did she mean to Jared—if anything?

The school bus pulled to a stop. Dylan jumped off and
waved. A smaller dark-haired boy was with him. Although a grade separated the two boys, Dylan and Miguel
Morales had become inseparable because they attended
the same school.

Rachel and the boys walked back up the farm road. At
a junction, Miguel went on his way, calling, "See you
later."

Dylan asked, "Can Miguel come over to play?"

"Homework first," Rachel said automatically.

"Aw, Mom."

When they walked into the house, Ira was ranting,
"What happened to it?" He glared at Dylan. "Did you
eat my pie!" He pointed at the table. "It's gone!"

An empty plate sat on the table. A smudge of apple pie
filling and a few crumbs told the tale. Someone had eaten
the piece Ira had set aside for his afternoon treat.

Rachel put Dylan behind her back. "Dylan hasn't been
here all afternoon—he just got home from school."

"Someone ate it!" Looking for a target, Ira's rage fell
on Dylan's dog. "The dog must have done it."

Digger was too small to reach the table top, but Rachel
couldn't be sure if Sunny was innocent. She'd left the dog
behind to go meet Dylan. Hoping to appease Ira, she said,
"I know pets can be a nuisance. But Dylan loves his dog.

If you'll just give her a second chance, I'll keep a closer eye in the future.''

Ira snapped, ''I want her out!''

A tearful Dylan wrapped his arms around the dog's thick neck. ''Sunny didn't do it.''

The dog sat back, wagged its tail and grinned.

The tail wagging must have done it. Ira threw the dog a disgusted look. ''I want that animal out of this house! From now on, she can sleep in the barn.''

Although Rachel drew herself up tall, she was no match for her father-in-law. From day one, she'd done everything to please this difficult man. Today's lunch was an example. Fair or unfair, she could tolerate a certain amount of mistreatment, but not when Ira directed his anger at Dylan.

It was time to make a stand. ''If Sunny goes, we go.''

At her ultimatum, Ira's lips rounded in surprise, then hardened in anger. ''You won't go. You got exactly what you wanted from my son—a wedding ring and a piece of Stones End. I know your kind—always out for what you can get.''

''That's not true,'' she said hotly.

He fixed her with a look. ''Do you love him?''

''Well, I...'' She didn't know Jared well enough to come up with a comprehensive answer...one that would satisfy Ira. A small inner voice scoffed at that reasoning.

''I rest my case.'' Ira stomped off, leaving Rachel fuming at the injustice of his accusation. Since the wedding, he'd set up one impossible obstacle after another.

Well, Ira did not ''know her kind.'' Determined to prove him wrong, she said impulsively, ''Let's go home.''

Dylan looked confused. ''We are home.''

''Our other home. We never moved out, remember?''

Suddenly, it all seemed so simple, so logical. She was

simply correcting a mistake. She should never have entered into a marriage of convenience. It wasn't working. Dylan wasn't happy. Rachel wasn't happy. Jared certainly wasn't jumping for joy. It was high time to end this before their relationship went any further. An annulment was the obvious answer. The marriage had failed. Rachel put the blame squarely where it belonged—on Jared.

For days, he'd left her at Ira's mercy while he disappeared for hours on end, claiming the necessity of work. If he wasn't at the clinic, he was out lending a hand with the harvest. Then there was Olivia.

Another woman?

Why endure this behavior from a man who avoided her at every turn? Why stay where they were barely tolerated, where there was no love? Was that what she wanted for Dylan? For herself? No! There was no real place for them at Stones End. Not a secure one. She refused to settle for less.

Luckily, she hadn't brought much with her. She packed the few items, and they were ready. Somehow, she couldn't bear the thought of telling Jared, so she took the cowardly way out and wrote him a note explaining that she wanted their brief marriage annulled. She would be in town if he wanted to come and discuss the situation. Like two sensible adults, they could come to some sort of agreement over Dylan.

She was not giving him up!

Rachel stared down at the note. Wondering how to end it, she chewed on the end of the pen. She could have written pages and pages of complaints, but she settled for one...a child needed to grow up in a house of love. From what she'd seen so far, Stones End didn't come close!

Chapter Eleven

"Dylan, get in the car."

"But, Mom...what about..."

Rachel held the door open. "Never mind. Everything's going to be fine." Praying she was right, she dropped a kiss on the top of his head. "I promise."

With a troubled frown, Dylan climbed into the car and attached his seat belt. "Jared's not going to like this."

She wanted to scream. "I don't care what Jared likes," she said in a tight determined voice. "I have to do what's best for us—you and me. We're a team, remember?"

"Yeah, but..."

Rachel shut the passenger door on the rest. She was through listening to the males in her life. Drew, Jared, Ira—they'd had her jumping through hoops long enough. She tossed the luggage into the back seat. Digger was safe in his box. "Sit!" she told Sunny and Digger, and the dogs obeyed. The fish were sloshing around in their bowl, and various animals were safely caged. They were only going a few miles into town for now. She'd plan their next move later. She'd get a map and plan the rest of her life—this time with no detours!

For now, she felt free. She climbed in and turned the key in the ignition. The engine roared to life. She bit her lip, feeling guilty. Jared had repaired her car, and now she was using it to run away. She stiffened her spine. This was no time to weaken her resolve. Rachel put the car in Reverse and backed out of the driveway.

A huge brownish-black shadow loomed out of nowhere.

Rachel slammed on the brakes—mere inches from the gangling beast. She couldn't believe it! A moose was in the driveway. It didn't blink an eye. Not a twitch. She blew the horn. When he didn't budge, Rachel got out and tried to shoo him away with a wave of her hands. Nothing happened. She was red-faced and furious when Ira came out on the porch.

"What the hell are you doing?" he shouted.

"Watch your language," she shot back. "There is a young impressionable child present!"

Although intimidated by the animal's size, she pushed his hard stump-tailed rump. At that, he twisted his head, swirling six feet of antlers in a wide arc, as he looked at her with a hangdog expression. With long droopy ears and a muzzle that hung four inches lower than his chin, how else could he look?

"Now listen here, young woman."

"Don't you 'young woman' me." Rachel looked at the moose and wanted to cry—better yet, she wanted a shotgun. Crying never accomplished a damn thing! She glared at Ira—her father-in-law. Good God—how had she gotten herself into this mess! "This is all your fault!"

Now, Ira was as red-faced as Rachel.

Naturally, Jared would pick that exact moment to appear. When his pickup turned into the driveway, Rachel groaned.

Jared got out of the truck. At the sight of Rachel locking horns with a moose, he smiled. "I see you've met Beauregard. He's practically—"

With an audible sigh, she interrupted, "I know—he's practically family."

Jared smiled. "He's just a lovesick moose. Beau turns up every summer to court one of our cows. And he's taken a serious liking to Jessie's herb garden." At a glance, he took in the entire scene, including the suitcases haphazardly tossed into the back seat of Rachel's car. She wasn't just out for a joyride—she was leaving him—and taking Dylan along with her.

Jared felt a sharp stab of disappointment. He'd always known it would take someone special to deal with his father. At some point, he'd begun to hope that Rachel might be the one. He knew all about women who up and left at the first sign of trouble—like his mother. He hated to admit his father might be right about Rachel.

Standing on the porch steps, Ira looked prepared to wage battle, and Rachel looked furious.

Well, Jared had wanted to see fireworks.

After getting some of the details, he calmed his father down and suggested Dylan wait in the house.

"Your mother and I have to talk," Jared said in a reasonable tone, leaving Rachel no room to argue.

Once they were alone, she put all her frustration into words. Facing Jared, she flung out her hands. "It's obvious your father doesn't want us. The situation is impossible. Dylan and I can't stay here." With those words hanging in the air between them, she looked away—as if she didn't want to see Jared's reaction. "I think an annulment is the answer," she said with a firm set to her mouth. "Dylan needs a mother and a father. But he also needs stability. And a sense of security. He's not getting that here."

Jared looked at her delicate profile, the stubborn tilt of her chin, and searched for the right answer. "I know my father takes some getting used to." With a harsh laugh, he ran his hand through his hair. "God knows being his son hasn't always been easy. But his heart's usually in the right place."

She glanced at him, still openly doubtful, but perhaps willing to be convinced. "I suppose."

"Maybe if I talk to him," he suggested, knowing that words alone would never move his father.

Frowning at his suggestion, Rachel folded her arms across her waist. "I'd rather you didn't."

"I thought that was what you wanted."

"I want him to accept me and Dylan on his own, without any interference. Relationships can't be forced."

Jared raised an eyebrow. "Are you talking about you and my father, or you and me?"

She shrugged. "A bit of both, I suppose."

He looked at her in silence for a long moment. "You're not going to make this easy, are you?"

"Is that what you want?" she parried.

He smiled warily. "So, where exactly are we going with this conversation?"

"I'm not sure." Her smooth brow wrinkled in confusion. "I have to decide."

Heartened by her apparent indecision, Jared wondered if there was any chance to save their marriage before it even began on any intimate level. He'd never given a thought to annulment, but apparently she had.

"Look," he said finally, "it's too late to leave now.

Dylan is upset, and so are you. Don't make any hasty decisions. What harm can there be in staying the night and looking at the situation more clearly in the morning? I can't force you to stay. This marriage might not be typical, but it does have to be built on something besides obligation.''

Her eyes widened, as if surprised, and relieved. "I'm glad you agree.''

"I'm not agreeing to anything," he warned her. "But if you decide to leave, I won't try to stop you. And as far as Dylan's concerned, I know the boy's place is with you.''

Later, Rachel lay awake in the big brass bed at Stones End, trying to figure out why she was still there. With a few words, Jared had defused the situation by simply agreeing with everything she said.

Only hours ago, she'd been so fed up and angry with Ira, herself and Jared. With a sigh, she sat up, hugging her knees tight to her chest. Now that she was free to go, she wasn't sure she should.

What if there was no turning back from this decision? Any action she took would decide her fate as well as Dylan's. Did she have the right to take him from his father? Could she turn her back on Stones End, and a chance to give Dylan a family, a chance to make Jared love her? The answer, if there was one, eluded her. Rachel wasn't a gambler. Life had conditioned her to be too cautious, frightened of losing.

She'd lost her temper with Jared's father.

Ira was probably gloating—he'd won. He'd made his low opinion clear from the moment he set eyes on her. She'd meant to prove him wrong—and somehow forgotten her resolve. Why? To escape her growing feelings for

Jared? At what point had thoughts of an annulment begun to appeal? When Jared continued to avoid her? When Olivia called?

Eventually, Rachel drifted into sleep. Around midnight, she woke. Something had disturbed her, she thought in some confusion. Then she heard Digger whining. The puppy slept in a box at the foot of Dylan's bed. Apparently, Digger wanted out. The whining continued.

Rachel got out of bed and pulled on her robe, then slid her bare feet into a pair of slippers. She yawned as she crossed the narrow hall. Jared had left a night light on, yet she was conscious of every shadow, every squeak, every loose floorboard. She silently opened the door to Dylan's bedroom. He'd gone to sleep upset because Ira refused to back down. As ordered, Sunny was banished to the barn for stealing Ira's pie.

"Shh," Rachel whispered to the small puppy hanging over the side of the box. She scratched the silky head. "What's wrong, sweetie?"

Digger licked her hand. Tail wagging like a white flag, he sat back in the box, and yipped.

"Hush, you're going to wake everyone," she murmured as a few facts registered. Where was Dylan? A glance at the empty bed told its own story.

For one sick moment, Rachel imagined the worst—Dylan was gone. She'd failed to protect him, and he'd run away.

She rushed down the stairs. A thorough search of the rooms didn't turn him up.

That left outdoors. She looked into the black night. Dylan could be out there anywhere. The farm was huge, filled with hazards, particularly at night, when animals hunted for prey. Panic struck at the thought.

But maybe she was overreacting. Maybe Dylan had

gone to find his dog. She could only hope, but there were several barns, and she had no idea where to start. She tried to think.

Of course, Jared would know. He knew every square inch of Stones End. Rachel closed her eyes. Although she had no choice, she hated asking for Jared's assistance, especially since she was determined to put an end to their marriage. He didn't seem brokenhearted. Neither was she. That was the problem—neither of their hearts were irreparably invested in this relationship.

Soon their marriage would be over, he was probably relieved—just as she was. Wasn't that hollow feeling in the pit of her stomach relief?

Unable to face that now, Rachel took a flashlight from a hook by the back door, then let herself out of the house. The night was warm, but the breeze was surprisingly cool as she left the protection of the house and struck out along the long driveway for the clinic where she hoped to find Jared. She shivered in her thin silk robe but didn't go back for something warmer. When something large dived for her head, she started to run, clearing the thick cover of overhanging trees before she reached the clinic. She ran up the steps, raised her hand to knock on the door....

When it swung open abruptly, she fell forward and landed against Jared's chest. His face registered shock. "Rachel!"

It all happened so fast.

She felt his hands against her waist. Breathless, she said, "How did you know it was me?"

"I didn't." His voice sounded husky, and his breathing felt heavy against her—as if he'd been running, too. He glanced down at the flashlight clutched in her hand. "I was awake and saw a light wavering up and down the road."

"Oh." She flicked off the light, adding to the aura of intimacy.

His face broke into a warm smile that shocked her—along with his shirtless physique. His tan ended abruptly where a pair of blue-and-white striped pajama bottoms rode low on his hips. The hair on his arms and chest was pale and gold, giving the sleek defined muscles a gilded appearance. Behind him was a small cot with the covers thrown back in haste.

"You've changed your mind about leaving," he said, clearly coming to all the wrong conclusions.

"No!" she said in high tones, her breath suddenly nonexistent. As his gaze scored over her, she felt underdressed in her peach-colored robe. The silk clung to her, but at least she was decently covered—unlike Jared. "No, that is, I'm still leaving in the morning. It's Dylan. He's gone."

Jared released her. "Gone?"

"He's not in his room. I was hoping he might be here."

"He's not here." Apparently, her concern communicated itself to him. His smile fled. "You think he's run away?"

"He was upset about Sunny sleeping in the barn. He might be with her, but I don't know where to look."

"Give me a minute." Jared reached for his clothes.

While he dressed, Rachel turned away and pretended to be absorbed in a graphic display of a cow's gestation period as she heard the rustle of clothing, the rasp of a zipper…

Moments later, they stepped outside. Rachel looked up at the night sky. "Something flew at me before."

"Probably a bat. They help keep the mosquito population down. Believe me, they're far more frightened of you than you are of them."

"Mmm," Rachel murmured, not reassured.

When they walked up the black road, she stayed close to Jared's side. Her heart pounded. When Jared reached for her hand, she knew another kind of anxiety—the fear of learning to rely on this, on him....

They found Dylan in the cow barn.

Although the building was occupied with about twenty dairy cows, it smelled surprisingly sweet and clean with fresh hay scattered around the occupied stalls. Dylan had found an empty one. He was sound asleep, curled up next to Sunny with an arm curled tight around the dog's neck.

Relieved at the sight, Jared switched off the light. When Rachel remained silent, he suddenly realized she was shaking. He wasn't sure how to comfort her, but he drew her into his arms. "Listen, he's all right. It's over."

"It's just that if anything happened to him, I...."

Jared took a deep breath. "Being a parent is never easy." She nodded, so he kept talking. "I suppose worrying goes with the job description."

With a deep sigh, she pulled away. "He's normally so cooperative. I never dreamed he'd run away like that."

"He didn't run very far," Jared reminded her.

She laughed shakily. "No, he didn't, did he?"

When she made a move toward the stall, Jared stopped her. His hand on her arm was firm and persuasive. So was his voice. "Why don't we just leave them? They'll be safe until morning."

Rachel looked around the cavernous barn. "But won't Dylan be cold?"

Jared didn't argue with her—she'd already been through a difficult day. She needed reassurance, not a debate. "How about if I carry him inside?"

Rachel felt relieved.

Then, she sighed, aware of the surrounding night, and

her empty bedroom waiting. If she left in the morning, they might never have another chance to be alone.

"You've been very kind," she said. "Thank you."

"I don't expect thanks."

"No, I don't suppose you do." She curled her arms around her waist. "I'm sorry things haven't worked out."

"Are you?" He raised a skeptical eyebrow.

"Well, of course."

He braced his legs apart, with the direct challenge, "Then prove it."

"How?" She clenched her hands, afraid of the answer.

"Stay."

Rachel laughed shakily. "Just like that?"

"Why not?" His gaze held hers, leaving no room for evasion. "A marriage can be fixed as well as broken."

She couldn't look away. "Do you honestly believe that?"

"No. Not really." He laughed harshly. "But let's give ours a test—at least six months."

"Six months?"

He was willing to negotiate. "All right, how about three? Don't you think a marriage deserves that much?"

Weighing her answer, she looked toward Dylan. If the decision was so wrenching at this early stage, how would it be in three months when she and Dylan were more firmly entrenched at Stones End? Knowing that was exactly what Jared counted on, she shook her head. "I can't think now."

He didn't hide his disappointment. "We can't postpone this discussion indefinitely."

"I thought we agreed to wait until morning." She was going to hold him to that.

"All right." Jared lifted the boy and carried him from

the stall. He whistled for Sunny to follow. "Don't worry, I'll square it with Dad tomorrow."

In silence, they walked back to the house. Rachel climbed the stairs, her tension mounting with each step. In Dylan's bedroom, she drew back the bed covers.

Aware of her unease, Jared moved around her and carefully placed the boy on the bed.

Dylan stirred. "Where's Sunny?" The boy's eyes were red and puffy—he'd obviously shed some tears earlier.

Something tightened in Jared's chest. "Don't worry, Sunny's not going anywhere. She's right here. Right where she belongs."

Dylan's smile trembled a bit. "Thanks."

"Hey, it's after midnight. Isn't it about time you got some sleep?" Jared ruffled Dylan's hair.

"Right." Dylan hesitated; then, just as Jared moved away, he tacked on a very deliberate, "Good night, Dad."

Dad.

The word had never once fallen from Dylan's lips. It was a first for Jared, as well. He'd begun to wonder if Dylan would ever say it. And yet, he wasn't prepared for the impact. A small crack in his heart opened, and Dylan filled it. Being a father meant responsibility, joy and pain, in equal measures. After spending time with Dylan, it came as a shock to realize how little he knew about eight-year-old boys. At that age, Jared was into sports, all kinds—Dylan had an artistic streak. Animals, however, appeared to be a common ground. He was only beginning to grasp the meaning of being a parent. Fatherhood had less to do with sperm, and more to do with changing diapers, walking the floor at night, watching a baby's first step, or seeing him off to his first day at school. Jared had missed all those.

He saw the anxiety in Dylan's eyes as the boy waited

for a response. Acting on instinct rather than experience, Jared said, "Good night...son."

He heard Rachel's small suppressed gasp, but had no time to react because Dylan sat up and threw his arms around him.

The move caught Jared off guard. His response was a little slow and awkward as he gathered the small warm body to his chest. This emotion was new and raw—a gentle ache. Jared glanced over Dylan's head and encountered Rachel's stricken expression. They both knew the time for discussion was over. Dylan had settled the matter.

Rachel would stay.

She walked out without a word.

After tucking Dylan into bed, Jared went in search of Rachel. She'd left her bedroom door open. He found her there, leaning against the windowsill, looking out into the empty night, with her forehead pressed against the glass.

She looked lost and alone—as alone as he felt. With her face reflected in the black glass, he watched one solitary tear slowly trickle down. He handed her a tissue.

"Thank you." She wiped her eyes and tried to smile through her tears. "I don't know why I'm doing this."

More than the unshed tears, her brave smile tore at his heart. He raised his hands, intending to comfort her, but dropped them when he saw her shoulders stiffen in open rejection. Taking a breath, Jared slipped his hands into his pockets. "Are you all right?"

She nodded. "I'm actually glad that Dylan feels the way he does. It's what I wanted for him. It's just that..." Her voice drifted off. She took a fortifying breath and started again, putting her thoughts into words, revealing her soul to him. "It's just that I wasn't prepared for how I would feel."

What could he say, except, "I'm sorry."

"Don't be," she returned, startling him with a fierce show of spirit. "You've won."

Somehow, Jared didn't feel like cheering, nor did he want to cause her any more anguish. Nevertheless, he wanted to hear her say it. "Does that mean you're not leaving in the morning?"

"Dylan is my son, I'll stay for as long as he needs me."

Although it wasn't what Jared wanted to hear, he had to accept it. A niggling reminder of his own needs made him fear for his own welfare. What if he let himself love her? She wouldn't leave until Dylan grew up, but then what? How could he bind Rachel to him?

Despite all the remaining doubts, coupled with his own disappointment in her answer—which clearly didn't include him—the simple beauty and generosity of her love for Dylan moved him deeply. For as long as he lived, he would remember this moment—with Rachel in her silk robe, her bright hair tangled, her eyes bright with unshed tears.

Yes, he would remember this moment when he was old and gray. The day Rachel shook his heart and made him weak with wanting her. The day he knew he'd wasted so much time with her and wondered if a lifetime would be too short to learn to love her as she deserved.

Her nearness affected him as it always did.

He'd avoided being alone with her since their wedding, hoping the gnawing ache would wear off, but it hadn't. He wanted her more than ever. And all of a sudden it seemed so simple. Perhaps avoiding Rachel was all wrong. Together, they'd dealt with this crisis over Dylan. Perhaps it was time to test their wedding vows and seal their bargain by putting an end to any remote possibility of annulment.

Besides, the thought of his lone narrow cot at the clinic seemed unappealing compared to the double brass bed. The quilt was turned down invitingly. He had only to take Rachel by the hand and lead her there. And if she rejected him? Could he deal with that?

He'd never know the answer unless he tried. With the thought, Jared turned her toward him.

Her eyes held a thousand questions, for which he had only one answer. He kissed her, drawing her against him, letting her feel his hunger, his need.

Pulling away, she drew in a shaky breath. "This is still too soon."

"Way, way too soon," he agreed, nibbling at her ear. He moved to her throat. "Don't say anything."

"What about the annulment?" she whispered, searching his eyes for the truth. "What if you fall in love with someone else? You might want your freedom someday."

"To hell with the annulment!"

Her hands rose in protest, then fell against his chest. "We still should talk about this."

He shook his head. "That only leads to more talk and more problems. I want you, Rachel. No words can change that. You're my wife, and I want to make love to you."

His mouth stopped any further protest. At the touch of her lips against his, he groaned, betraying his need to possess her. He dragged her closer, felt her collapse and press against him. There was nothing tentative or slow.

From beginning to end, the kiss was an act of possession—a touch desperate because he knew he wasn't the reason she'd agreed to stay. She'd stayed because Dylan needed a father, and Jared just happened to be the guy.

He wanted so much more from Rachel.

Slowly, he drew off her silk robe—it was the same color as her skin. When she'd come to him at the clinic earlier, he'd first thought she was naked—until he saw the edges of her robe fluttering like butterfly wings.

When he ran his hands lightly down her arms, she shuddered, unknowingly betraying her physical response. And once he knew she wanted him, there was no going back...for either of them.

The moment for objections came and went. The bed sank beneath them. "I want you," he gently reminded her, then amply demonstrated what he meant.

And this time, Rachel heard the tenderness. Not that it was any comfort when her heart was racing and she couldn't catch her breath. She couldn't get close enough. He released her for a brief moment.

"Where are you going?" she said, shocked at her immediate sense of loss. Without him, she felt cold.

"Not far. I'm going to close the door." While he was at it, he turned off the overhead light, plunging the room into darkness.

She couldn't see him—just a faint outline moving against a blacker wall. "Where are you?"

He laughed softly. He was closer than she thought. She felt the air stir as he bent to remove his shoes. She heard him undress, then felt the bed give as he climbed back in.

The touch of his hands in the dark thrilled her as he slowly peeled away her nightgown, shimmering peach silk trailing along her skin. He kissed each inch unveiled.

Only one question remained.

For a second, Jared froze at the sight of the locket. He didn't need a reminder of Laurel. The memories were indelibly etched in vivid detail—pale skin, and vivid red hair against a pillow...a locket glowing in the moonlight, and a woman's mocking laughter.

Yes, he remembered it all, but this time he refused to let it stop him. Rachel was innocent, vulnerable.

His eyes softened and he said, "If you don't mind."

Jared held her gaze as he carefully reached around and untangled a strand of her hair from the clasp. He freed the chain and removed it, holding it in his hand for a second. As if scorched, he dropped it onto the bedside table.

As the weight left her throat, Rachel pressed a hand to it and felt the loss. She felt naked. And free. As if a shadow had lifted. With a pang, she knew a moment's unease. Jared had deliberately removed any reminder of Laurel. Why?

What did Laurel mean to him?

Before she could voice her fears, Jared kissed her again. Lost in his touch, she swallowed her objections, unwilling to let Laurel destroy this moment, as she had so many others in Rachel's life. The thought made her feel guilty. She silenced that too and wondered—at what price?

Then, he was there, drawing her to him, and into a journey of discovery. Deciding it was time, she warned him of her lack of experience, she whispered, "I've never...."

"I know." How did he know, Jared wondered. Was it the soft tremor in her voice, the small gasp when he touched her breast, the artless search for his mouth when he stroked her intimately—any or all of those things?

His last rational thought was that he was glad to be the first. And he honestly wished he'd met Rachel, instead of her twin, that night at the Stillwater Inn. But the past, with all his regrets, couldn't be undone.

There was only now, this moment and Rachel. Their bodies meshed, their breaths and sighs mingled, and time spun itself out. The act of possession became an act of mutual surrender. Jared felt her surrounding him, and he moved gently, in awe of what she made him feel.

Perhaps for the first time in his life, he was willing to look no further than this magical gift—this mystery of mysteries—that he could no longer deny. Rachel not only held him enthralled, she felt as if she were made for him.

They captured the night.

Tomorrow would take care of itself.

Chapter Twelve

In the morning, Ira wasn't pleased to find the dog in the house. However, he kept quiet about it until Dylan left for school. "The dog has no manners," he said bluntly.

Jared had stayed to talk to his father. "We'll try to keep her out of your way. But Dylan's had to make a lot of adjustments lately without asking him to give up his dog."

Rachel held her breath and waited for Ira's reply.

"Well, when you put it like that—" he started to say when Fred arrived in the middle of the discussion.

Apparently, Fred had heard enough to voice an opinion. "Course the dog can stay. Why not?"

Exasperated, Ira said, "Because she stole my pie!" And the rest came out—all about Rachel's threatening to leave. She blushed when Ira said, "Course Jared changed her mind."

Rachel was amused to see Jared's face turn red as well.

"Well, I'll be darned." Fred removed his hat and scratched his head. "Don't know what all the fuss is about. Sunny couldn't have eaten that pie, 'cause I ate it."

Obviously hoping he'd heard wrong, Ira glowered at his oldest and dearest friend. "You ate my pie?"

Fred twirled his hat in his hand. "Well, it was just sitting there, didn't have your name on it, so I ate it." He looked sheepish. "Always did have a weakness for Jessie's apple pie. Sorry if it caused a spot of trouble."

Ira demanded, "Well, why didn't you tell anyone?"

Fred shrugged. "No one asked."

Rachel felt like laughing at Fred's account. She caught Jared's expression. He looked relieved, and vaguely amused. Ira, on the other hand, looked ready to burst. He sputtered something unintelligible.

Fred frowned. "What's that you say?"

Ira threw him an irritated glance and enunciated clearly, "All right. When I'm in the wrong, I can admit it."

"Go ahead, and do it then." Fred's eyes filled with mischief. "Apologize."

When prodded, Ira grit his teeth. "I'm sorry."

Fred chuckled. "Well, don't say it to me. Rachel's the one you owe, and Dylan. And Sunny," he tagged on at the end.

When Ira's face got beet red, Rachel said, "I accept your apology. It was a misunderstanding, and now it's over."

She was amazed when Ira said, "No, it was my mistake. I jumped to conclusions. The dog can stay. I never meant it to be permanent—just until she learned some manners."

It was a gracious apology, and Rachel accepted it with

an open heart. "Thank you. And I apologize, too. I might have overreacted just a little."

"Ha!" Ira's gray eyes were twinkling.

At that moment, he looked a lot like Jared. Rachel saw the resemblance. In his prime, Ira Carlisle must have been a proud, handsome man. Tall and straight, with that devilish grin, he probably turned the ladies' heads. Jared certainly turned Rachel's head. That probably explained why she hadn't formed a clear, coherent thought, or made a sound decision since the day she met him. Her attempt to escape Stones End had resulted in total failure. Instead of freeing herself, she'd spent a passionate night with her husband and turned her farcical marriage into something physical.

And real.

Now, Rachel felt hot as she recalled the night she'd spent in Jared's arms. She should be exhausted, but she felt exhilarated, forced to admit how desperately she wanted to stay at Stones End. Dylan's acceptance of Jared had given her an excuse. She'd tried to save herself. And failed. Now she was out of ammunition; she was through fighting Jared, and herself.

Ira left, claiming he had paperwork to get done.

Jared said, "I have to get back to work." His gaze was warm with approval when he bent and kissed her mouth. Only their lips touched, yet she felt the helpless urge to cling. "See you later," he whispered, then walked out.

Her gaze followed him across the room. The sound of the door closing released her. Aware of Fred's attention, she started to gather the breakfast dishes.

Fred helped. "I just wanted to apologize again for all the commotion." He scraped, then piled the plates together.

"It wasn't your fault." Rachel capped a bottle of catsup, which Ira poured over everything she cooked.

"Doesn't matter whose fault it is. Sounds to me like that piece of pie almost ended your marriage. Sometimes it's the small things that cause the most trouble."

Rachel smiled. "I suppose you're right."

"Folks are prepared for the big stuff, but little things sort of sneak up on you. Now I know Ira isn't small stuff. Don't let him rile you. He's good at it."

"I'll remember that," she said, assuming that was all.

But Fred wasn't through. He pulled something out of his jacket pocket. "Been meaning to give you this." He held out the wreath of flowers Rachel had worn on her wedding day. "Found these on the floor under a chair the other day, so I saved them—just in case you decided you wanted them back."

Rachel stared at the wilted flowers for a moment before accepting them. She had no idea what to do with them, but she wanted to cry. She'd tossed Jared's flowers away as if they meant nothing. She knew a moment's shame. "Thank you."

He tucked his hands in his back pockets. "Should be a family Bible around here somewhere. Seems to me, Jessie said something about pressing some of her bridal bouquet between the pages. Kind of a family tradition."

Rachel traced the rose; its edges had turned brown, but a delicate scent lingered. The blue flowers had closed their petals tight. "I'll do that," she said, not sure she had the right. She was a Carlisle bride, but not a chosen one.

Fred cleared his throat. "You know, my wife and I never had kids. Helping Ira raise his was the closest we got. That boy of yours reminds me of Jared when he was young—always was taken with every living creature, and couldn't stand to see something hurting."

Rachel smiled. "So he became a vet."

"Reckon that's what he wanted." Fred looked at the flowers in her hand. "He's a good man. Just give him a chance." He chuckled. "Don't mean to be preaching." He looked around the room. "This house has known a lot of unhappiness. The right woman could change all that." He set his hat on his head. "Guess I should be going to work. You need anything, anything at all, just ask."

Rachel was curious. "There is one thing. I know it's none of my business. No one ever mentions her name aloud. But why did Ira's wife leave?"

Fred smiled sadly, reminiscing. "The question is, why did she come to Stones End in the first place?"

Rachel tilted her head. "All right, why?"

"That's simple—'cause Ira wanted her." When Rachel couldn't hide her skepticism, he chuckled. "Oh, you should have seen him back then. Ira was never shy. He met Avis on a trip, took one look, and that was that. He married her. She was a city girl, young, pretty. She loved to sing and paint pictures, and get all dressed up in her fancy clothes and go out dancing all night." He lifted his shoulders. "Trouble is—you don't get much of that around Henderson, or Stones End, in case you haven't noticed."

"I've noticed." Rachel understood all too well; her sister had been the same. Some men found that type of woman irresistible. Apparently, Ira had. What about Jared? What attracted Jared to Laurel? No matter how shallow and brief, there must have been something.

Fred continued, "Ira hoped she'd grow to like it here. They had their babies. I suppose she tried, but it just wasn't in her to settle down. They got to arguing. So, one day, Avis decided she'd had enough. She up and left, with another man." His expression held sympathy for his friend. "Ira loved her, so he could forgive her almost anything. But not that. She wanted a divorce, and she wanted her kids. She got one, but not the other. Well, Ira got his revenge, he made sure she never saw Jared and Jessie again. She went away, and never did come back." He shook his head. "Heard she died last year."

Rachel took a deep breath. "I'm sorry to hear that."

He sighed. "Well, I'd best be going."

After he'd left, Rachel looked down at the flowers.

With a resigned sigh, she decided to look for that Bible. She found it on a table in the living room, as if it waited for her. When she opened it, a faded rose fell out. Weddings, births, funerals were all recorded on the first page. Some names were faded, along with the pressed flowers, but some were newer. Rachel's name was there, next to Jared. She was the latest Carlisle bride.

Selecting a rose from her bridal wreath, she placed it between the thin pages. Then, with a whimsical smile, she added a sprig of faded chicory. Suddenly, she didn't feel so alone. She squared her shoulders; she was one of the Carlisle brides. If they survived, so could she.

Rachel's new resolve was put to the test sooner than expected. Jared didn't make it home for lunch. He didn't make it to supper either, which left Rachel alone to cope with Ira. After the pie incident, she tried to dispel the lingering awkwardness. She and Ira had clashed, with no clear winner—they'd both said too much. She hoped it would clear the air and open the door to mutual understanding.

After the meal, as if to confirm that, Ira said, "Since you're family now, you can call me Dad."

Stunned by the extended olive branch, Rachel didn't dare refuse. Nevertheless, she nearly choked on the words, "All right—Dad."

They'd finished eating, the dishes were done, the long evening stretched ahead. Ira put on some taped music. He raised an eyebrow. "Don't suppose you play cribbage?"

At the invitation, she looked up. "Cribbage? Um, no." She set out a fresh tablecloth, smoothing out the corners.

"I could teach you," he suggested.

Rachel shook her head. "I don't think so."

Ira's mouth turned down with the words, "That's a shame." He obviously thought she was a coward.

Well, she was. She'd had all the excitement she could stand for one day.

Until then, Dylan was silent. When he spoke up, he surprised both Rachel and Ira. "I'd like to play."

Rachel's heart quaked. She didn't want Dylan exposed to Ira's biting tongue. "Don't you have some homework to do?"

"But it's Friday. There's no school tomorrow."

"Stop mollycoddling the boy! He's got to grow up sometime." Ira peered down at Dylan with a faint smile of approval. "I'm not going to bite if he makes a wrong move."

Mollycoddling—was that what she was doing? Rachel wondered. Naturally, she felt protective. Letting go and watching him grow into a Carlisle was full of pitfalls.

Ira pulled out a small wooden game board. He sat at the wooden table and motioned to Dylan. "Take a seat."

"Yes, sir." Dylan sat opposite.

"I'm your grandpa. Think you can say that?"

Dylan grinned, testing the word, "Sure…Grandpa."

Ira nodded in approval. "Well, about cribbage. It's a two-man game." He shuffled some cards.

Rachel hid a smile when Dylan sat up straighter. "How about if I make a bowl of popcorn?" she asked.

"Sounds good," Ira agreed.

This was a side of Ira she'd never seen—or perhaps she hadn't wanted to see Jared and his family as anything but adversaries. She'd erected a wall, making it easier to hold on to her resentment of their interference in her life. After listening to Fred's account of the family history, she knew Ira wasn't an ogre—just an unhappy man disappointed in life. Jared and Jessie had felt the loss of their mother. Rachel's heart ached at the thought of two motherless children growing up with only their father's harsh brand of love.

To her amazement, Ira's explanation of the game was patient, yet he didn't talk down to Dylan.

Dylan listened with rapt attention and caught on quickly. The evening passed with the two locked in a contest of wits over a cribbage board. Scottish reels played in the background. By the time Rachel went to bed, her head was reeling with the sound of bagpipes, flutes and drums.

Jared hadn't come home.

She kissed Dylan good-night, then went to her own room.

Her room?

After last night, was it hers alone? Did Jared intend to share more than a third of the closet and a couple of dresser drawers? They hadn't discussed any new sleeping arrangements. Was he waiting for her to make the next move? If so, he would wait a long time because she didn't feel confident enough to go in search of her husband.

Nevertheless, she showered, put on a pale green lace-trimmed nightgown, brushed her hair until it shone, and dabbed perfume in a few strategic spots. Then, she went to bed. When she couldn't sleep, she picked up a magazine—when she couldn't read, she got up and paced....

Jared had spent the entire night in her bed, but she had

no idea where he intended to sleep tonight, here or at the clinic, now that they had consummated their marriage.

It was after ten; she assumed he must be working late. Some tall trees blocked her view of the clinic.

She pressed her hand to her throat and felt the missing locket. It was still on the bedside stand where Jared had placed it after removing it from her throat the night before. Putting it back on would amount to nothing less than throwing down a gauntlet and making a huge issue of the past. And Laurel. Maybe it was time to let go.

No matter how painful, she couldn't hide behind Laurel's shadow. With a deep sigh, Rachel carefully placed the locket in a small velvet-lined box where it would be safe—and out of sight. She'd discovered that only two people belonged in a marriage. There was no room for a third.

When Jared got home, the house was dark—except for a light burning in an upstairs window. About to turn his footsteps toward the clinic, where he had every intention of sleeping, he hesitated. Until that moment, his decision had been firm. He was going to leave the next move up to Rachel. Last night, he'd made love to her, perhaps unfairly, knowing she was upset and overwrought about Dylan.

She had responded, but no words were exchanged—no whispered words of mutual need and want—much less love. And without those, he wasn't sure of his own feelings, much less Rachel's. Despite the sated passion, she remained stubbornly mysterious and elusive. He'd touched her body, and made her his, but had he touched Rachel's heart?

And now, hours later, he wanted her again. No matter how much he tried to deny it, the thought of coming home to Rachel had been eating at him all day, wearing down his resistance and making a joke of his determination to slow down and give her more time. She'd left the light on—was she waiting for him? Or was he reading too much into the situation? He rubbed his hand over his face, wishing he had the answer. Rachel had turned his life upside down.

When Rachel heard the stairs creak, she spun from the window. Jared. She stared at her closed bedroom door. Realizing she didn't want to be caught waiting up for him, she dived for the bed, pulled up the covers, and reached for the magazine she'd discarded earlier.

When he walked in, she was out of breath.

"Hi," he said with a wary smile.

"Hi." Instead of sounding casual, the word came out sounding soft and breathy. Sexy.

Her husband had just come in. Shouldn't she be asking about his day? The words didn't come. Instead, Rachel sat speechless and entranced when he unbuttoned his shirt.

"I'm sorry I'm late," he said, moving toward the dresser. "I had an emergency."

She cleared her throat. "What kind?"

"A cow with milk fever." With his back turned, he reached into a drawer for striped pajama bottoms, then proceeded to undress. "It took awhile, but she'll make it."

She watched, entranced, as he slowly removed his shirt, his pants, and the rest. Trying to hide her unease at his total lack of inhibition, Rachel tried to remain cool and calm. "You must be hungry. I can get you something to eat."

"No, thanks. The farmer's wife insisted on feeding me."

"Oh?"

At the undisguised tone of possession, he turned. "She went to grade school with Fred."

"Oh." Rachel smiled into his twinkling eyes, relieved that the imagined threat of a buxom farm wife had aged a bit.

But then, he walked toward her, wearing a smile and nothing else. Apparently, the pajama bottoms were to remain neatly folded and unused. Rachel stared, unable to look away, which didn't seem to discomfit him at all— nor did her blushes stop him from joining her.

She felt the bed dip and barely managed to hang on to the shreds of her dignity when his hot gaze ran over her bare shoulders and pale green nightgown. The silk dipped at the bodice in a dazzling display of ecru lace, revealing a modest glimpse of pale flesh that seemed more erotic than total nudity. After leaving a scorched trail, his gaze dropped to the magazine in her lap.

"Are you reading that?" he murmured.

She'd forgotten all about the magazine. Now she stared at it blindly. "No."

His eyes grew tender. He gently pried it from her frozen fingers. "Good."

Rachel finally let go. She leaned back against the pillows and released a deep tortured sigh as he followed— as if linked by gossamer threads, finer than silk, stronger than steel. His mouth found hers. Bliss.

Hours later, Jared woke and discovered Rachel in his arms. With her head resting against his shoulder, she felt warm and luscious, like something out of a dream. Her hair tickled his nose. He smoothed it down, and somehow his hand got tangled in the bright curling tresses.

Smoothing the silk fineness between his fingers, he marvelled at the texture of a woman. There was so much he wanted to know about Rachel. He drew her closer, and felt her stir, fitting her curves to conform to his body, as if seeking his warmth. She sighed. Jared closed his eyes, aware of a sense of peace, wishing there were a way to make it last, and knowing that daylight would only bring more dissension, more adjustments.

Luckily, all the adjustments weren't painful. Making love to Rachel, for instance, was as natural as breathing. Getting cut off might prove life-threatening.

At the reminder, he eased away from her. Turning aside, and punching his pillow into a ball, he lowered his head and stared into the dark night—picking out every small detail of the room he now shared with his wife, and wondering how in the hell he was going to fit into it— now that he'd made his move and taken possession. Without a doubt, Rachel was a force to be reckoned with. Only one sure thing remained—there was no going back.

With a mutual cessation of hostilities and the white flag out on all sides, life at Stones End began to lose its bitter edge. Something new was happening. Jared wasn't quite sure what it was, but it threatened his heart and put his will to resist Rachel's invasion through test after test.

He won some, lost some. Who was keeping score? Not Jared. One day, he came home and she was planting tulips.

Tulips.

He took that as a hopeful sign that she was planning on watching them bloom come spring.

That led to taking the next step. Jared helped Rachel carefully pack boxes of fine and everyday china, glassware and books from the cottage in town. There were several handmade rugs. Clothes and practical household items made up the rest. She didn't own much.

In fact, Jared was amazed at how little. Stones End had accumulated an attic full, but Rachel had inherited very little from her parents—except insecurity. For the first time, he understood what Rachel wanted for Dylan—and why. And he wondered, as he had once before…what did Rachel want for herself? With everything packed, he looked around the still-furnished living room, searching for the key.

Despite the sofa and chairs, it looked barren without the small touches she'd added to make it homelike. She'd left the curtains, and he wondered how many other bits and pieces of herself she'd left behind during a transient childhood. She carried the scars. In his zeal to right old wrongs, he'd uprooted her again. And he wondered—how could he put Rachel back together again?

"I guess that's it," Rachel said, without any evidence of regret, and he wondered what she was really feeling.

Aware that she'd done her best to make a home for herself and her nephew—his son, Jared felt a stab of guilt that was all too familiar. He'd taken something precious and irreplaceable from Rachel…besides her virginity.

Every item Rachel owned fit into the back of the pickup. Jared tied down the hatch. He'd forgotten all about Drew's car. When Rachel climbed into the sports car, Jared's mouth tightened with anger.

He didn't even try to restrain his irritation. "You don't seriously think I'm going to let you take that home."

At the challenge, Rachel said, "I can't leave it here to be vandalized or repossessed with the house."

"Let Evan take care of it."

"Evan is gone. I don't intend to drive it, just store it in a safe place until Drew comes home. He'll need a car. I thought there might be room in one of the barns."

Obviously annoyed at this sign of loyalty to a man he despised, Jared dipped his head. "If you insist."

Rachel turned the key in the ignition. "I think it's only right," she said, forced to raise her voice over the dull roar.

Jared's eyes flashed at her stubborn insistence, but he said nothing more, and neither did she.

When Rachel drove away, she didn't look back at the home she and Dylan had shared for such a brief time. She'd learned at a very young age that there was never any going back to the places she'd been. Picking up stakes and moving on—that had been her father's creed.

At Stones End, Rachel turned at the familiar mailbox. She followed Jared's pickup at a distance, then stopped when he parked by an abandoned barn on the property.

He got out and opened the large doors. She drove the car into the dim interior. Then, before her vision could adjust, Jared was there opening the car door. She climbed out. The barn was cool. Silent. Shadowed. Shafts of light filtered through the boarded-up windows.

It wasn't the ideal place for a confrontation, but in that short drive home, Rachel's irritation had built.

Picking up the argument where they'd left off, she lifted her chin. "I know Drew made mistakes, but why can't you forgive him?"

At her directness, Jared drew back. "It's not all personal. Drew uses people whenever it suits him. He tried to marry Jessie to get his hands on Stones End."

Rachel couldn't hide her shock. "But Ben and Jessie...."

He dipped his head. "Right. Jessie was crazy about Ben, but that didn't stop Drew from interfering. Or trying to."

Rachel frowned. "But why?"

Jared shrugged. "The Pierces wanted the timber rights to Stones End, and Drew was willing to go to any lengths to get it. Luckily, he didn't succeed."

Noting the satisfaction in his voice, Rachel said, "Would that have been so terrible?"

"I could never stomach Drew as a brother-in-law."

Still, she persisted. "You grew up as neighbors. Weren't you ever friends?"

Jared hesitated. "I suppose the rivalry was friendly at first—kid stuff. Sports. Girls. Drew didn't like to lose." He smiled, admitting, "But then, neither did I. Once, we got caught drag-racing down Main Street. I got a fine and lost my license for six months. Drew's father hired a lawyer who got him off free and clear, without even a slap on the wrist. That's when I realized we weren't playing on a level field. The odds were always in Drew's favor."

"Maybe you were lucky. You learned your lesson, but Drew never did. In the end, the Pierce money didn't save him."

"I suppose you're right." His expression hardened. "But that doesn't excuse the fact that he kept Dylan's existence from me for eight years."

"No, it doesn't," Rachel admitted. "In some crazy way, I think he was trying to protect Laurel. And he did provide generously for Dylan all those years."

"Financially," Jared pointed out, disapproval evident in the hard set of his jaw. "He provided money. That's all."

"Maybe that's all he thinks he has to give."

For a long moment, Jared remained silent, apparently weighing all her words, one by one, until they added up to something worth his consideration. Finally, he heaved a sigh, admitting, "Maybe you're right." It was faint endorsement, and Rachel tried to hide her disappointment.

But then, Jared met her eyes. He laughed softly. "I suppose I do owe Drew. In the end, he gave me Dylan…and you. But don't expect me to like him."

Her breath caught when he leaned forward and trapped her against the car. He took her mouth in a hard, silent act of ownership.

Over the next weeks, Jared redoubled his efforts to make Rachel content to stay at Stones End.

The exterior house painting got done…which only made the interior look shabbier. Like a lot of old farmhouses, Stones End had a large country kitchen that served as a combination eating and sitting room. Next to this was a smaller room, a pantry, where the food was actually prepared. The room was small but sunny, the wallpaper dingy. At one time, it might have been attractive—trellised ivy green against a neutral background, but now it was an eyesore.

One day, Rachel simply couldn't live with it a moment longer. When she pulled at a seam, a long strip came off. The next one was a little more difficult. She fetched a scraper. Before she knew it, the room was half stripped.

"What do you think you're doing?" Ira's voice startled her. He glowered at Rachel, then at the bare walls, the littered floor where the paper lay in torn strips. "My mother put this up." His voice choked on the words. "We had chickens back then. She saved her egg money and ordered the paper from a Sears catalog."

Rachel gasped. She'd never guessed the wallpaper was a family heirloom. "I'm sorry. Maybe I can piece it together." She reached for a strip. When it crumbled in her fingers, she looked at him helplessly. "I'm sorry."

At her distress, Ira cleared his throat. "That was more than sixty years ago. Maybe it's time for a change."

Change?

She needed more convincing. "If you're sure?"

"Of course, I'm sure." Ira offered to help.

Together, they stripped the remaining paper. Sensitive to her father-in-law's feelings, Rachel replaced it with similar paper—green ivy and red strawberries climbing a white background.

The kitchen cabinets needed a face-lift. Fresh white paint and new black cast iron hardware did wonders. Everyone got into the act. Ramon offered to replace the worn linoleum floor with red ceramic tiles.

What about a new stove and refrigerator, Ira asked. Why not? When it was finished, Jared shook his head in amazement. Somehow, Rachel had wormed her way into his father's affection. Was he missing something here? Rachel had given up her freedom to keep Dylan. Her love for the boy was that strong. Jared wondered what it would be like to be loved by Rachel that way—without reservation, without hesitation, without persuasion, but freely? What then? Could he love her back?

She saw him in the doorway. "Do you like it?"

He laughed when she tapped her foot on the linoleum floor. Ah yes, he should have guessed what that look meant—she hadn't forgotten their wedding night—or the hardwood floors under the tacky old linoleum. For better or worse, he'd married a nest-builder, which meant that like all peacocky males, more interested in cohabiting a nest, rather than actually building one, he had to do his part and feather her nest. So, he refinished the hardwood floors.

Luckily, a light sanding and a good coat of sealer did the job. The walls went from faded blue to warm gold; a rust and brown hooked rug added color to the gleaming floor.

September days dwindled into October.

As the days grew colder, the house grew warmer.

Outside, a hillside covered in pine trees stood like a stern silent sentinel, guarding the house against invasion; but here and there, a stand of birch trees turned giddy yellow. By the corner of the house, an oak tree went from green to gold. A tunnel of maple trees turned to flame.

And the leaves fell.

One by one.

Chapter Thirteen

A whole new world opened up for Dylan and held him enthralled—just as Rachel's world was shrinking.

With all its space, animals and a male role model thrown in, Stones End held an irresistible allure to an eight-year-old boy. To Dylan's delight, Jared took him on rounds. Soon, they were communicating about goats and pigs, cows and horses, not to mention the animal wildlife, which was abundant at Stones End. Unfortunately, Rachel couldn't bridge the gap between her and Jared.

Physically, they were in tune, but emotionally, they were a million years apart. She could feel her close ties to Dylan breaking—or stretching—to include the boy's father. Dylan was happy—wasn't that what mattered? Maybe he didn't need her as much as she wanted to believe. The feeling wasn't new. It was all mixed up with maternal instincts and losing control of her life—ceding authority over Dylan, and finding herself locked in a sensuous haze where a word or a look from Jared could have her yearning to be alone with him.

Sometimes, when he went off with Dylan, she ached for Jared to turn around and invite her along. But he never did.

Why couldn't they be a threesome—a family?

While Stones End came together, Rachel's life continued to unravel. And in all that emotional chaos, something rare took place. With Dylan and Jared preoccupied, Rachel needed someone to care for, and Ira desperately needed attention.

She trimmed his hair and brewed special teas, which she knew he only pretended to like.

When a visiting nurse dropped in for Ira's routine check up, Rachel learned that Dora Cummings had nursed Ira through a heart attack.

"How's he doing?" Dora asked, as she removed her coat.

"See for yourself." Ira made his appearance in a bright red corduroy shirt with his thinning white hair slicked down.

The elderly woman laughed. "I can see you're in fine mettle. Let's check your vital signs and make sure they agree."

Smiling at the interchange, Rachel said, "I was just about to make some cranberry tea. Would you like a cup?"

When Dora accepted, Ira followed Rachel into the kitchen, sputtering, "What did you do that for?"

"Because I like her. You don't have to join us."

"Humph."

Rachel wasn't surprised when he sat through tea. Ira preened when Dora expressed amazement at his progress. After that day, Wednesday afternoon tea became a ritual.

More confident after her success with Ira, Rachel felt braver, ready to tackle something bigger. Jared. The first opportunity came a few days later when she came home from a trip into town to stock up on food supplies. She found Jared and Dylan busily working on an outdoor project.

"We're putting up a swing," Dylan explained. His face beamed with pride. He held down a length of pine board while Jared applied a handsaw. Rachel had never allowed Dylan close to anything sharp; she felt a moment's alarm as the saw made a clean cut, and two pieces fell away.

Relieved to find Dylan still had ten fingers, she smiled weakly. "That looks great."

With a length of rope already strung in the oak tree, attaching the seat took only a few minutes. They had a swing. Jared turned to Rachel. "How about giving it a try?"

"All right." Rachel wanted to refuse, but didn't dare. Jared offered her so little. She slid onto the swing and hung on. Her heart skipped a beat when Jared placed strong hands at her waist and gave her a push, then another. She drew in a shaky breath when his thumb brushed the underside of her breast. Had he done it deliberately? With a laugh, he pushed. She swung—arcing into the vivid blue sky like an arrow shot from a bow—straight into the sun.

Some bright gold leaves fluttered and fell around her, carpeting the ground, and it seemed as if joy was trapped in that golden moment. She wished she could find a way to hold on to it. Rachel had never played at life. She was always the sensible twin, forced to grow up fast when her parents died. For a moment, she felt young, unafraid, seeking adventure, but when she looked at Jared, she didn't feel childlike. So, instead of looking at him, she looked up, surprised to discover the oak tree branches were almost bare.

Autumn progressed.

Halloween came. Jared helped Dylan carve a pumpkin; that used to be Rachel's job. And more leaves fell. Soon, the yard was a carpet of gold. One cold autumn day, raking leaves turned into a game.

From the kitchen window, Rachel watched as Jared raked them into a huge pile. Then Dylan and Miguel romped around, scattering leaves to the four winds. The dogs—one big and one small—barked and gave chase.

The day was crisp and cool, bright with sun, blue as only an autumn sky in Maine can be. And suddenly, Rachel felt confined. On impulse, she grabbed a sturdy jacket from a hook by the back door, and slipped it on as she went out to join them. Her footsteps felt light, crunching in the dry leaves. She was halfway across the yard when she realized she hadn't waited for an invitation. The thought stopped her midstep. What if Jared had been waiting for her to show an interest? What if they both waited too long, and never broke through the barrier of pride? At the thought, she hastened to get to Jared, suddenly aware that time wouldn't wait.

At her arrival, Jared seemed surprised, but he said nothing. Dylan's eyes lit up.

"Have you got an extra rake?" she asked.

Jared handed her one. Digger was on a leash. In his excitement, the puppy barked and danced in circles around Rachel and Jared, wrapping his leash around, until they toppled into the mound of leaves.

Rachel laughed at Jared's look of consternation. "Have you forgotten what leaves are for?" she asked.

Jared chuckled. "Not quite." The boys tossed a basket

of leaves, then dived on top, joining in the fun. Rachel sneezed. Jared could feel her warm breath against his ear. He took the opportunity to steal a kiss, and Rachel smiled into his eyes, wrapping her arms around his neck. He pulled her closer, noting the exact fit, and wishing there weren't so many layers of clothing between them. She was wearing his denim barn jacket. The rough fabric emphasized her softness, her femininity. A sheepskin collar framed her face.

Freckles marched along her nose; her cheeks were flushed with color. He traced the heat in her cheek with his thumb.

For a moment, Jared forgot everything. All he saw was Rachel, her blue-violet eyes. Slowly, drowning and lost in her eyes, he lowered his head and kissed her smiling mouth. She released a small surprised gasp, allowing him entry. He drank deep, sinking deeper and deeper....

A ripple of boyish giggles slowly intruded.

Jared came out of it in a daze, and slowly raised his head, his eyes rueful as they held hers.

"Oh no," Dylan groaned, "they're kissing!" He buried his face against his dog's neck.

With a soft careless laugh that belied his aroused state, Jared pulled himself off Rachel, then reached for her hand. With one pull, she landed on her feet.

"Back to work," Jared ordered, aware that his heartbeat was still unsteady. And that worried him. A heart could get a man in a lot of trouble. Just look at where it had gotten him. He was feeling all mushy and sentimental about a boy and his dog—and a woman. A thin-skinned, red-haired woman who filled his bed and threatened his heart. A woman who feared attachments—almost as much as he did.

He wasn't prepared to admit an emotional tie. Women

always left—just like his mother; they lied—just like Laurel. Was Rachel different? Did it matter that she touched him as no other woman had? Why wasn't that enough? Perhaps because he had no real ties to her. She'd agreed to stay, but their marriage was built on making the most of a bad situation. If she tired of it, she could walk out at any time. There was nothing to stop her. Was there?

Making his marriage work had become a mission. He wanted Rachel. And no matter how much he might like to deny it, he knew it wasn't only for Dylan's sake.

Later, Jared went out on call immediately after supper. He was surprised to find Rachel up when he came home.

"You never finished your meal." She set some crocheting aside and rose from her chair by the window. "Can I fix you something?"

Jared dropped his medical bag on the floor. At the sight of her, all the day's frustration collided with his seemingly unquenchable desire for this woman who just happened to be legally tied to him.

He said huskily, "I'm not hungry for food." Despite every effort, he'd lost a mare and her foal. Defeat still clung to him. He knew only one cure—even though it was only a temporary fix. Night after night, he reached for Rachel, but it was never enough. Now, he took her hand, using it to drag her closer until she fell against him. "I want you."

In this one area they were compatible. If only sex could solve all their other problems. It added heat and tension to a strained relationship, but nothing more, certainly not trust.

For the second time in his life, as if he needed a lesson, Jared had discovered that sex alone left a void. But it was all he'd asked from Rachel, all she gave of herself; and so, he took it. Love wasn't part of their marriage bargain.

They'd both dismissed it. Sometimes, he wondered if it was too late to change the terms.

That night, they made love, but in the morning Rachel woke alone in the big bed. With a sigh, she rose.

Weeks ago, she'd moved the rest of her things from the cottage, and Jared had gradually taken up a fair share of space. It was now *their* bedroom. They shared the closet. She felt an odd little thrill when she saw his dress and casual shirts lined up next to her blouses, his slacks next to her skirts. He had a collection of ties, some colorful, some staid.

Sometimes, when he walked around the room half-dressed, she couldn't control her blushes. He'd laugh and pull her into his arms. They usually wound up in bed. It was all so new, so exciting, so natural…could it last?

The phone rang somewhere in the house.

Pulled out of her fanciful daydreams, Rachel closed the closet door and went downstairs.

The phone was still ringing.

Rachel picked up the receiver. She recognized the feminine voice immediately, Olivia, who asked for Jared.

Rachel's fingers clenched. "He isn't in right now."

"When can I reach him? It's sort of important."

Rachel wanted to hang up, but she couldn't. A reminder of Jared's reaction the last time Olivia called made her say, "He should be here around noon."

"I'll be asleep by then," Olivia informed her lightly. "I just got off a night shift, west coast time."

"I see. Where are you calling from?"

"California…I'll try and call later. You're Rachel, right? I think we spoke once before."

"Yes, that's right."

"I was wondering if Jared told anyone about me."

"No, no he didn't." Rachel took a deep breath. What was there to tell? "Perhaps you'd like to tell me?"

There was a long pause. "It can wait."

Aware that pretending Olivia didn't exist hadn't gotten her anywhere in the past, Rachel asked, "Could I have a phone number and an address where he can reach you?"

After that exchange, Rachel hung up the receiver. No longer able to deny the evidence of another woman in Jared's life, she faced another painful fact. They might be married in every sense of the word, but that didn't mean there wasn't another woman...someone he loved.

Olivia?

How could the mere thought hurt so much? Suddenly, she had to confront Jared. She pulled on a warm knit sweater and slipped out of the house.

At the clinic, Rachel walked into a hectic scene.

Jessie struggled to hold on to a small lamb. "Jared's busy, but we could use some help."

The place was crawling—jumping—with lambs. There were about a dozen, although Rachel couldn't get an accurate count with them milling about in confusion. Rachel asked, "What in the world is going on?"

"I'm afraid we've got a major emergency on our hands. A sheep farm was attacked by coyotes last night," Jessie said. "This little one isn't too badly hurt, but some couldn't be saved, and some are just suffering from panic."

"I don't know anything about lambs, but how can I help?"

"Ramon and his wife are assisting me in the treatment room, and his daughter took Nathaniel home with her. Most of the injuries are minor, but a border collie was badly mauled."

"Is the dog going to be all right?"

"I don't know. Jared's getting ready to operate." When the lamb flailed its legs, Jessie calmed it with a few soothing words. "As you can see, I've got my hands full at the moment. If you can manage the phones for a while, that would be a big help."

"That I can do."

Jessie disappeared around a corner. Aware that the clinic was obviously a family affair, with any available body drafted for emergencies, Rachel sat behind the desk.

She'd scarcely been there five minutes when a firm masculine voice came through the intercom.

"Jessie, I need some help." Jared added an urgent, "Stat!" There was some static, and then the voice was gone.

Rachel pushed several buttons, trying to get it back. When that failed, she went in search of Jared. She went down the hall, and followed a trail of bloody pawprints. It stopped at a door marked Surgery. Rachel pushed it open.

Obviously expecting his sister, Jared's eyebrows rose at the sight of Rachel. "Good, we can use some help."

Rachel apologized. "Jessie's busy."

"You'll do."

"Do what?" Rachel realized no one was listening to her.

The owner of the dog was there. Obviously distressed, he patted the dog's head, over and over. The dog whimpered.

The man said, "Will my dog be okay?"

Jared popped a vial of anesthetic. "I think so. He's got a couple of bad gashes. I think we can sew the ear back where it belongs, and his front leg needs some stitches. The worst is the gut. He's bleeding badly. I won't know what's involved until I get in there."

Jared changed the subject, breaking the growing tension before it could affect the medium-size black-and-white dog. "Rachel, this is Barney and Max—short for Maximillian IV. Max is a prize-winning border collie. And one plucky little dog going up against coyotes." He patted the dog's rough coat. "Aren't you, boy?"

Barney put in, "Best sheepdog I ever had." His eyes were red. He cleared his throat. "I'd sure hate to lose him." At the sound of his master's voice, Max wagged his tail, once, twice.

"We're going to make sure you don't," Jared said, with a sympathetic smile. "If you can stay, we can use your help."

"Sure thing."

Jared threw Rachel a glance. "Are you ready?"

Rachel shook her head. "I don't know where to begin."

"If you'll put on those gloves, I need someone to hand me the instruments." A nod of his head indicated a table with everything set up. "First, I'm going to administer anesthesia. Then, I can guide you through the rest."

"All right." Rachel didn't feel confident. She had no experience with this sort of situation. "I'll try."

He nodded in approval. "You'll do fine."

When Jared moved around the dog, Rachel got her first unobstructed view of Max's injuries. At the sight of exposed flesh, she felt the room recede. She hadn't realized that Jared was aware of her distress.

He spoke sharply, "Rachel, are you all right?" His words sounded fuzzy. Couldn't he see she was not all right?

"No, I'm not," she mumbled, suddenly wanting to lie down. The floor would do in a pinch.

She didn't see what was so damned funny when he

grasped her hand and laughed softly. "Don't faint on me now."

At the bracing words, she came out of a spin. "I'm all right." She still felt weak. When Jared handed her a glass, his hand on her brow felt soothing. When she took a sip of brandy, she opened her eyes wide and met his gray glance.

He smiled reassuringly. "You'll do."

Focusing on the fact that Max needed immediate attention and there was no one else to help, Rachel listened carefully to Jared's instructions. Nevertheless, she blanched at the first incision. After that, a certain rhythm took over. Jared's hands were skilled and sure. Rachel felt his tension when Max's breathing got erratic. He glanced at her, and she met the concern in his eyes with her own— then, his relief when the dog stabilized. It was an odd moment of perfect communication. Later, she wondered if she'd dreamed it.

Hours later, she was quite proud of herself when Jared said, "That's it," and pulled off his rubber gloves. "The punctures weren't as deep as I expected. I'm going to start him on antibiotics. We'll need to keep him. Barring any complications, he can go home at the end of the week."

"Thanks, Doc," Barney said. "You did some good work today. Thought sure the dog was a goner. I'm going to spread the word, and send some business your way."

Jared smiled. "I'd appreciate that."

"Well, guess I'd better check on my lambs." Barney tipped his hat at Rachel. "Good to meet you."

After he'd left, Jared administered the antibiotic. He then glanced at Rachel. "Thanks for your help today. I hope it wasn't too traumatic." He tossed the used syringe away.

Rachel started gathering up used utensils. "I'm not sure if I was much help."

"You did fine. We make a good team."

"You did all the work," she said, but couldn't deny a warm inner glow at his words. They did make a good team, in so many ways, which held promise. Marvelling at that small piece of enlightment, she slipped her hands in her pockets.

When her fingers encountered a small folded piece of paper, she remembered—Olivia. She'd come, prepared for a confrontation, but now she hesitated, afraid of his reaction.

She'd just witnessed Jared handling a hurt dog and the owner with medical skill and compassion. The problem was that Rachel didn't want to be handled. She wanted to be loved, which made the truth vital. If there was another woman in Jared's life, she needed to know.

Rachel waited while he checked and recorded Max's vital signs, then said, "There is something I wanted to see you about."

Jared looked up from the chart, apparently surprised at her tone. "So, tell me."

Rachel hadn't meant to blurt it out, but that's exactly what she did. "Olivia called again."

"Olivia called?" His stunned reaction only added to Rachel's fears. "The same Olivia who called before?"

How many were there? she wondered in confusion. "Who is she?" She couldn't disguise the accusation in her voice, the jealous impulse to hear the truth, an admission or a denial, from his lips. She hoped his explanation would be simple, honest, direct.

"You think there's another woman." His incredulous tone made her want to scream.

Rachel answered in a tight voice, "Her name is Olivia,

and she's called twice, all the way from California, asking for you…no one else. What am I supposed to think?''

He tossed the chart aside. "I don't expect you to leap to the conclusion that I'm carrying on a long-distance relationship. Apart from everything else, don't you think I could find a more convenient arrangement?''

"I don't know what to think. Tell me.''

He sighed. "I don't know what there is to tell. My mother left us. She never told my father when she gave birth to a baby girl eight months later.'' He ran a hand across the back of his neck. "When she died twenty years later, she left a diary, and some snapshots, but there was no trace of the girl's whereabouts.''

All Rachel could think of was, "How old is she?''

"Nineteen, almost twenty.'' He took a deep breath before adding, "My father claims he never knew.''

Seeing his struggle to remain unmoved by what was obviously a delicate, painful family situation, Rachel wanted to comfort Jared, but didn't know how. The limits of their relationship seemed glaringly obvious—a shallow mockery.

Marriage should be a haven against the outside world, a coat of armor to protect against pain and disappointment, an anchor in a storm-tossed sea. Though bound by marriage and a mutual duty to raise a child, Rachel and Jared remained separate and alone.

A few pieces were still missing from the puzzle. "I don't understand,'' Rachel asked. "How did she locate you?''

"We hired a detective a year ago. After a lot of false leads, he narrowed the search down to the west coast, the Seattle area and southern California. He suggested posters in supermarkets and laundromats. She's college age, so universities made the list. We've had a couple of calls that went nowhere. This woman might not be her,'' Jared said, revealing his skepticism.

''But it could be.'' Rachel said, willing him to hope. ''I'm sorry for misjudging the situation.'' She reached into her pocket. ''This might help find her.''

Frowning, he accepted the small slip of paper.

Rachel slid her hands in her pockets to hide their trembling. She was very sorry, and willing to make amends— if only he would let her. The note was a small offering; nevertheless, it was a beginning.

He looked at it blankly. ''What's this?''

''It's all there—Olivia's address in San Francisco and her phone number. There's also her work address.''

Jared read it over carefully. She wondered if he was taking the time to memorize it, but when he pinned her with a glance, she knew he wasn't thinking about Olivia.

He looked puzzled. ''If you thought I was involved with this woman, why did you go to all the trouble of getting the information so I could get in touch?''

Felling horribly exposed, but unable to hide behind evasion, Rachel said, ''Because since the first phone call, I knew she meant something to you.''

He said quietly, ''What if she wasn't my sister?''

''I don't know,'' she whispered, glad she hadn't had to face that possibility.

Her words fell between them—an ever-widening whirlpool of doubts, dragging them down. Jared said, ''I wish you'd come to me with your suspicions earlier.''

She looked at him, her eyes deep purple with remorse and confusion. ''I'm sorry, I couldn't do that.''

With that admission, Jared faced the painful fact that Rachel's doubts had led her here today. She obviously didn't trust him, any more than he trusted her. Perhaps they didn't trust in happiness. The incident, one among many, exposed the flawed, weak structure of their relationship. They were virtual strangers. So, where did they go from here?

Chapter Fourteen

That evening, Jared called Olivia.

Rachel never knew exactly what they said to each other, but later Jared said simply, "I'm not sure it's her, but I have to find out."

"Yes, of course." Rachel set her own concerns aside. Like Jared, she was worried about Ira's health. He'd lived with the knowledge of Olivia's existence since Jared came home a year and a half ago with the sad news of his mother's death. With Ira's full approval, Jared had hired a private detective. Hopefully the long search would end in San Francisco.

Ira slumped in his chair. "What's next?"

"I can get someone to cover, take a few days off, go and meet her." Jared shrugged, but Rachel recognized the tension in the firm set of his lips. "Then, we'll see."

Ira obviously hoped for more conclusive news. "Sounds like another wild-goose chase."

Jared had his own misgivings. He wanted to hope and believe in happy endings and reuniting his family, but he'd been disappointed several times before. In the last year he'd traced several promising leads, each time hoping this was it, this was Olivia.

His mother had remarried at least twice that they knew of, which meant that Olivia's last name probably wasn't Carlisle. This one called herself Olivia DeAngelis from San Francisco. The last one had come from Seattle...not to mention others in Tampa, Dallas, Santa Barbara, Vallejo, even a remote desert spot call Needles. He'd met young women, some independent and strong, some sad and disconnected. All were looking for a family they'd lost. And so was he.

He remembered his parents as two separate people. He recalled them fighting, then his mother leaving. At the age of seven, Jared learned that his life could fall apart. He'd felt a lot of anger; he'd buried it until he turned eighteen when he discovered his mother had sent cards and gifts for years—his father had sent them back. It was just one more betrayal. So how could he trust in happy endings?

And yet, he wanted to believe in Rachel. At some point, he had to move past the hurts, or carry anger and bitterness into the next Carlisle generation.

Jared stood, he looked across the table at Rachel. "Max is improving," he said, reminding her of the injured border collie. "But I can't leave him unattended overnight. I'll see you in the morning."

Rachel whispered, "Good night," and felt at a loss as she watched him go out the door. Her life had become a series of emotional highs and lows. She tried to steer a straight course in between, reminding herself that a little distance would do them both good.

Ira had been oddly silent, but after Jared left, he clearly needed to talk. "Guess we made a mess of things."

Rachel couldn't argue. "People make mistakes."

"Avis was restless; but the final break wasn't all her fault," he admitted, sitting down heavily in his favorite chair by the window. "I promised her a fancy vacation. But when the time came, a new piece of equipment cost more than I had set aside. Avis was mad." He shook his head, as if recalling the scene. "She cleaned out our savings account and went on the trip. She came home two weeks later."

Unsure if he was aware of her presence, Rachel didn't interrupt, but she took a chair nearby.

The anger built in his voice, as he revealed more. "It was Jared's birthday. The boy waited all day for her—so sure that she'd come with the special present she'd promised. He fell asleep and I put him to bed." He looked out the window, as if he could still see Jared and Avis. "She turned up late. She was wearing this fancy blue silk dress, high heels and a silly hat—looked like a million dollars." His face darkened. "She'd met this man; she'd spent my hard-earned money on clothes to impress him."

His body slumped as he turned back to Rachel. "I refused to let her see Jared, or Jessie. She never told me she was pregnant. There was no question of paternity. She'd never set eyes on the other man before that trip."

"I'm so sorry," Rachel murmured, when he stopped. Her eyes felt dry and scratchy with unshed tears.

"Me, too," Ira said glumly. "If I'd taken her on that trip—" His shoulders rose and fell. "Who knows? Things might have turned out different. She said I was married to Stones End, not to her. That I always put it first. And maybe she was right."

Rachel looked at his gnarled, calloused hands resting

empty in his lap. All his life Ira had tended to Stones End, and made things grow. He'd put the farm first, before his wife and children. It was terribly sad, and Rachel wanted to weep for all of them. Ira, Jessie, Jared. Avis.

Instead, she took his large hand between hers. "It's not too late to change things, Ira. Your children want to love you, you just have to let them."

He sighed heavily. "Maybe," he murmured, but he didn't sound convinced.

She had to let it go at that.

"I kept her from them, thought it was best if they forgot they had a Ma." He sighed. "Course I was dead wrong. When Jared found out, he was angry; Jessie's more forgiving." Ira shook his head in regret. "Sorta took the heart out of the boy." He smiled wistfully at Rachel. "Now looks like it's up to you to get it back."

Rachel laughed nervously. "I don't think I can."

"If he's capable of loving anyone, it's you. I've seen the way he looks at you. He's wearing himself out, trying to run away from you and the way he feels."

Over the next few days, Rachel wondered if Jared would give her a chance to test Ira's theory—not that she was that anxious to try. Without trust, they'd failed each other, and now each knew how much it could hurt.

Jared used the injured border collie as a reason to sleep at the clinic. Rachel wasn't sure that was his only reason. She sensed his anger and disappointment. But as long as he deliberately continued to avoid her, how could they get past it?

While they'd reached an impasse, other events moved swiftly. Jessie volunteered to make plane reservations. When the confirmation arrived, Jared opened the envelope.

Two tickets fell out.

"There's a mistake," Jared said. "We only need one."

Jessie looked over his shoulder. "No, it's no mistake, Dad said to order two—one for you, and one for Rachel."

Ira said firmly, "You were planning to take Rachel?"

Jared turned red. "Not exactly."

"I can't leave Dylan," Rachel said. Five days on a trip alone with Jared seemed daunting. His lack of enthusiasm wasn't exactly flattering. She wanted that laughing, teasing, aggravating male back—even if he was a stranger.

"Dylan can stay with us," Jessie said, "Nathaniel will love the company." And that was that.

Rachel's troubled gaze drifted to her husband seated across the room. As if connected, Jared glanced up and met her look. His eyes were dark and distant. Had his eyes ever lit up for her—or had that been her imagination? Had it all been for public display—making the best of a bad bargain?

Did he regret their marriage? Did she?

Rachel didn't have the answer, but she intended to find out. Later, when she kissed Ira good-night on his ruddy cheek, she whispered, "Thank you."

The following day, Rachel and Jared got a late flight out of Bangor. They were going to find Olivia. Hopefully, along the way, they would find each other.

Seated side by side in the narrow seats, Rachel could feel Jared's tension. She'd dressed for warmth in a black turtleneck and matching slacks, layered with a wheat-colored blazer, but she felt chilled.

The next few days could mean the end of a long search for Jared's sister. Or it could mean nothing.

Jared seemed unapproachable. He even looked different, more formal, in businesslike gray dress slacks, white shirt and tie. A charcoal sport coat deepened the color of his eyes. How would she survive the next few days when they'd hardly exchanged a word in over a week?

The attendant served a light snack. On a whim, Jared ordered wine. "To Olivia," he said. She'd arranged to meet them at the airport. But first, they had to get through this late-night flight to Chicago where they would change planes and land in San Francisco in the morning.

Rachel sipped from her glass. "I hope she's all you want."

"To happy endings?" And new beginnings? Jared didn't voice the latter, but he was wishing for a fresh start with his wife.

Later, the attendant collected the empty containers and glasses. Jared replaced his tray, then Rachel's. Their hands collided. Her wedding band gleamed bright gold in the dim light. Jared remembered placing it on her finger with some reluctance. Now he never wanted it to come off.

When had that transition occurred? He wasn't sure. But since the early days of his marriage, he'd had plenty of time to reflect and time to regret the way he rushed Rachel to the altar. He was so confused about her.

Thanks to his father's interference, he'd been granted a few days with his reluctant wife—time enough to sort out his marriage? What if he started now? He could reach for her hand, and murmur something like, "Your hand is cold," and raise the tips of her fingers to his lips…then note with a small sense of triumph that she didn't draw back.

What if they were meeting for the first time? It was the middle of the night. The drone of the engines had lulled most of the other passengers to sleep. Outside, the sky was dark; lights appeared in small clusters far below, then disappeared.

If they were two strangers on a plane, with the same destination, he would be bowled over by her. Would he ask her out? Would she accept? Oddly enough, they'd never flirted, never gone through any preliminary stages of courtship. What if they started now?

He turned. Before he could make a move, or utter a single word, Rachel reached for the in-flight magazine and turned to the crossword puzzle.

The airline attendant came through. "Please fasten your seat belts. I'm afraid we've run into a little bad weather. For the next hour or so, we're in for a bumpy ride."

And a bumpier landing.

Several hours later, Rachel looked around a drab, dimly lit hotel room. At least it looked clean.

"I'm sorry, it's nothing fancy," Jared apologized once again as he pocketed the key.

She set her overnight bag on the bed. "The storm isn't your fault." Due to sleet and strong gusty winds, all flights out of Chicago were indefinitely delayed.

They'd been told to check back in the morning.

"I should let Olivia know we won't be on time." He picked up the phone and dialled her number. "There's no answer," he said, hanging up after letting it ring awhile.

Rachel felt his frustration. She rubbed heat into her arms. "At least this place is warm."

Jared checked the thermostat. "Or it soon will be. I'm starved, how about you?"

When she nodded, he glanced at his watch. "It's almost midnight, too late to find a restaurant open. I could check room service. How about a sandwich?"

"Anything, as long as it's on the light side." Rachel unpacked a few items from a small bag. "I'd like to shower and change first."

The king-size bed took up most of the room.

Jared averted his eyes, trying to get the tempting image of Rachel out of his mind. He'd vowed not to seduce his wife until she came to him...which would probably be a cold day in hell judging from her cool responses so far.

Jared picked up the phone. "I'll order." Luckily, the hotel kitchen was still open. "Two sliced turkey sandwiches on rye, lettuce, tomato. Pasta salad on the side. Apple pie. And coffee for two. No, make that one coffee and one tea—herbal if you've got it." They did. "Thanks." Jared hung up.

Rachel disappeared.

With the sound of running water in the background, he pulled off his tie, then loosened his shirt collar. Was it getting warm, or were thoughts of Rachel taking a shower only feet away making it difficult to breathe?

He slumped down in the chair and stared out the window. Chicago was all lit up, tall buildings slicing a taller black sky. Still hours until dawn, it promised to be a long night. Even longer, he thought several moments later when Rachel emerged from the bathroom with her skin flushed and pink and smelling like lilies of the valley. There was that peach robe again, just a shade darker than her skin.

As if it had lost its moorings, his heart knocked around in his chest. She'd tied her damp hair on top of her head. He'd like to remove the ribbon, set her hair free....

A knock at the door announced the waiter's arrival and pulled Jared out of his fascination with the way her throat met the angle of her shoulder...she usually shuddered when he kissed her there.

Smothering the thought before it got completely out of control, he tipped the waiter who had left the tray on a small table placed near the window. The food looked appetizing, but suddenly Jared wasn't hungry—at least not for food.

He pulled up a couple of chairs, and invited Rachel to join him. "We even have a view."

With the drapes open, they looked out on the damp stormy night. Sleet and freezing rain struck the glass.

With a grateful sigh, Rachel poured tea and took a sip.

Jared picked up a sandwich. They ate in silence for a minute or two. "We need to talk, make some plans," he said, trying to dispel the intimacy of the moment.

"Yes." With a clatter, Rachel set the cup into the matching saucer. She sat up straight and tilted her chin at a defensive angle.

With a twitch of his lips, Jared raised an eyebrow. "I was thinking of discussing plane schedules for tomorrow. What were you thinking?"

Looking startled, she took a deep breath and slowly released it. "I don't know where to start."

"We aren't going anywhere...we've got all night." It wasn't how he'd hoped to spend it; nevertheless, she was probably right. "Let's clear the air," he said, deciding to do more than that. How about blowing this pretence of a marriage to kingdom come and starting from scratch? "You don't trust me. That's been made fairly clear recently. I think I can guess—this is still about Laurel."

Jared wanted a confrontation; nevertheless, he wasn't prepared when the first volley came from Rachel. "That's the problem. You keep confusing me for my sister."

Dealt a direct blow, he went very still. "Is that what you really think?"

She spoke in frustration. "I don't know how you feel about her, or me. You never tell me anything."

She was right, of course. How could he tell the truth

without marring Laurel's image? "I'm not sure this is the best time to discuss this."

She tilted her head. "Will there ever be a good time?"

"All right, what would you like to know?" He pulled off his jacket and tossed it on the bed.

Rachel watched it land, then turned back to him. "This isn't an inquisition."

At that, he lifted an eyebrow. "You're right. I don't want this to stand between us. I tried to tell you before, but you weren't ready to listen."

Of course, he was right, she had refused to let him explain. "I still don't want details of your affair," she said. "But I do need to know if you loved her."

"I hardly knew her," he said gently.

She frowned. "You said that once before."

"And you didn't believe me."

"No, I just assumed that there had to be more."

He said starkly, "There wasn't. We met that one night and I never saw her again. It was all a mistake. I think we were both looking for something that wasn't there. For what it's worth, I'm not very proud of my behavior. And I'm sure Laurel regretted it as well."

Rachel said quietly, "I know she did. She was terribly unhappy when she found she was pregnant."

Jared's face suddenly looked lined where it had been smooth. "Dylan's the only good thing that came out of it. I'm sorry she went through the pregnancy alone, and for all the years I missed with my son. I've tried to make things right. If there was a way to undo the past, I'd grab at it in a second," he admitted in a voice filled with old regrets, layer upon layer built over time. "But all we have is now, and what we make of it. I can't promise more than that."

Rachel listened, searching for hidden meanings to the

past that might present answers to the future. But as far as reassurance went, his explanation fell short of her hopes. In fact, every word confirmed her belief that she was part of Jared's atonement for guilt. She had to face the fact that her twin was no innocent victim. Laurel and Jared shared a one-night stand, with no strings attached. But that one night had resulted in the birth of a child nine months later, and a seemingly endless round of repercussions. Despite Jared's admission that he'd never loved Laurel, he'd clearly been attracted. By now, Rachel knew him well enough to realize that if he'd known about the pregnancy, his code of honor would have compelled him to marry Laurel.

Rachel was his wife by an accident of fate—clearly not by his choice. He'd made no effort to pretend that he loved her. For that she had to be grateful, she supposed.

Before their wedding, he'd pointed out that love didn't have to be part of the setup—as long as they both agreed to share Dylan. And Rachel, ever practical, had agreed. But that was before she'd fallen in love and broken the terms of their bargain.

They went to bed, clearly divided. The bed was wide enough for half a dozen. Keeping a distance took no effort.

At least, it shouldn't have.

During the night, Jared turned to Rachel in his sleep and pulled her into his arms. Surprised to find her there, he woke her with a ragged groan as he ran his hand down the curve of her spine.

"I've missed you," he rasped against her throat, and felt her voluptuous sigh—a whisper shuddered against his ear. Jared closed his eyes. If he was dreaming, he didn't want to wake up. He'd hardly slept in days—not since he left her bed. He gave her no room to evade his searching kisses, the touch of his hand as it slid down the length of her and made her shudder and cling to him.

But it still wasn't enough. He wanted more.

Even in their most intimate moments, man to woman, skin to skin, flesh to flesh, he could never penetrate Rachel's reserve—that small part of her that remained maddeningly elusive. She was strong, not hard. She was soft and feminine, with a warm generous heart...the only woman he could ever love—if there was such a thing.

She had this thing about attachments; she was fighting her feelings, protecting herself from him. They were well-matched, he had his defenses, she had hers.

But his were crumbling.

Fast.

The following morning, Rachel woke in a sheet-tangled bed to the sound of Jared humming some aimless tune in the shower. He sounded so pleased with himself, so...so masculine! She buried her head in the pillow, wishing she could as easily drown out her memories of the previous night.

When the phone rang, she hitched the sheet under her arms and reached for the receiver. She listened to the operator, but was fully aware of the moment when the shower stopped. A moment later, Jared came out. He was buttoning a fresh white shirt, tucking it into a dark pair of slacks.

Feeling his gaze rake over her from head to toe, Rachel couldn't prevent a blush. She tried to concentrate on the phone. "Thank you," she said, then hung up after writing down the man's instructions.

The edge of the bed gave when Jared sat. "Who was it?"

"The airline returning your call. They have a cancellation—if we can get there by eleven this morning."

Jared glanced at his watch, and said, "We've got exactly one hour and thirty-four minutes," which didn't give her much room to argue when he added, "We've talked about giving this marriage a real chance. We have four days left. I know it's not long, but can we put all our problems on hold—just until we get back to Stones End?"

"All right." Rachel had her reasons for cooperating. It seemed odd to be learning about the man she'd married this late in the game. But perhaps they were just getting started. Why not face the rest when they got home?

They had four days left.

The delay in Chicago had cost them a whole day.

When they landed in California, the travel delay and forced change of plans complicated their arrangements with Olivia. She was working and couldn't meet them.

After settling into their hotel, Jared said, "There's no point in waiting until tomorrow. It shouldn't be too difficult to find the place where she works."

The Blue Lagoon Restaurant was easy to find.

It was a cozy family restaurant; the decor was tropical, with pirate lore and fishnets strung from heavy wooden beams. Seafood was the specialty.

Jared gazed at the menu. They'd eaten earlier. "How about dessert? The chocolate cheesecake sounds good."

Rachel thought of the calories. "Oh, why not?"

He raised an eyebrow. "What?"

"It's loaded with calories."

His gaze swept over her. "On you, they look good."

"Thanks." She took a sip of water. "I think."

He laughed. "Have I said something wrong?"

"You're supposed to say that I'm wasting away."

"You're perfect, just the way you are."

She flushed. "Thank you." She felt self-conscious—until his attention shifted to their waitress.

The name tag on her uniform said it all—Olivia.

Jared recognized her. He'd seen her before—a plucky little girl posing with palm trees swaying in the background. But then, she turned and he wasn't sure. If this was his Olivia, she hadn't grown very tall. She was small, delicate, with short fair hair curling around a heart-shaped face.

She was dressed in a drab beige uniform, but when she smiled, she lit up the room. "Hi, what can I get for you?" Her gray eyes twinkled when she leaned closer and confided, "Just don't order today's special, the shrimp is rubbery."

When Jared didn't respond at once, she said, "Do you need more time? I can come back."

"No," Jared said hoarsely, unable to get another word out. He was already twenty years too late.

Olivia's eyes grew wide. "You're Jared," she said softly. "Oh my God, I can't believe it; I recognize your voice!" She turned to Rachel. "And you must be…"

"Rachel."

Olivia laughed. "Of course, we spoke on the phone."

Jared rose awkwardly, his movements slow. Olivia had no such inhibitions. She threw her arms around him, "This is unreal! You're here. I can't believe it."

Jared hugged her back. He closed his eyes, in apparent disbelief. Rachel saw his expression and swallowed a hard lump in her throat.

A bell went off nearby. Olivia's boss, a big, beefy man, shouted across the counter, "Hey, Livvie."

Livvie—of course. There was nothing remotely formal or stiff about her.

"How about serving food?" The man continued, "I'm trying to run a business here. People are hungry."

Apparently not intimidated by his gruff manner, Olivia turned to him with a laugh. "Hank, this is him. My brother! This is Jared. I missed him at the airport yesterday, but, well, here he is!"

Hank wiped his hands on his white apron. "Well, I'll be damned. And you said he'd probably changed his mind."

Olivia shrugged. "Looks like I was wrong."

Hank grinned at her apparent delight. Rachel couldn't hold back a grin of her own. Hank joined in the reunion. So did several of Olivia's regular customers. With handshakes and hugs all around, a little bit of California sunshine rubbed off on Jared.

Hank grabbed him in a huge bear hug. "So, you're Livvie's brother, imagine that!" He pumped Jared's hand, as if he were visiting royalty. "She's talked of nothing else since she found that poster at the university and called that detective. Up and down like a roller coaster, deciding to call, not to call. Finally, I dialled the number for her."

Jared smiled. "Then, I have you to thank."

"It was nothing. Livvie's a good kid." Then, Hank shooed them away. "Go home, go home. You have a lot of catching up."

Olivia blew Hank a breezy kiss. "Thanks, I'll see you tomorrow." Her smile included Rachel and Jared when she said, "Let's go before he changes his mind."

Once they were outside, Rachel insisted, "Why don't you two go ahead? You have a lot to say to each other. You don't need me along."

Jared said, "What will you do?"

"I'll get a cab—go back to the hotel." Rachel backed

away. "Maybe I'll have an early night and catch up on some sleep." For some reason, she blushed at the words.

"I'd rather you came." At the silent appeal in his gray eyes, she realized this next phase, perhaps the end of a long search for Olivia, could prove difficult for Jared. "The situation's delicate," he added when Rachel hesitated. "It could use a woman's touch."

"All right." What about Jared, she wondered. Did he need a woman's touch? He'd lost his mother at an early stage—did it make him invincible?

Obviously unaware of the tension between them, Olivia chattered away, "I share an apartment with friends from my art class. It's close enough to walk."

So, they walked—uphill.

Olivia explained that she shared an off-campus apartment with three roommates, fellow art students at the university. She stopped at a Victorian house—a painted lady—resplendent in gray and coral and teal. There were stairs.

Olivia lived in an attic apartment. She bounded up the steep winding staircase. Rachel and Jared followed more slowly. The door was open.

"Come in, come in." Olivia went around, stashing items under the sofa cushions. "Please excuse the mess." She shooed an orange cat off the coffee table.

Apparently trying not to get carried along by the girl's bubbliness, Jared said, "I don't want to put a damper on things, but I also don't want to build up anyone's hopes. In the last year, I've followed several leads, and each one turned out to be the wrong Olivia. This time, the detective said you had proof positive. He didn't say what it was."

"Oh, yes, of course." Olivia laughed self-consciously. "And here I am, carrying on like you're my long-lost brother, and you haven't got a clue. I'm sorry, I thought you knew."

Jared said gently, "Maybe it would be simpler if you just showed me what you have for evidence."

If his hesitation disappointed Olivia, she hid it well. "I'll be just a minute. Why don't you both sit down?" She waved them toward a table and chairs. "Would you like coffee, tea?"

"I can make it," Rachel said, sensing Jared's growing impatience. Besides, she needed something to do. The tension was almost unbearable. Jared had waited so long for this moment. She wondered how he could be so outwardly calm.

Now that she'd met Olivia, she felt a sympathetic tug in the girl's direction. If Avis was the girl's mother, her childhood couldn't have been easy. Rachel knew what Avis was like—a woman desperately searching for love, but basically incapable of loving anyone back. A woman like Laurel.

Rachel also understood why Jared's experience had made him cynical about women. He obviously couldn't tell true love from false. Perhaps he never would.

When Jared got up and started pacing, she realized he wasn't as unperturbed as she imagined. He stopped to examine a painting of a desert sunset. The colors were neutral—except for a blazing red sun blending into the sand. With the artist's name, Olivia, inked into the canvas, the painting was partially finished, set up on an easel.

Rachel found the kitchen. It was stocked with typical college student fare—peanut butter and crackers, potato chips, popcorn. A tired banana sat in a bowl. There wasn't any milk. The coffee was instant. Rachel found a tea kettle and put water on to heat. When it was ready, she set three mugs on the table. By then, Olivia had returned.

She set a medium-size suitcase on the table. Her eyes held Jared's. Her voice was soft, yet filled with conviction when she said, "I am your sister."

Chapter Fifteen

Jared saw the candor in her eyes, and remembered an old snapshot of a little girl in a dress that was too big, with eyes that knew too much. Despite Olivia's determined lighthearted manner, there was something so vulnerable about her. She was only nineteen—young to be on her own.

He suspected she hadn't had much of a life.

"I hope you're right," he said, from some place deep inside, and discovered he meant it.

Olivia's smile wobbled a bit. "It's all in here."

The answers Jared needed were in a battered suitcase decorated with gaudy tourist stickers that read like a travelogue of hot spots—New York, Miami, Reno, Las Vegas, Hollywood. "Open it," Olivia said when he stared at it—as if it held a time bomb.

Rachel wondered—was he afraid of what he'd uncover? Old secrets? Lies? She'd heard enough from Ira and Fred to know there would be pain.

As if tearing away a curtain to the past, Jared opened the suitcase. Inside, he found a shoebox with collages glued and lacquered onto the surface. His mother had always liked pretty things, he recalled. The box contained snapshots, a copy of a birth certificate—Olivia Carlisle, born eight months after his mother left. The birth certificate shocked him.

Jared cleared his throat. "Why do you call yourself DeAngelis?"

Olivia shrugged. "My mother married several times, but I guess that name stuck. Mike was a cop, a good one. When the marriage ended, I stayed. Mom came and went."

"What happened to him?"

Her eyes grew shadowed as she explained briefly, "He was on duty. There was a robbery—a high-speed chase. Hank is his brother." That explained quite a lot.

Realizing he owed a huge debt of gratitude to Hank, Jared turned back to the contents of the box. Though he couldn't bear to read them, the details were all there in his mother's private diaries—handwritten, penned in ink, faded and blue—a woman's sad little memories of life gone wrong. The box held all the family secrets—answers to the riddles that still plagued him. Even as a child, he'd recognized his mother's weakness, her need to be protected.

After she left, he often worried about her. He'd spent years trying to find her with the help of a hired detective—the best he could afford, which wasn't much. Sadly, the investigation had turned up little more than a death certificate. Apparently, after losing touch with Olivia and Mike DeAngelis, Avis had died alone in a charity hospital in San Diego. However, she'd left a trail that led to her daughter. And for that, Jared had to be grateful.

"There's something else." Olivia held out a package. "It's addressed to you. I believe she tried to send it to you. I'm sorry, it's a little late."

Twenty years too late.

The package was dated and stamped, "Return to sender."

Jared stared at it. Oh God, it couldn't be—not after all this time. Slowly, he set the diary down and reached for the package. It wasn't very large. Of course, he knew what it was.

Life had taught Jared to believe in a woman's ultimate treachery. He'd learned that at an early age. He'd come home from school one day and discovered his mother was gone—two weeks before his seventh birthday. In his child's mind, he'd known it was all a terrible mistake; she'd never miss his birthday. Besides, she'd promised him a Spiderman watch—just like the superhero in the comics. So, on his birthday, he'd taken a bath, put on his best shirt—the one with the stiff collar for special occasions—then combed his hair and waited.

All day, he sat by the window and waited, knowing she would come. Eventually, his father silently carried him up to bed. Ira never said anything about the gift.

The day after his seventh birthday, Jared decided he simply wouldn't love his mother anymore. He put her out of his heart. And so, the boy grew into the man.

Now, twenty years later, he opened the package, lifted the lid of a small box and stared at the watch. "She didn't forget." His entire life had been shaped by this one missing piece of the puzzle. His mother had remembered her promise, she had loved him. He'd based his opinion of women on one betrayal, and now he knew it was all a mistake.

He'd never let another woman close enough to find out if he was wrong, he'd never let Rachel close enough to love him. He'd been wrong about his mother. Was he wrong about Rachel?

He looked at her and found her eyes filled with unshed tears. For him? She smiled through the moisture, and he knew that somehow she understood all he was feeling.

Could she love him?

A noisy interruption put an end to the nostalgic moment, for which Jared was grateful. He didn't think he could take many more emotional breakthroughs at the moment.

Olivia's friends arrived; they brought more friends who had even more friends. They had pizza and were planning to make a night of it. Everyone was pleased to meet Olivia's brother. Someone turned the music up.

At that point, Jared looked at Rachel—she looked exhausted. "Shall we go?"

"Yes," she whispered.

Before they left, Olivia hugged them both, but her eyes clung to Jared—as if she still couldn't believe he actually existed. "I'll see you tomorrow."

Jared smiled in open agreement. "That sounds good."

Rachel and Jared went back to the hotel.

With the drapes drawn, the room was dark. Rachel switched on a lamp. All the way back in the cab, Jared had remained silent. She'd waited for him to mention Olivia.

He pocketed the room key. "What did you think of her?"

"She's charming." Rachel smiled, easing into the

topic. "She's so bubbly and bright; she makes me feel terribly old."

Jared chuckled. "Me, too. I don't know why, but I expected her to be more like Jessie. They look a lot alike, but it's all on the surface."

"She's her own person."

"She's my sister, and I don't even know her. We're strangers," he said, revealing his inner turmoil.

Rachel said gently, "You have a lot of years to catch up, but you have time on your side."

And only time would heal.

They'd been up for hours, and the jet lag had finally caught up with them. Rachel took a shower, then Jared. When he came out, and found her sound asleep, he climbed into bed beside her and drew her against him.

With a deep contented sigh, he closed his eyes.

They slept late, catching up on some much-needed rest. After a leisurely breakfast in the room, Jared pushed his plate aside. "We're supposed to meet Olivia for lunch."

Rachel said, "It's almost that now. Why don't you go? You should get to know each other without a third party."

Jared nodded. "I suppose you have a point. Olivia has an art class later, then she has to work. This hotel has a decent restaurant. How about meeting me downstairs for dinner—around seven?"

"I'd like that," Rachel said. And then, there was just his mouth searching for hers, stealing her breath and sending her hurtling through space, lost in his arms, his kiss.

At last, he drew in a breath. "I have to go," he said, burning her with a hot glance. "I'll see you later."

His eyes promised more than dinner.

They'd agreed to meet for cocktails in the downstairs lounge. While he waited, Jared ordered scotch on the rocks. He was on his second when he raised the short glass to his mouth, the movement arrested at the sight of a tall redhead poised in the entry. A slim black skirt and a beaded black sweater outlined her luscious body to perfection. He slowly lowered the glass. He'd never seen Rachel look so out-and-out sexy. In fact, he'd forgotten how exquisite she was.

She looked around, then smiled with apparent relief when she spotted him at the bar. As she made her way across the crowded room, he could see the avid expressions on the other men's faces—which she ignored. No doubt about it, Rachel was a knockout. She had no conceit, no concept, of her own perfection—and perhaps that's what made her unique. She was beyond the perfect alignment of facial features, the graceful lines and generous curves of her body. She was Rachel.

Their eyes met and held in the reflected glass, and she flushed—her composure obviously shaken by the warmth in his gaze. She was out of breath by the time she reached him.

She slid onto the barstool next to him.

At her request, he ordered white wine, then smiled at her. "You know, it just occurred to me that this wasn't such a good idea after all." Jared leaned close and murmured. "I want to feed you, then take you to bed."

A direct hit, her answer nearly knocked him off the barstool. "I want that too," Rachel said, fully aware of all she was inviting. He'd asked her to temporarily put their problems aside, she was cooperating—at least, that was the excuse she gave herself.

He laughed. "You're always full of surprises."

And he was always predictable, she thought. Appar-

ently, they were still playing a game. Perhaps that's all
she meant to him…nevertheless, she didn't want it to end.

Although the place was crowded, a waiter found them
a small table for two. There was live entertainment—a
piano. It was just the sort of intimate setting for lovers
Rachel had always imagined and never experienced. She
felt out of her depth and kept reminding herself that this
was Jared, her husband, which didn't help ease her discomfort at all.

They ordered dinner, shrimp in a pesto sauce served
over spinach linguini with baked broccoli and mushrooms
on the side. A dish of raspberry sorbet completed the delicious meal, washed down by a fine vintage wine.

They talked about Olivia, Dylan, Stones End. Anything
but what they were feeling.

The band was playing jazz. "Do you think we can
dance to this?" Jared asked, impatient with the conversation. He wanted to hold her.

"We can try." Rachel was wearing heels which
brought her almost up to his height. When they danced,
she couldn't avoid his eyes. His eyes drank her up, swallowed her whole. Their bodies fit, moving slowly to the
music, a prelude to another dance. When his hand slid to
the small of her back and drew her closer, a small gasp
escaped her. She couldn't contain a shudder of pleasure.

Jared nuzzled her ear and felt the heat in her face as
she flushed deliciously. "This feels nice," he said huskily,
not making any effort to hide the effect she had on him.
It was too late for pretence now, far too late. "But I think
we should call it a night."

"Mmm," Rachel agreed, but she knew it wasn't over.

The elevator was empty.

Jared pressed a number, then pulled Rachel against him.
His kiss was hungry. It ended on the twenty-third floor.

Their room was down a long hall. It seemed miles long. But at last, they were in the room, with the door firmly closed and locked behind them. He pulled her against him and leaned back against the door, drawing her into him as their lips met in a long slow heady kiss.

When he raised his head to draw in a breath, her eyes were closed, her long silky eyelashes a dark smudge against her fair skin. Her eyes flew open when he flipped on the light switch. Her eyes were dark, almost purple. He saw the naked hunger there, and knew his eyes must betray the same dazed expression. He ran his hand through the silk of her hair, freeing any constraint. "You are so lovely."

When he reached for the first button on her sweater, she drew in a breath. "Please…the light," she whispered.

He shook his head. "I want to see you…all of you. I want to touch you." To his surprise, she drew away, stepping back into the room. A bright light shone overhead. "Tonight, in that bar, I was so damned glad that I was the lucky guy who got to take you home." His possessive gaze drifted over her. "And I'm glad I'm the man who gets to take you to bed. Can you live with that?"

"Can you?" she asked, her eyes full of him.

"I'm not going to let you build walls, Rachel. This is just about you and me." This time, Jared didn't wait for her answer. He kissed her until she had no resistance left. And this time, when he reached for the first button on her sweater, she let him.

Rachel dropped her hands, unable to deny him anything, because she wanted it, too. She wanted to lose herself in him, forget all the caution and reasons why she should hold back. There was no reason—only this. The touch of his hands, the taste of his mouth, the heat generated by two.

Moments later, the sheets on the bed felt cold against her naked skin, but not for long.

Jared tasted the wine on her lips; she went to his head. Somehow, he had to convince her that they belonged together, that what they had was good. They had a future together, if only she could envision it.

When he reached for her, without words, she felt his need, and welcomed him to her. Their loving was slow and gentle, laced with desire, slowly unfurling, until it grew and grew and grew, then turned to pleasure—more intense than ever before. Because he needed her. It was something she understood, at long last, because she could finally admit—she needed him. She wasn't cold, or distant, or emotionless, she was a woman in love. They made love, giving and taking, expressing what they felt while the words remained unspoken, locked in their hearts.

The days flew, and then there were none—they were leaving, going home in less than twenty-four hours.

Their last stop was the Blue Lagoon.

In the brief time Jared had known Olivia, he'd caught only a glimpse of her, as if through a prism, and then, only the parts she allowed. But he began to know her and recognize a family trait. She'd learned to protect herself. She filled her life with activities, instead of people. Her life was hectic, disorganized and full. She had friends, too many to count, and none of them close.

She had Hank, but she didn't have family.

She didn't think she needed one.

On the last day, Rachel and Jared stopped at the diner to say goodbye. Jared had purchased a farewell gift.

He'd obviously put some thought into it, and he couldn't have chosen anything more appropriate, nor one that would hold so much meaning. As Rachel watched, he handed Olivia a small velvet box. "I hope you'll wear this to remember you're a Carlisle."

Olivia lifted a gold chain and pendant from inside. "It's wonderful," she said softly, her head bent.

"It's a Celtic knot," Jared explained, clearly pleased at her reaction. "The knotwork is interlaced in a continuous line symbolizing eternity. Jessie has one; I have the ring."

Though touched by the thoughtfulness behind his gift, Rachel denied an inner stab of pain. He meant to bind Olivia to him and Jessie. With so few words, he'd left Rachel out. What feat of magic or sorcerer's trick could she perform to transform herself into a Carlisle? If the answer existed, she didn't know it.

Olivia clutched the pendant in her hand. "Thank you, I'll always treasure this. I can't believe you're actually leaving tomorrow. The time has gone so fast."

His eyes held regret. "I could only arrange a short visit. If you could come back with us, it would mean a lot to Dad and Jessie," he said, using the opening to state his case for bringing Olivia home, even temporarily.

The girl's eyes widened in dismay. "I can't. There's my job, my friends, my classes."

"They'll be here when you come back," he pointed out.

"I'm sorry, that's impossible," she whispered, twisting her hands together. "I just can't."

"Maybe some other time." Jared said, to which Olivia made no reply. To Rachel's surprise, Jared didn't argue.

Instead, he reached into his pocket. "Here's the plane ticket—in case you change your mind. Or you can turn it in for another flight. It's good for the next six months."

Olivia placed her hands behind her back. "I'm sorry."

With a deep sigh, he placed the ticket on the table. "I

guess this is goodbye.'' He hugged his sister awkwardly, she clung to his broad shoulders. "Take care,'' he said huskily. "I'll be back sometime.''

"Yeah, sometime.'' She blinked back a tear. "I'm so glad you came...you and Rachel.''

She gave Rachel a fierce hug. Rachel could feel the younger woman trembling and knew this must be wrenching for both brother and sister. They'd found each other only to be parted. Who knew when Jared and Olivia would see each other again? They lived on opposite coasts, which wasn't an insurmountable span. But sometimes distance was measured in more than miles.

As they left the restaurant, Rachel saw the defeat in Jared's eyes. He'd succeeded in finding Olivia, but he'd failed to reach her. Jared walked out of the Blue Lagoon without looking back.

Outside, Jared hailed a cab and put Rachel into it. "I need to stretch my legs,'' he said, after giving the driver directions. "I'll see you back at the hotel.''

Before Rachel could object, the cab pulled away from the curb. She watched Jared stride off—as if he had someplace to go. Or perhaps he simply needed to escape. He always seemed so sure, so confident, so alone. There was always a part of him that couldn't be reached. Obviously, he could take care of himself; and yet, she hated to think of him wandering around San Francisco in this mood.

With a weary sigh, she rested her head back against the car seat, forced to admit that Jared didn't want wifely concern or comfort from her. He'd never indicated the slightest emotional weakness or need. Was that what she wanted from him? If nothing else, this trip had emphasized how much she craved more than a physical relationship with her husband.

Despite the confidence and surface charm, Jared was a

loner. At an early age, he'd obviously learned to rely on himself. No one had softened the blows. No wonder he had so little faith in a happy ending. Rachel despaired of ever breaking through all the barriers.

Suddenly sure of what she had to do, she said, "Please, stop." When the driver squealed to a stop in heavy traffic, she asked, "Can you turn around?"

The driver looked at the bumper-to-bumper traffic. "Not anytime soon. Maybe in the next block."

Rachel got out and walked.

The Blue Lagoon was a distance. When Rachel got there, the dinner crowd had dwindled. Olivia was taking a break.

She was visibly surprised to see Rachel. "Did you forget something?"

Rachel took a seat. "I'd like to talk to you."

The girl's expression grew shuttered. "There's nothing left to say. Did Jared send you?"

"No, he didn't. There are some things you should know."

"If it's about meeting my father, I'm not interested."

Rachel sighed, admitting, "It's about Ira. He's waiting to meet you. He's seventy-one years old. Don't waste the remaining years you have left with him."

"I didn't create this situation."

"I'm not going to sit here and make excuses for him. I don't know what went on between him and your mother. Neither do you. But there's one thing you should know—he never knew about you. Your mother never told him."

Olivia's eyes flashed with pain. "That's not true."

"But it is," Rachel insisted gently. "Your parents both made mistakes. And now, it's up to their children to make repairs. It's the only way to put an end to it."

Olivia rubbed her forehead. "It's all so old. Why should it matter so much? Why are you doing this?"

"I'm doing it for Jared, and Ira and Jessie. And you. I really like you, Olivia, and I'm so sorry. I wish I could make all this go away. If you can't do this for Ira, try and think of Jessie and Jared. You lost a father, but they lost their mother. They never got those letters she sent...not one. They thought she didn't care. You need to go see them. Don't you see? You're their only tie, the only one who can give her back to them."

Obviously moved, Olivia swallowed hard, but she said, "I have to think. I can't just drop everything and go to Maine. What's it like at Stones End? It's cold in Maine, right? And there's lots of seacoast. That's about all I know."

"Unfortunately, it's on the cool side now, and it gets colder in winter. But spring is lovely, and we do have a summer. I'm afraid you won't see the seacoast in northern Maine. But we do have rivers and lakes." Rachel smiled ruefully. "I must sound like a real estate agent."

"Or a travel agent," Olivia said. "Remember, I haven't agreed to anything."

Rachel nodded. "Anyway, about Stones End." She tried to find words to explain. "The house is old; generations of Carlisles have left their mark on it. It's isolated, and it can be lonely. When you look outside, there's nothing but space, acres and acres of it. If you listen, you hear the birds singing, and a stream trickling down, and the sound of a tractor nearby lets you know someone's around. It's big," she ended, "and you find yourself stretching to fit."

Olivia smiled. "And you love it there."

Rachel laughed in genuine surprise. "I suppose I do. So, will you come? Jared's taken the first step, now it's up to you. It's taken twenty years to open this door, please don't close it without giving it a lot of thought.''

Olivia still looked troubled, obviously torn. "It would be so disloyal to my mother's memory.''

"Of course,'' Rachel said. "And I understand how you feel. But your mother's gone, and nothing you do can hurt her. You have a family waiting for you. Don't you think she'd want you to be happy?'' Rachel gave her a moment to think about that before going on. "Do you know that Jared has taken six other trips to meet someone named Olivia? Now that he's found you, please don't let him down.''

Rachel saw the answer in the stubborn set of Olivia's chin. The girl was a Carlisle through and through. "I'll think about it.''

Rachel had to leave it at that.

For the last time, she left the Blue Lagoon. The sun was setting. The breeze felt almost tropical. It would be cold back home. At a crosswalk, she stopped, not sure of her direction, then she saw a cab. She hailed it and gave the name of the hotel.

With a weary sigh, Rachel settled back in the cab, watching the city go past, block by block. When the driver pointed out a tourist attraction, she murmured, "That's lovely,'' and it was, but it was also crowded and noisy, unlike Maine and Stones End. She hoped Olivia would come.

Their conversation played over in Rachel's head. Oddly enough, in attempting to convince Jared's sister to forgive and forget the past, she'd discovered the answer to her own soul-searching. For months, Rachel had struggled between divided loyalties, with her growing love for Jared competing with her loyalty to Laurel. She'd felt torn in two, but in the end, none of it mattered. Love had its way.

She and Laurel were twins, they'd shared their mother's heartbeat and come into the world together. As children, they'd loved and laughed and fought for the same place in the sun.

And then they grew up.

And everything changed, except for one thing—they always accepted and forgave their differences because their love for each other was stronger than any division. Rachel sighed. Yes, Laurel would want her to be happy. With a newfound sense of peace, Rachel realized she didn't have to choose. She loved Jared with a deep, abiding love, free of shadows and doubts. She'd tried hard not to love him—as if love gave her a choice.

Jared seemed self-sufficient. What did he want, besides a woman to warm his bed? It wasn't enough for Rachel. Once passion wore off, what would they have? Nothing. She had her pride. She wanted to give in this marriage, not just get.

Half an hour later, Rachel walked into the hotel room.

Jared was at the window, he turned abruptly at the sound of her entry. His eyes flickered over her in relief. "Where have you been? I was worried." His voice was soft, but she could see the tension in the set of his shoulders.

"I went back to talk to Olivia."

He crossed the gray carpeted space. "I didn't realize you were going to see her."

Rachel slowly removed her jacket. "I talked to her, though I'm not sure she was listening."

Jared took the jacket from her and tossed it on the bed. "You are the most stubborn woman I've ever met."

His eyes gleamed with admiration. He drew her close. It felt like the most natural thing in the world.

Rachel whispered, "I'm so sorry about Olivia."

He interrupted with a firm shake of his head. "Let's not talk about it. This is our last day before we go back. I don't want anything to spoil it." So he felt it, too.

They'd put their problems on hold; but tomorrow, they were going back to Stones End. Reality awaited. Perhaps he was right. Why let family problems intrude? They'd catch up with them soon enough.

He pulled the pins from her hair, then started to undo her blouse. "We only have tonight, and I know how I want to spend it."

"But we leave tomorrow. We have to make plane reservations, and pack, and...." Her blouse came off, then her skirt.

When she couldn't think of another thing to add to her list, he said in an amused tone, "And we will do all those things, but first, we need to take care of a more urgent matter." He drew her close, demonstrating how urgent it was. There was laughter and relief when she mumbled something unintelligible and sank against him, her resistance gone.

Once he'd removed the rest of her clothes, and his, he found the bed, leaning over her, and shocking her with the words, "Have you ever thought of having a baby?"

"A baby?" She froze.

Jared groaned. "I need to know. Now. Because in a minute it will be too late to do anything about it." He was laughing when he said it, but suddenly Jared knew that children, several in fact, were very much in the future he envisioned with Rachel.

"Yes," Rachel whispered, wondering why she'd never thought of it before. How perfect. Children. Love was a seed. To grow into something real and lasting, love had to be nurtured, not hidden in some dark secret place where fear of rejection smothered it. "If you're sure?" she asked, hardly daring to breathe because his answer meant so much.

"I'm sure," Jared said, knowing she'd never leave him if they had a child. Why hadn't he thought of it before?

Although Olivia had made no promises, Rachel expected a phone call later that evening. She was so sure, but the phone remained silent. She hardly slept. The following morning, she kept looking for Olivia—in the lobby as they checked out…outside when they found a cab…at the airport…right up to the last moment when the flight attendant called their seat number.

"We have to go," Jared said firmly.

They boarded the plane, slowly making their way down the narrow aisle. The plane was nearly full to capacity.

Jared stored their luggage overhead. Rachel had brought just one small suitcase. He took the window seat.

Rachel preferred the middle; the seat beside her was conspicuously empty—as empty as she felt. She felt some of Jared's defeat. The plane was minutes from takeoff.

Olivia wasn't coming.

Rachel turned to Jared. "I was so sure that if I talked to her, I could convince her." She lifted her shoulders with a small shrug that felt heavier—as if she felt the weight of Jared's pain and sense of loss. And in a way she did.

Jared reached for her hand. "It's not your fault." His attention shifted, then his face broke into a smile when he caught a movement in the aisle.

"Hi," a breathless voice said.

Rachel turned, afraid to believe her ears.

Olivia sank into the empty seat with a sigh. She slid one small piece of luggage under the seat in front.

Jared looked at the soft carry-on bag with an ironic

smile. One thing could be said for the women in his life—they travelled light.

Olivia was dressed in black leather—her warmest clothes, she claimed. "Rachel said it could get cold in Maine." The words tumbled out in her usual rush to crowd everything into the moment. "Sorry I'm late. I was afraid the plane would take off without me. My cab got stuck in traffic."

Chapter Sixteen

It was snowing when they got to Stones End. With the temperature just above freezing, it fell in fat wet flakes and melted when it hit the blacktop. Nevertheless, the road was slick in places. Easing into the curve, Jared turned at the signpost and drove the remaining way. The tires crunched onto the driveway.

Every window in the house was lit up.

He heard Olivia's gasp of delight.

Although exhausted, she'd stayed awake the entire trip, fascinated by this vast northern landscape. The fields at Stones End were covered in a pure white blanket; hills and valleys flowed one into the other.

Olivia stared out the window. "I've never seen snow before." She climbed out of the car and simply stood there. She raised her face to the sky, snowflakes caught on her eyelashes. She blinked in surprise and laughed—a sound of pure enjoyment. "It's awesome!"

Turning full circle, she stared at the snowcapped trees, the hills, the barns, the house. "It's perfect," she whispered. "Just like a Christmas card."

Seeing Stones End through her eyes, Jared smiled at her reaction, and rediscovered that sense of wonder. He'd come and gone from his boyhood home so many times, but something always drew him back. For the first time in recent memory, he felt a true sense of homecoming.

Everything he loved was here.

"Welcome home," he said, including Rachel in his smile.

They still had issues to deal with, but he'd asked her to put them off until they got back to Stones End. With their return, all the problems came rushing back. Rachel had tried, he'd tried, but she clearly wasn't happy. At first, he'd hoped she'd adjust, but expecting her to do all the adjusting in this marriage wasn't fair.

But what was fair in love?

The door opened. A light came from inside. Ira stood there, stern, large and formidable, framed in the doorway. He peered into the darkness. "What's holding things up?"

His long shadow fell across the white snow.

Jared saw Olivia stiffen and knew she wasn't nearly as confident as she pretended. "Let's go inside." He took her hand and started up the walk.

As they approached, the deep wrinkled frown on Ira's face slowly ironed out. He drew a deep shudder of a breath that seemed to come from the hidden depths of him.

"You're Olivia," he murmured, his voice harsh, breaking with emotion. "That was my grandmother's name. You look like her somewhat, around the eyes."

Olivia froze. "Yes, well—" Her voice cracked. For the

first time, Jared saw her run out of words. A tear trickled down her cheek.

Awkwardly, like a rusty hinged gate, Ira opened his arms, and she simply walked into her father's embrace.

Ira wept, his shoulders heaving. "My God, it is you."

Olivia's head nodded up and down against his thick chest. She gulped out a small laugh. "Yes, it's me."

Witnessing the miracle of love, Rachel wiped a tear from her eye. These people—these Carlisles—she hadn't meant to love them, but they'd worn down her resistance until she literally ached to be one of them.

She'd come to love Stones End. She wondered if she would ever feel as if she belonged there. For so long, she'd searched for a place to belong, only to learn it wasn't a place; home meant Jared and she wasn't there yet. Not quite.

The day before, they'd made love. When he spoke of their future including children, she'd let her heart speak for her. She'd agreed, knowing how much family meant to him. While she loved him for that, she could see so plainly why Jared had married her. She'd always regret that he didn't have a choice. Could she learn to live with that?

Without further ceremony, they all went inside where Ben and Jessie, Nathaniel and Dylan waited.

Dylan ran to hug Rachel, then ran to his father.

Jared hugged him hard. Rachel watched as the family crowded around each other, hugging, kissing, talking, laughing and crying all at once. They had so many years to catch up and seemed bent on cramming as much as they possibly could into these precious moments. Rachel felt such joy at their reunion. Only one thing was missing—she wasn't part of it.

At that moment, Jared looked around and found Rachel

missing. She was still standing by the door—as if she wasn't sure of herself. His valiant, courageous Rachel, who never hid behind pretence, wasn't sure of her place. And that was his fault. He'd married her, but he'd never given her a special place that was hers alone.

They were quite a pair, he thought wryly. Life hadn't given either of them much faith in this thing called love.

And suddenly, Jared knew what he had to do. He'd been thinking about it for days.

He reached Rachel in two strides. "Come," he murmured. "Grab a warm jacket and some boots."

When she just stood there, he bundled her into his barn jacket. "Where are we going?" she asked.

He took her hand and led her out the door, back the way they'd come. "We won't be missed for a few minutes. I need to check on a couple of things."

"Now?"

"Mmm," he murmured with a twinkle in his eyes, stealing her objections by simply sealing her lips with a kiss. "Come with me. This won't wait."

They walked down the driveway, then through the trees, cutting across a path between two fields. Their footsteps left tracks in the slushy snow.

"What about your family?" she said, catching her breath at his haste. "Won't they miss you?"

He slowed down. "This won't take long. I want to show you something." He stopped in a clearing near the long low clinic building. "Here we are. This is it."

Frowning, Rachel said, "If this is your idea of a joke!"

He laughed. "Can't you see it?"

She looked around. "What? There's nothing here."

"Our house. We're going to build right here." He staked out the place with his gaze. "I hope you won't mind being so close to my work, but I thought this way,

I'll be nearby. Jessie will be leaving soon, going back to Virginia. I could use an assistant.''

When she remained speechless, he began to worry.

''In any case,'' he said, ''you're standing in the middle of the kitchen, with a view of the valley so you won't feel confined.'' Jared watched her facial expression undergo several emotions—from disbelief to amazement to joy.

She tilted her head. ''But why?''

He smiled cautiously. ''I know walls won't hold you, if you want to go. But I intend to build them. Maybe I didn't go about this marriage business in the right way, but you are mine, Rachel.''

Always practical, she had to remind him, ''You only asked me to marry you because of Dylan.''

Crossing that hurdle suddenly seemed almost impossible. But Jared reached for her hand. ''And you only agreed because of him. Are we going to spend the next fifty years arguing about it, or will you believe that I love you now?'' His voice softened and his eyes darkened with intensity. ''I don't know when or where it started to be love. Maybe it was always there. But I love you, more than life itself. What we have is something I've never had before. It's coming home and finding you waiting, or watching you with Dylan, or my father. And it's knowing that you need a home to call your own. This is it.''

She smiled tremulously. ''How did you know?''

He tugged gently on her hand, drawing her close. ''I know you.'' He placed the palm of his hand against her heart and felt the beat—strong and a little unsteady at his touch. The way she responded to him made him smile and gave him the courage to say the rest. But first, he placed the palm of her hand against his heart. Heart to heart, he said, "I know you—here. Deep inside. I never knew I could love someone as much as I love you."

At last, Rachel saw through all the layers to the man beneath. She looked into his wary gray eyes and saw so many things—sorrow and regret, and a firm determination to make it up to her, somehow. She saw beneath the surface to the sad little boy watching at the window, waiting in vain for his mother to turn up…and the idealistic youth whose values had hardened…and finally the uncompromising man she'd vowed to love, honor and cherish a few short months ago.

Rachel saw all this, yet she suspected she'd barely skimmed the surface. Yes, Jared expected a lot from those around him, but he was hardest on himself. And he gave as good as he got. From the first, he'd never hesitated in his obligations to Dylan. How many men would have turned away? He'd married her out of duty. It was part of him, deeply ingrained—just like his height, the gray of his eyes or the burnished gold in his hair—it was part of the man she loved. She had to accept all of him—that was the key to what love was all about. Acceptance.

She had a troubling thought. "But what about Ira?"

"We'll be within shouting distance. Besides, I suspect Dora's going to become a permanent fixture. And if Olivia stays, the house won't be big enough for all of us. But all that can wait. Let's talk about us."

"All right," she said slowly.

He cleared his throat. "Some time ago, I took something from you—a locket. I know how much it meant to you, and how much it meant to give it up. You did it for me."

"For us."

He stopped for a moment, as if his heart had skipped a beat. "Thank you for that." His smile warmed her.

"When I was in San Francisco, I found this to replace it. I hope you'll wear it." He held out a pendant on a long gold chain. "It's like the one I gave Olivia. But there's a difference." He placed it around her neck. "I wanted to wait and give it to you when we were alone."

When he stepped back, Rachel felt the cold metal against her throat, but it warmed quickly. "It's shaped like a heart," she said in a soft voice as she studied the delicate handiwork. Instead of a round shape, the Celtic knotwork wove together in an unbroken line to form a heart.

Jared said huskily, "It means eternal love."

Rachel whispered, "I don't know what to say."

He drew in a breath. "That's good, because I'm not done yet. I want you to know that I never wanted to hurt anyone. Yet, I hurt Laurel, and Dylan. When I tried to correct that, I hurt you. Can you ever forgive me?"

"Yes," Rachel said without hesitation.

Nine years ago, two very young people had hurt each other. No one was to blame, except fate. That same fate had brought her and Dylan and Jared together—with a little help from Drew Pierce. She felt like laughing—how odd to think of Drew playing Cupid! Some day she would have to thank him. She was suddenly fiercely glad. For the first time in her life, she felt fully alive, free of shadows, free of the past. She wished Jared could feel the same.

"I forgave you some time ago," she said softly. "But maybe you need to forgive yourself first."

The words fell gently from her lips...and lodged in Jared's heart—like a healing balm. "Ah—there you go again," he said with a smile. "Throwing the ball back to my corner." He kissed her.

When he lifted his head, she smiled mistily, deeply

moved by his tenderness. The warm, funny, human side of Jared never failed to arouse a response in her. She tilted her head to look up at him, amused to see that his hair was white with snow, and she thought of the years and years ahead of them. Oh, she knew him now.

"I know you did your best, and you never intended to hurt anyone. You always want to save everyone and refuse to admit a weakness, but guess what, Jared?"

He frowned warily. "What?"

She smiled. "You're not perfect." He was close—but why add to his conceit? Women fell for that wounded genteel knight in him. He could have had anyone, but he'd chosen her. And she was deeply grateful. She felt like laughing, shouting it to the winds. Instead, she wrapped her arms around him, all of him, and leaned against him because she recognized his strength even if he didn't, and because he would always be Jared—her knight in shining armor—rescuing fair maidens who didn't want to be rescued, and placing personal honor and family tradition above all else.

"I love you anyway," she murmured.

The words felt like a gift he'd never expected. He gazed into her eyes and saw love. Some people said it was like a rose, but Jared knew they were wrong. Love was like a chicory weed.

It grew wild along the roadside, where concrete met earth, where the ground was frequently disturbed. Wherever its tentacles could grab hold and set roots deep into the ground, it thrived. And nothing could destroy it. It grew unprotected, hardy and indestructible, year after year after year. When in bloom, the delicate blue-violet blossoms rivalled a cloudless blue sky.

They were the color of Rachel's eyes.

"I love you, too." He smiled, and the gray glitter in

his eyes wasn't hard, it splintered into a trillion stars in a black heaven. "I think you're perfect."

"No, I'm not."

"Yes, you are."

"No," she sputtered when Jared silenced her objections with a searing kiss. She was wrong, he was right.

Only a perfect woman could love an imperfect man. Wait a minute, did he have that right? he wondered. Oh well, at least they'd stopped arguing. They'd work out all the details later. For now, Rachel was content to be in his arms—right where he wanted her. They had the rest of their lives. Eternity.

There was no beginning, and no end, to all they could be, as long as they had each other....

*   *   *   *   *

Be sure to watch for
Drew and Olivia's romance,
coming soon to
Silhouette Special Edition.

Feel like a star with Silhouette.

We will fly you and a guest to New York City for an exciting weekend stay at a glamorous 5-star hotel. Experience a refreshing day at one of New York's trendiest spas and have your photo taken by a professional. Plus, receive $1,000 U.S. spending money!

Flowers...long walks...dinner for two... how does Silhouette Books make romance come alive for you?

Send us a script, with 500 words or less, along with visuals (only drawings, magazine cutouts or photographs or combination thereof). Show us how Silhouette Makes Your Love Come Alive. Be creative and have fun. No purchase necessary. All entries must be clearly marked with your name, address and telephone number. All entries will become property of Silhouette and are not returnable. **Contest closes September 28, 2001.**

Please send your entry to: **Silhouette Makes You a Star!**

In U.S.A.	In Canada
P.O. Box 9069	P.O. Box 637
Buffalo, NY, 14269-9069	Fort Erie, ON, L2A 5X3

Look for contest details on the next page, by visiting www.eHarlequin.com or request a copy by sending a self-addressed envelope to the applicable address above. Contest open to Canadian and U.S. residents who are 18 or over. Void where prohibited.

Our lucky winner's photo will appear in a Silhouette ad. Join the fun!

SRMYAS1

HARLEQUIN "SILHOUETTE MAKES YOU A STAR!" CONTEST 1308
OFFICIAL RULES
NO PURCHASE NECESSARY TO ENTER

1. To enter, follow directions published in the offer to which you are responding. Contest begins June 1, 2001, and ends on September 28, 2001. Entries must be postmarked by September 28, 2001, and received by October 5, 2001. Enter by hand-printing (or typing) on an 8 ½" x 11" piece of paper your name, address (including zip code), contest number/name and attaching a script containing <u>500 words</u> or less, <u>along with drawings, photographs or magazine cutouts, or combinations thereof</u> (i.e., collage) <u>on no larger than 9" x 12"</u> piece of paper, describing how the <u>Silhouette books make romance come alive for you</u>. Mail via first-class mail to: Harlequin "Silhouette Makes You a Star!" Contest 1308, (in the U.S.) P.O. Box 9069, Buffalo, NY 14269-9069, (in Canada) P.O. Box 637, Fort Erie, Ontario, Canada L2A 5X3. Limit one entry per person, household or organization.

2. Contests will be judged by a panel of members of the Harlequin editorial, marketing and public relations staff. Fifty percent of criteria will be judged against script and fifty percent will be judged against drawing, photographs and/or magazine cutouts. Judging criteria will be based on the following:

   - Sincerity—25%
   - Originality and Creativity—50%
   - Emotionally Compelling—25%

   In the event of a tie, duplicate prizes will be awarded. Decisions of the judges are final.

3. All entries become the property of Torstar Corp. and may be used for future promotional purposes. Entries will not be returned. No responsibility is assumed for lost, late, illegible, incomplete, inaccurate, nondelivered or misdirected mail.

4. Contest open only to residents of the U.S. <u>(except Puerto Rico)</u> and Canada who are 18 years of age or older, and is void wherever prohibited by law; all applicable laws and regulations apply. Any litigation within the Province of Quebec respecting the conduct or organization of a publicity contest may be submitted to the Régie des alcools, des courses et des jeux for a ruling. Any litigation respecting the awarding of a prize may be submitted to the Régie des alcools, des courses et des jeux only for the purpose of helping the parties reach a settlement. Employees and immediate family members of Torstar Corp. and D. L. Blair, Inc., their affiliates, subsidiaries and all other agencies, entities and persons connected with the use, marketing or conduct of this contest are not eligible to enter. Taxes on prizes are the sole responsibility of the winner. Acceptance of any prize offered constitutes permission to use winner's name, photograph or other likeness for the purposes of advertising, trade and promotion on behalf of Torstar Corp., its affiliates and subsidiaries without further compensation to the winner, unless prohibited by law.

5. Winner will be determined no later than November 30, 2001, and will be notified by mail. Winner will be required to sign and return an Affidavit of Eligibility/Release of Liability/Publicity Release form within 15 days after winner notification. Noncompliance within that time period may result in disqualification and an alternative winner may be selected. All travelers must execute a Release of Liability prior to ticketing and must possess required travel documents (e.g., passport, photo ID) where applicable. Trip must be booked by December 31, 2001, and completed within one year of notification. No substitution of prize permitted by winner. Torstar Corp. and D. L. Blair, Inc., their parents, affiliates and subsidiaries are not responsible for errors in printing of contest, entries and/or game pieces. In the event of printing or other errors that may result in unintended prize values or duplication of prizes, all affected game pieces or entries shall be null and void. **Purchase or acceptance of a product offer does not improve your chances of winning.**

6. Prizes: (1) Grand Prize—A 2-night/3-day trip for two (2) to New York City, including round-trip coach air transportation nearest winner's home and hotel accommodations (double occupancy) at The Plaza Hotel, a glamorous afternoon makeover at <u>a trendy New York spa</u>, $1,000 in U.S. spending money and an opportunity to <u>have a professional photo taken and appear in a Silhouette advertisement</u> (approximate retail value: $7,000). (10) Ten Runner-Up Prizes of gift packages (retail value $50 ea.). Prizes consist of only those items listed as part of the prize. Limit one prize per person. Prize is valued in U.S. currency.

7. For the name of the winner (available after December 31, 2001) send a self-addressed, stamped envelope to: Harlequin "Silhouette Makes You a Star!" Contest 1197 Winners, P.O. Box 4200 Blair, NE 68009-4200 or you may access the www.eHarlequin.com Web site through February 28, 2002.

Contest sponsored by Torstar Corp., P.O Box 9042, Buffalo, NY 14269-9042.